# The Good Twin

## by

## Suzanne Rossi

**The Good Twin**

Cover Art by *Kim Mendoza*

The Wild Rose Press, Inc.
PO Box 708
Adams Basin, NY 14410-0708
Visit us at www.thewildrosepress.com

Publishing History
First Crimson Rose Edition, 2015
Print ISBN 978-1-5092-0259-1
Digital ISBN 978-1-5092-0260-7

Published in the United States of America

**My arms broke out in goosebumps. Someone** was living here, although not home at the moment. I needed to get the hell out and call the police.

I whirled and ran out the front door not bothering to even close it behind me. The thought of returning to that narrow pathway gave me the shivers. I headed straight for the neglected driveway. This was little more than an overgrown path, too. The deep ruts made walking difficult, so I moved to the side trying to avoid the roots of trees and vines that had encroached for years. A tree had fallen ages ago blocking access. Getting a car up this thing would be impossible.

I stepped over the fallen tree, and then stopped. There in the dirt were several faint tire tracks. I stooped to inspect them closer. Behind me a twig snapped and footsteps rushed toward me.

Before I could rise and turn, pain exploded in my head. I toppled over as my world went black.

## Praise for Suzanne Rossi

"What a GREAT book this is! I absolutely adored several things about *DEATH IS THE PITS*, first of which is the murder mystery/whodunit storyline. The pace was quick and the wit was sharp and Ms. Rossi kept the twists and turns going. Every 5 minutes I could see another character being the culprit, and though I thought I figured out the real story, the truth kept me guessing until the very end."

~*Delta, TheRomanceReviews.com*

~\*~

"Ms Rossi kept me intrigued in this mysterious murder mystery. The pace of this [*THE REUNION*] is good and the storyline flowed well. The characters were well developed and the emotions of the characters were so real. I loved how one of the characters was the drama queen of the bunch, and I especially loved how she was retelling what had happened."

~*CozyReader, TheRomanceReviews.com*

~\*~

"Suzanne Rossi writes fabulous romantic suspense…I am such a suspicious person when reading romantic suspense but [the hero] got through my defenses very quickly…If you are looking for a mystery reminiscent of the classics with a touch of heat then [*DEADLY INHERITANCE*] is a fabulous choice. I admit I enjoyed the look into the lives of the uber-wealthy and as always am looking forward to the next story by this author because she never disappoints."

~*Night Owl Reviews*

## Dedication

Writing is hard work. Ask any author. It takes desire, discipline, dedication, and a little bit of luck.

~*~

I dedicate this story
to all the unpublished authors out there.

~*~

Follow your dreams—they are what you desire.

~*~

Adhere to my theory of BICHOK
Butt in Chair, Hands on Keyboard—it's part of discipline.

~*~

And finally, dedicate yourself to succeed.

~*~

These three things will bring the luck.

~*~

I hope I see your first novels on the racks soon.

Prologue

*Diary of Amy Margaret Wallace*

Ten years ago, I killed Abby, my identical twin. Oh, the authorities deemed it an accident, but that didn't lessen the guilt. Taking the boat had been her idea, but I was at the controls when the storm hit.

I didn't see the object in the water until it was too late. We impacted hard. The boat flipped upside down and exploded with a deafening roar. Terrified, I grasped a flotation pillow and screamed Abby's name. She never answered.

No body was ever found. The theory was Abby had been sitting directly over the gas tanks, and what remained fed the fish.

I held out hope she was alive, suffering from amnesia and wandering from place to place. Sometimes in my dreams of churning water and tossing boats, I find Abby and pull her to safety. At other times, she finds me and sucks me into a watery grave. I spent six months in a sanitarium before finally admitting Abby was dead.

I hate the Fourth of July, yet live at the lake house during the summers as penance.

Then, a miracle occurred—a miracle that has proven me right all along.

While sitting on the dock this afternoon, I saw her.

She whipped past fifty yards away, skimming the water in a blur, at the controls of a red runabout.

Abby is alive, and she's come back.

## Chapter One

"Jenny, Mr. Grayson would like to see you."

I lifted my head from reading a law reference book and gazed at one of the clerks.

"What about?" I was in the midst of working on an intricate contract, and hated being interrupted, even by a request from the senior partner of the Grayson, Banks, & Wilkes Law Firm.

"I have no idea, but he said pronto."

I sighed, marked the place in the book, and strode down the hall to the corner office all the while wondering what the hell I'd done now.

"Go on in," his secretary said when I entered. "He's expecting you."

I nodded and opened the door to the inner sanctum.

"Miss Devlin, please come in and have a seat," Mr. Grayson invited.

Nervous and uncertain, I took a seat in the plush leather chair in front of his desk. A man in his late fifties to early sixties sat in another nursing a glass of pale amber liquid, which I assumed was scotch. Grayson, Banks, & Wilkes wasn't a bourbon kind of establishment. A cut glass decanter sat on the desk. Grayson didn't offer me anything to drink. Why should he? He was a big muckedy-muck, and I was a contract law attorney, specifically literary contracts.

"I'd like to introduce you to Mark Bridges, Miss

Devlin." We murmured briefly and shook hands. "Mr. Bridges is the brother of the late Constance Wallace. I believe you are familiar with the family, are you not?"

I thought hard. "The name sounds familiar, but I can't place it."

"I believe you lived next door to them."

My memory fumbled for identification before hitting on the fact my boss wasn't referring to my home in St. Louis.

"If you're talking about the people who lived next door to us on Lake Wildwood, then yes, I remember them."

"Then I assume you were also acquainted with the children."

I remembered the twins. The one always in trouble had died in an accident of some sort several years ago. "I babysat a few times."

My boss nodded as if in approval. "So, you know about the terrible tragedy."

I shifted uncomfortably in my chair, curious as to what this was all about. "Vaguely. I was in my last year of law school when it happened." The girls may have looked alike, but that was it. One had courted trouble, while the other cringed at the thought of displeasing anyone. "One was killed in some kind of car accident, wasn't she?"

"Boating. Abby died," Bridges said. "Amy was at the helm."

"That's right. I sort of remember. Amy must have been devastated at causing her sister's death, even if it was accident."

"Were you aware that my niece was in a sanitarium for a while after the accident?" Bridges asked. He stared into the glass before raising it to his lips.

"I didn't know that, but I'm not surprised. I imagine she took the death very hard. May I ask what this is all about?"

"Does your family still use the lake house?" Bridges inquired, ignoring my question.

"My parents live in Kansas City now and try to get there as often as possible, although I don't think they've stayed for any longer than a week in several years. They sometimes rent it out for the season." I paused. "I don't mean to be pushy, but why are you asking me all of this?"

"A couple of weeks ago, I got a call from Amy— very excited and babbling that she'd seen Abby," Bridges said.

"But that's not possible. Abby's dead."

"I know. I thought perhaps she had seen someone who looked like Abby, but she claimed to have seen her again a few days later while walking in the woods." He bolted the rest of his drink and set the glass on Grayson's antique mahogany desk. "I'm worried. Her behavior isn't normal. I was wondering if you would go with me to Vermillion for a few days and see her, talk to her, as an old friend."

I sat back confused by the request. "Mr. Bridges, how on earth can I help? If your niece is having a breakdown, she needs a doctor, not a lawyer."

"If I show up with a psychiatrist in tow, she might go from mildly disturbed to over the edge."

"But, I haven't seen or spoken to her in—well, in years. I didn't attend the funeral, and to be honest, I didn't see her much before that. Won't she find it strange that I come knocking on the door with you right behind me?"

"We'd go separately. You arrive first and renew acquaintances, and then I'll come a day or so later."

"I'm sorry, but I don't think I need to be involved in this. I knew the twins as children, and I'm not that well versed in how the accident happened. Besides, it's none of my business."

"It's because you *don't* know all the details that I'm asking. Amy has almost no friends to confide in. She never did. Her refusal to sell the lake house and returning summer after summer isn't healthy. I begged her to get rid of the property years ago. Please, Miss Devlin, I need help. Your presence might trigger memories of old times, when she was a child."

"Seems to me that would just make matters worse. She'd be remembering the accident."

Bridges shook his head. "I don't agree. I'd think it might help to remember the good times rather than dwelling on Abby's death. Since you knew the girls before the accident, your presence may bring back those good memories. I want so badly for her to be happy."

I hesitated, not wanting to give in, and yet not wanting to refuse help to a woman who was tortured by the past.

"For all I know, my parents rented the house this summer," I protested. "And I have work to do."

Bridges stared with narrowed eyes. "The house is empty. I've already checked."

Was he that sure of me? I didn't like it.

"My parents don't always go through an agency to rent, Mr. Bridges. They could have rented it privately for a short term."

"A simple phone call to them should answer that question."

"And I'm sure you can use a week or so away from the heat and humidity of St. Louis," Grayson added in a smooth tone. "I understand you're doing exceptional work in your department. And such a dedicated employee—in early and often working late. Hand off your case load to a clerk."

Something didn't smell right. Grayson, who didn't know me from Adam, laid it on thick, buttering me up. And Bridges—well, why he didn't just have a doctor accompany him and introduce him to Amy as a friend? That sounded sensible. Certainly more sensible than what he suggested.

Grayson cleared his throat. "Think of it as a gesture of goodwill, a case of showing a willingness to go that extra yard for the company, Miss Devlin."

Rah, rah, sis-boom-baa. Since when did Grayson, Banks & Wilkes need a cheerleader—and a very junior one at that? *What the hell is going on here?*

"As the family attorney, Mr. Bridges is the trustee of the Wallace family funds. He oversees everything, but is finding it a bit cumbersome, isn't that right, Mark?"

"Yes, my sister and her husband left everything to Amy in a trust. She lives off of it. My niece is a wildlife illustrator. She only does it to keep busy and donates all her earnings to charity. I've found that over the last few years, keeping abreast of the investments and such has been a strain. I also negotiate contracts for the family businesses, including the literary ones involving Amy and her illustrations."

"Mr. Bridges is thinking about transferring this

enormous responsibility to our firm. It's a very lucrative account, and the literary portion is yours if you just do him this little favor," Grayson said with a wolfish smile.

Now I understood. What would the world be like without lawyers and twisted motives? He had both bribed and blackmailed me in the same sentence. It was an offer I couldn't refuse.

"Before I say yes to this, I need to know more about the accident. I don't want to say the wrong thing to Amy."

Bridges sighed, reached for the decanter, poured another glass of liquor, and took a generous gulp.

"I only know what Amy told the authorities. It was just after the July 4$^{th}$ weekend. One night the two of them took a joy ride on a neighbor's thirty-five-foot cabin cruiser. Amy was at the controls when a storm blew up. They hit something in the water, the boat overturned and exploded." He shivered and gulped more scotch. "Amy's blood alcohol came back at point-oh-six. Impaired, but not drunk. Amy admitted they'd killed a bottle of wine."

I heaved a breath. No wonder the poor woman had ended up in a sanitarium. "Any charges filed?"

"No. To the police it was an unfortunate accident. The neighbors were good friends and couldn't bring themselves to press charges. Trust me. It was Abby's idea to steal the boat. Amy went along for the ride. She's a follower, not a leader."

"Which neighbor?"

"The Howards, two lots to the east."

"I remember them. Do they still live there?"

Bridges shook his head. "They sold the house a

few years ago and moved to Florida."

I hadn't been to the lake house in years. My work schedule hadn't allowed anything other than vacations built around family holidays like Thanksgiving and Christmas.

"Why doesn't Amy sell the place? It can't have good memories."

"I've begged her to do just that ever since my sister passed away. She refuses. It's not healthy, if you ask me."

I agreed. "Won't my showing up at Lake Wildwood look odd after all these years?"

My boss answered as if anticipating my refusal. "Not at all. Just say you had some free time and wanted to get away from the city for a few weeks. Mark's niece sounds like a trusting sort. Why would she question it?"

"Exactly!" Bridges concurred.

"I've always seen you as a team player, Miss Devlin," my boss said, his voice still smooth just like the one he used in court.

A team player, huh? I had the feeling I was about to be tackled for a loss.

Amy's uncle tossed the rest of the liquor down his throat in a jerky motion. I wouldn't have minded a belt at this point in time, but the offer wasn't forthcoming. Instead, I took a deep breath, not liking what I was about to say, but saying it anyway. When in doubt, punt.

"Very well, Mr. Bridges, when do I leave?"

"As soon as possible."

I turned to Grayson. "I'm in the middle of drawing up the Williams contract with Wind River Publishing."

He smiled a satisfied smirk. "Hand it off to

Howard Mills. He can finish it."

I stood. "I'll need a couple of days to attend to personal matters. I can arrive on Thursday afternoon. Fourth of July is over a week away."

Bridges beamed. "Perfect. That'll give you some time to reacquaint yourself with Amy. She occasionally returns to St. Louis for business during the week, but is always at the lake on weekends. Thank you, Miss Devlin. I appreciate your help."

He waved a hand in dismissal. I nodded to Mr. Grayson and swept from the room, not particularly liking Mark Bridges, my boss, or the feel of this. I brushed my hands over my arms as if to remove dirt. I should have refused, but the lure of a big, fat commission suggested that maybe I should leave the dirt on.

A chill rolled down my spine and back up again. I believed strongly in following intuition. It wasn't too late to back out. Something smelled, and the stench was overpowering.

Chapter Two

I dodged another pothole in the lake house driveway and winced. I didn't remember it as having been this bumpy. Mom and Dad needed to do something. A quick phone call to my parents had confirmed there were no renters this season, nor had there been for three years, which explained the condition of the drive. Mother, however, had assured me the house was in good shape and relatively clean. She and Dad had spent a weekend in late April sprucing the place up. I didn't enlighten them as to why I suddenly felt the urge to spend time at the lake.

The three-hour journey west from St. Louis had proven uneventful, and I had stopped at the local grocery store to pick up enough food and drinks to last a couple of days.

I pulled up in front of the house. It sat on a slight elevation and the view from the porch was of rolling hills. The deck out back overlooked the lake. A series of steps—a hundred and two to be exact—led down the steep hillside to the dock. As a kid, I hadn't been much into panoramas. I didn't appreciate the scenery until later.

The place didn't look much different than it had ten or twelve years ago. The sight of the white clapboard brought on a wave of nostalgia. At some point in time, the forest green shutters had changed to black and the front door from black to cranberry.

A sense of uneasiness rolled over me. I'm basically an insecure person. I put in long hours because I fear my bosses will think my work isn't good enough and in turn strive to prove it is. I abandoned personal relationships six years ago. I don't like being out of my comfort zone. And what I was about to do was definitely outside that perimeter.

I exited the car and glanced toward the Wallace property on my left. A late model silver car in the drive told me someone was there. I assumed it belonged to Amy.

The sound of hammering came from the property on my right where I observed a man crouching by the front steps. He tossed a weathered board aside replacing it with a new one and pounding it secure. From the looks of the rest of the house, the man had a lot of work to do.

This would be the Forrester lake house. During my call to Mom, she'd told me the Forresters had passed away a few years ago. I seemed to remember they had several children, all older than me, but had no idea if the repairperson was one of them. He saw me and waved, and then returned to his task, shifting his weight from leg to leg, the denim of his cut-offs stretching across his derriere.

It was a fine rear end. I paused to stare a moment longer. Something inside me stirred. So those nerve endings weren't so atrophied after all. I speculated about the rest of his anatomy.

*Oh, for God's sake, Devlin. Get a grip. You came here for a specific purpose and gazing at your neighbor's ass isn't it. Besides, this kind of thinking can only lead to trouble. And we all know what happened the last time you let your urges override common sense.*

Tired and hoping to pop a frozen dinner into the microwave for an early meal, I grabbed several plastic grocery bags, fumbled with the lock and key, opened the door, and walked in.

The inside hadn't changed much. The furniture was new, but the placement the same. Memories of those long forgotten summers spent here with my parents and three older brothers swamped me. God, we'd had fun—the boating, the fishing, the water skiing—not to mention barbeques with neighbors, including the Wallaces, and visiting friends on the weekends.

*Why does time have to march on?*

I needed no direction back to the kitchen. Mom said she'd had it remodeled. The new cabinets and countertops were an improvement, as was the breakfast bar. A newer, smaller kitchen table in the eating area replaced the rustic one that had provided plenty of space for a family of six plus assorted friends.

It only took a few minutes to put the groceries away. Finished, I returned to the car for the rest of my luggage. I was lifting my computer case from behind the front seat when the sound of crunching gravel made me turn.

A slim woman paused a few feet away. I'm five-feet-six-inches. She stood just short of that. Her dark hair brushed her collarbone in a bob, the center part giving her a Madonna-like appearance. She wore beige slacks, a white top, and white canvas shoes. Even though it had been years, I recognized Amy Wallace.

"Hello," she said in a light voice. "Are you renting for the rest of the summer?"

"Actually, no, my parents own the place and I'm just here for a few weeks. You're Amy, right? I'm Jenny Devlin." I advanced, my hand outstretched.

"Oh, my goodness! Jenny, how good to see you. It's been forever." She shook my hand and smiled a welcome.

"It has indeed. You look well."

"Thank you. Here, let me help you with your bags." She walked to the open trunk, hefted the suitcase, climbed the steps, and walked inside.

I followed, surprised to see her. I'd gotten the impression she was shy, a loner.

"Just drop it here. I'll take them back to the bedroom later. Would you like something to drink? I have soft drinks and a bottle of wine, but no idea if there's any ice."

"Oh, no, don't bother. I just dropped by to say hello. Maybe tomorrow you'd like to come over for lunch. I do a mean chicken Caesar salad."

The invitation so soon after arriving caught me off guard. Her eager voice clutched at my heart. She sounded like a lonely child desperate for friends. Not what I'd been led to believe.

"I'd like that."

She smiled as if in relief and turned away. "Well, I'd better let you get settled in. I'll see you tomorrow. Is noon all right with you?"

"Noon is fine."

Amy waved and left. I carried the bags into the master bedroom and unpacked. That had been a quick re-acquaintance. *Quick and startling.* She appeared like magic, almost as if she'd been waiting for me—and had disappeared just as fast. I paused, reflecting on my thoughts. *It's almost as if she knew I was coming, but that's ridiculous.*

I shrugged. Maybe she'd been sitting in the screened-in portion of her front porch, had seen me arrive, and let her curiosity take over. I'd spent part of the time on my drive trying to think of how to approach Amy. She'd done it for me. Mark Bridges would be pleased when he arrived on Sunday.

On the surface, Amy hadn't shown any signs of a mental disturbance, but then maybe it was a fleeting thing—there one minute and gone the next. I sat on the edge of the bed. That feeling of something not being quite right slithered along my skin. Mark Bridges had all but painted his niece as a recluse, yet she'd showed up on my doorstep before the car engine had a chance to cool. I shrugged again, rose, and hung up another top. Whatever the problem, she'd looked normal enough to me—for all of the two minutes we'd talked.

My conscience gave me a kick in the rear end. I'd have made a lousy spy. I didn't like snooping into other people's lives. And the more I thought about this—for want of a better word—assignment, the more I wished I'd said no to the proposition. But I was committed now and had no choice but to move forward. Perhaps Amy's Uncle Mark would accept a simple report that all appeared to be normal.

Finished with my tasks, I wandered into the kitchen and opened the freezer door. My purchase of low-fat microwave dinners didn't sound appetizing. I wanted pizza. Mom had told me they'd had the place wired for Wi-Fi, but since my computer was still in its case, I reached for the phone book on top of the fridge repressing a smile. It had always been located there.

Before I could touch it, someone knocked on the front door. I hurried to answer, surprised to find the hunk I'd seen at the Forresters. The late afternoon sun glinted off his blond hair sending out shafts of yellow and gold. The awareness that had struck me earlier returned. I drew in a deep breath to steady my nerves.

"Hi, I'm sorry to bother you, but would you happen to have a basin wrench handy?" he asked.

"A what?"

He grinned, his blue eyes crinkling. "I didn't think so."

"What's a basin wrench?" I asked the question looking a long ways up. He stood at least two inches over six feet with a whip lean body.

"I'm replacing the kitchen sink and need to tighten the nut for the faucet. Thought I'd take a chance you might have one. Guess I'll have to make a trip into town. Are you renting for the rest of the summer?"

"No, I'm Jenny Devlin. My parents own the house. I'm just here for a few weeks. Are you one of the Forrester kids from years ago?"

"I'm Brad, the middle son."

I remembered him now. He'd been in college during my mid-teenage years. His mere presence had fueled my girlish imagination the few times he'd appeared at Lake Wildwood.

As I stepped back, I noticed Amy's car was gone from in front of the house. I hadn't heard her leave, and then reminded myself, I wasn't her keeper. I turned my attention to my other neighbor.

"Won't you come in? Can I get you a glass of water or a soda?"

He entered and held out his hands. "I'm a little on

16

the grubby side, but the water sounds great. Mind if I wash up?"

"Not at all," I said, gesturing toward the kitchen sink. His shorts and T-shirt were streaked with dirt.

While he washed, I opened two bottles of water. "Would you like to go out onto the deck?"

"Sounds fine."

He opened the door for me and brushed leaves from the chair before taking a seat at the round bar style table.

"Sorry, I just got here. Haven't had time to clean anything. Do you live at the house permanently or are you just here for the summer?" I asked, mimicking his actions.

"Can't decide. The past twelve years I've been living in Los Angeles. None of my brothers or sisters really wanted the place after Mom died, so I bought it from them. Don't know why. I haven't been here in seven or eight years. The place has kind of gone to seed."

"What do you do in Los Angeles?"

"I'm an author."

Of course, Brad Forrester. How silly of me not to catch it before—and me a literary contract attorney. "The mystery writer?"

"Guilty as charged."

"I love your books. When is the next installment of the Joe Archer series due out?"

He frowned and chugged most of his water. "Soon, I guess."

As an attorney, I found evasiveness intriguing. "So, what brings you here?"

He stared at the label on the bottle. "Oh, I needed

someplace quiet to work."

"Well, Lake Wildwood is certainly a quiet enough spot to write, but why trek two thousand miles for peace and quiet? Didn't any of your friends in California have a cabin or beach house where you could stay? At least, you wouldn't have to fix the place up," I said with a laugh.

He didn't elucidate, but instead raised his eyebrows and shrugged. "Where do you live?"

Okay, he obviously didn't consider it any of my business. Perhaps he didn't like imposing on friends or, given his good looks, maybe he was hiding from some predatory female. I moved on.

"St. Louis. I'm an attorney. Contract law a specialty."

"Ah."

I couldn't tell if that was a good "ah" or a bad one.

His gaze slipped past me toward the Wallace house. "Do the same people live there? Can't remember their name."

"The Wallaces. Only Amy lives there now."

"That's right. They had twins or something, didn't they? Didn't one of them die?"

I kept my answer vague. "Yes. Some kind of accident, I believe."

I found his interest in the Wallace family curious. Or maybe it was my conscience needling me again. Still, there was no need for him to know the circumstances of my presence. He finished his water and slid from the swiveling, high backed stool.

"Thanks for the drink, but I've got to finish that sink if I want to use it." He smiled and hesitated. "Would you be free for dinner tonight? I have no idea what kind of restaurants are in Vermillion, but I'm sure one of them must serve steaks."

The invitation, my second in a little over an hour, surprised me and my mind immediately slipped back to my teenage years. Such a request then would have turned me into a quivering mass. To my annoyance, it did now, too. For an instant, I was flustered. I kept to myself and didn't date much. God only knows what prompted the words to spill out of my mouth.

"I had a long drive today. I'm beat. How about tomorrow night? If you have to go into town for the thingamabob you need, why not pick up a couple of steaks and a bottle of red wine? I have salad makings here. We can fire up the grill and eat on the deck."

He gave me a lazy smile. "Now, that sounds like a good idea. What time?"

"Seven o'clock?"

"Great. See you then."

I followed him to the door and watched him cross the lawn toward his car. He waved as he sped off down the drive. I returned inside. Brad Forrester. Perhaps these next few weeks wouldn't be so dull after all.

Chapter Three

*Diary of Amy Margaret Wallace*

I have a new neighbor. Well, not really new. It's Jenny Devlin. Her family owns the house next door. It'll be nice having a neighbor again even if only for a few weeks. I remember she occasionally babysat for Abby and me. I invited her to lunch tomorrow. Hope she doesn't think I'm being pushy, but I do so long to talk to another woman.

Speaking of Abby, I saw her in town today. I was coming out of Baxter's Drug Store when she drove past in a little red convertible. Not a Miata like ten years ago, but something sleeker, more expensive. I wanted to yell, "Stop," but she zipped by before I had a chance to open my mouth.

I looked up and down the sidewalk. Nobody else seemed to notice. Of course, Vermillion has grown over the years, and many of the old guard no longer lived here. Perhaps, no one recognized her, or thought it was me.

I can't figure out why she doesn't come to the house. Is she angry with me for not having searched harder? Or is this punishment for almost killing her? And why would she return here? I'd always maintained my sister had amnesia. Could part of the veil have lifted allowing her a glimpse of the lake? Had some inner memory led her home to Vermillion, but not yet to me? Where was she staying?

Maybe if I spent more time on the dock, I'd see her in the boat again, and could wave. Or better yet, I'd ask at all the local motels and bed and breakfast places if someone looking like me has checked in. Yes, that's the ticket. I'll find her, hug her, and tell her how much I miss her. We'll talk into the wee hours of the morning, just like when we were teenagers.

I can visualize it. Abby's memory will return. We'll be best friends again, and the past ten years will be erased.

But first, I have to find her.

Chapter Four

I strolled up Amy's walk at noon the next day. A long porch spread across the front of the house. The right half was open to the outdoors with a porch swing and a couple of Adirondack chairs, while the left portion was enclosed. The Wallaces had used it as an overflow sleeping area and a playroom for the kids whenever it rained. Opening the screen door, I entered the protected area. Wicker set the tone. I imagined Amy used it to enjoy the view without benefit of mosquitoes. The official front doors were open to catch the breeze.

I rapped on one and called out, "Hello. Anybody home?"

Amy greeted me with a bright smile. "Jenny! Come on in. The salad's all made, and the Pinot Grigio is chilling in the fridge."

I stepped into the spacious living room. Not much had changed here either, at least not from what I remembered—new paint, new furniture—that was it. The room was a combination living-dining area. The carpeted living room sported a large, fieldstone corner fireplace, while the dining portion was tiled. The vaulted ceiling reached high and the patio doors on either side of the room angled outwards, reminding me of the prow of a ship. The open kitchen lay to the right of the front door with a staircase opposite leading down. I recalled the downstairs had been a large family/rec room with a wet bar and a couple of bedrooms.

My gaze was drawn to a huge painting of Abby and Amy above the fireplace. Its presence startled me. It wasn't hard to tell who was who. Amy was depicted in a sedate light blue blouse. Abby wore a form fitting scarlet sweater. Amy's hair was long, flowing over her shoulders, although at some time since the painting was done she'd had it trimmed to its present length. Abby's was cut in a hip, spiky fashion.

Amy caught my reaction and laughed. "Amazing, isn't it? I commissioned a friend and fellow artist to do it a couple of years ago. Other than the hairstyles, it's like looking in a mirror. Of course he had to work from photos. I gave him my college graduation picture and a snapshot of Abby Mother took that last weekend. I suppose I could have had us looking more like twins, but I wanted to remember Abby as she was when I last saw her."

I thought it must be a macabre reminder of a tragedy, and wondered how she could live with it. On the other hand, maybe its presence indicated Amy had no problem dealing with her sister's death. *Maybe* Mark Bridges was the one on the verge of a breakdown.

"I thought lunch on the deck would be nice," Amy said.

"That sounds lovely. It's not too hot today."

"And the trees give excellent shade." She stopped in the kitchen and opened the fridge where she extracted two large salad bowls. She nodded toward the island bar. "Would you grab the wine and the glasses? The table's already set."

I followed her out onto the deck. From a teak bar in

23

the corner, Amy found a corkscrew, opened the wine, and poured. She raised her glass in a salute.

"To renewing old friendships."

I clinked my glass to hers. "To old friendships."

I found the words odd since the twins and I had never been what I'd consider friends.

"Let's eat before the flies discover the Caesar dressing," she said, taking a sip.

I pulled out a chair and sat, my gaze sweeping over the lake. Years ago, the Wallaces had clear cut many of the trees from the slope toward the water for a better view. In their place, they'd terraced with stones and planted low, spreading evergreens. The evergreens had grown lush and full. Caladiums and impatiens brought a splash of color.

"This is beautiful, Amy. I remember how horrified one of the neighbors was when your father had the trees removed."

"That would have been our neighbor on the other side, Mr. Adams. He claimed we were despoiling the natural look, and that soil erosion would send our house down the hill."

"Obviously, he was wrong. Do you garden or have someone come in to plant?" I picked up my fork and speared a piece of lettuce.

"Oh, I do it. Mother was the gardener in the family. After she died, I kept up the tradition. Those beds look the same as the day she passed. I just don't have the heart to change anything."

Her words disturbed me, as had the painting, but had no idea why. A lot of people hated to let go of the familiar, seeking solace in it.

"So, Jenny, where do you live and what do you do?

Are you a hard-boiled career woman or married with children?"

"I'm divorced, no kids, and a lawyer in St. Louis. I specialize in contract law. Don't know if I'd characterize myself as hard-boiled, but I like what I do. What about you? I seem to remember a sketchpad and a pencil in your hands as a kid."

"I'm an illustrator. Mostly nature books, but occasionally I do children's literature. I'm between jobs at the moment. My last set of drawings went in to the editor a few weeks ago. I'm scheduled to begin a new batch in mid-September. I always try to keep the summer free, but every once in a while find my way into St. Louis for some shopping. How are your folks? Don't you have a couple of brothers, too?"

As we ate, I filled Amy in on my family. When I finished, she asked about my life in St. Louis. For an hour I talked, always at her prompting. I couldn't decide if she had nothing to say, or was truly interested. I finally pushed the salad bowl away and poured another glass of wine.

"I've monopolized the conversation enough. Do you live here year round or just in the summer?"

"I still live in the family home in Webster Groves, but usually spend the summers down here, although occasionally, I do make the drive during the other months. Fall is gorgeous what with the colors and all. Sometimes I get inspiration from it. And even the winter snow has a certain charm. I come when I need the peace and quiet to finish my drawings."

"I can see you now, sketching away with a fire snapping in the fireplace and the snow drifting down, a mug of hot chocolate in your hand."

Amy laughed. "I've been known to do that."

"Maybe we can get together in the city this fall. I know a terrific Irish pub. It's near downtown. Halloween is a big deal. Everybody, including the band, goes the costume route."

Her smile turned wistful. "That sounds like fun. I don't go out much. I always feel self-conscious in bars. That was more Abby's thing."

"Yes, I remember her as being the live wire. You were always more sedate." The mention of her sister's name made me uneasy, but since she brought it up I decided to probe. "She's been gone, what, ten or eleven years now, hasn't she?"

She cast her eyes down and nodded her head in jerky movements. "Yes, ten years. Funny, it doesn't seem that long. She'd come home to surprise us for the July Fourth holiday. It's amazing how much I still miss her."

Amy rose and gathered the bowls cutting off further conversation. I helped her clear up and finished my wine. If Mark Bridges thought his niece would confide in me about the Abby sightings, he was in for disappointment. I still had no clear idea of what I was supposed to do.

*Excuse me, Amy, seen Abby lately?*

She didn't appear unbalanced or delusional nor did I get the impression she was a recluse. Whatever Mark Bridges had handed me was not as explained in St. Louis. It was crap. I suspected there was more to this.

I thanked Amy for the lunch and suggested going into Vermillion in the next couple of days. This time lunch would be my treat.

"I'd like that. I'll get back to you," she replied.

I took my leave and returned home. A few minutes later while staring out the sliding glass doors to the deck, I saw Amy, sketchbook in hand walk down the steps to the dock. The view from my deck wasn't as good as from hers and I lost her in the foliage halfway down. Through a gap in the trees, I watched as motorboats zipped by on the water, many towing skiers.

A sudden memory surfaced of the Wallace family in their twenty-five-foot Sea-Ray. I'd been sunbathing on our dock and laughed as Abby had sent a huge spray of water toward me with her slalom ski. Later, Amy had passed by on two skis, hunched over, clinging to the tow rope with a death grip, and making no attempt to jump the wake into smoother water.

But then that was how I remembered the twins. Abby took chances. Amy didn't.

Earlier Amy had referred to renewing old friendships. I hoped she meant it. I found myself liking her, and if she had problems, wanting to help her chase the demons away.

****

I chose my clothing for dinner with Brad carefully. I wanted to look attractive, but not over-eager, finally settling on pair of black denim crop pants with a deep turquoise tank top. The color matched my eyes, and the mirror told me I looked great. Understated, but great.

Brad arrived at seven on the dot complete with two grocery bags.

"Hi. You look terrific. Redheads should always wear flamboyant colors."

Flamboyant? Had I gone overboard? "Uh, thanks."

I checked out his jeans and light blue polo shirt. Both were tight in all the right places. I peeked into the bag. He'd chosen steakhouse cut T-bones and included a bag of frozen French fries.

"Don't know about you, but I need my carbohydrates," he said with a killer smile.

I had to laugh. "From the look of things, I'd say you also have a yen for protein."

He laughed with me and placed bottles of vodka and vermouth on the kitchen counter along with two martini glasses and a cocktail shaker.

"Hope you don't mind, but I love a martini before dinner."

I hated martinis, but agreed to one now. He opened the bottle of Cabernet Sauvignon to breathe, and then mixed the cocktails.

"Now, where is your grill? I'll light the fire," he said, handing me a glass.

"I don't even know what kind of grill is out there, or if I have the proper things to start a fire. Should have thought to have you bring that, too."

We walked onto the deck and he uncovered an old Weber charcoal grill hiding in the corner. Lifting the cover of a deck box alongside, he pulled out half a bag of charcoal and some lighter fluid. I assumed Mom and Dad had grilled last spring.

"Hope the weather hasn't gotten to it," I commented, taking a sip of my drink. It tasted good—for a martini.

"We'll soon find out." Within minutes, a fire blazed. He grinned. "Excellent." He lifted his glass, touching it with mine. "Here's to neighbors."

"To neighbors."

Even though the light was still strong, I lit the candle on the table. I'd set it earlier and now slid onto one of the stools.

"So, tell me about Los Angeles. Am I having dinner with a married man?"

That thought had occurred to me this afternoon as I'd sat on the deck reading. A married man had cost me my marriage six years ago.

"Not any more. I've got two ex-wives floating around. One in Los Angeles and the other in Dallas. Only one still has me on the alimony hook."

"Sounds intense."

He shrugged. "I was a lousy husband. When I write, I tend to withdraw, sometimes not coming out of my office for days. They got bored. Not that I blame them. I don't do the social scene at all any more. Been there, did that when I was first published. Cocktail parties are a pain in the ass and I hate all the artificial good humor that accompanies them. I'm still friends with both exes."

"How long since you got divorced the second time?"

"Three years. What about you? Am I having dinner with a married woman?"

I sipped more of my martini. "No. I went the divorce route six years ago."

"Still friends?"

"Not even close."

"Oops. Sorry I asked."

"Me, too." I didn't want him to know what a total idiot I'd been. A change of subject sounded like a good move. "I can't remember. How many brothers and sisters do you have?"

He brought me up to date on his family, and while he grilled the steaks, I made the French fries and pulled the pre-made salad from the fridge.

The smell of meat on the grill made my mouth water and the hissing of juices hitting the coals sent a cloud of aromatic smoke skyward.

"So, tell me, where do you get ideas for your books?" I asked as he eased a steak from the grill to my plate.

He set it in front of me before doing the same for himself, and then poured the wine. "Here and there. Sometimes the inspiration comes straight out of the news."

I filled the salad bowls. "You mean you base your stories on real happenings?" I cut into the steak. Ah, medium rare—just the way I liked it—and popped a piece into my mouth.

"I might use the facts and twist the story a bit. How's your steak?"

"Fantastic. Perfectly done and delicious. You're quite domesticated."

He grinned and bit into a fry. "You don't do a bad job with French fries either."

"What's to screw up? Turn on the oven and bake for fifteen or twenty minutes." I sampled one, too. Not bad at all. "Do you also use people you know as characters?"

"All the time. I was recently at a conference of mystery writers where they auctioned off the privilege of having their names used in one of my books."

"You're kidding. People paid you to use their names?" Sounded odd to me, not to mention expensive.

"Three people paid five hundred bucks each to be mentioned once."

"How do you mention someone only once in

passing?" I don't know why, but this concept fascinated me.

Brad chuckled. "I used one guy's name on a street sign—So-and-so Lane. If nothing else, it guarantees they and all their relatives will buy the book just to see it." He sipped from his wine glass. "So, you're a lawyer. You said something about contracts."

During the rest of the meal, I tried to make contract law sound as interesting as writing novels. I probably didn't succeed, but he listened anyway. When we'd eaten the last morsel of meat and the final fry, he helped with the clean up—another point in his favor.

All in all, it was a pleasant evening that ended much too soon at ten o'clock. I walked him to the door where he turned and smiled.

"Thanks for hosting."

"Thanks for the steaks."

"Next time, my place."

"All right. I'm assuming you got the sink fixed."

"The sink is in perfect working order. I have things to do this weekend, but how about Monday or Tuesday?"

I hesitated. Mark Bridges was due on Sunday, and I had no idea what his agenda was regarding Amy.

"I'll let you know. I have a few things to do, too."

He nodded, leaned down, and kissed my cheek. "Thanks for dinner. See you soon."

He trotted down the steps and walked across the yard whistling off key.

I closed the door and decided Mark Bridges' agenda could take a back seat. I hadn't noticed anything radically wrong with Amy Wallace. Besides, I wanted to see a lot more of Brad Forrester.

Chapter Five

*Diary of Amy Margaret Wallace*

After hosting lunch with Jenny, I sketched by the dock for a while, and then drove into town determined to find Abby. She had to be staying somewhere. I eliminated the motels in town. The people running them had been there for years and knew us. If Abby had stayed with them, the whole town would know.

Instead, I checked out the newer B & Bs nearer the lake. While such places were more my style, for whatever reason, Abby could have chosen to stay in one of these converted older homes.

I drove home disheartened. I honestly thought I'd find my sister. But to every desk clerk I asked, "Do you have anybody who looks like me staying here?" the answer was no. I probably sounded crazy.

Could she be staying in a private home? A lot of people rented their houses during the summer. Maybe I was tackling this from the wrong angle. Why not try to trace the little red runabout I'd seen her in, or the sports car? Knowing Abby, she had to have at least one speeding ticket in the county. And unless she'd been stopped by a veteran of the sheriff's department, a new officer wouldn't recognize her, and the name Wallace wasn't unusual.

Yes, that sounded like a good idea. Tomorrow, I'd

check out the marinas and keep my eyes open for a little red sports car.

## Chapter Six

I awoke the next morning at the ungodly hour of five-thirty to the sound of reverberating thunder and rain hammering on the roof. The wind billowed the curtains at the open window, and I leapt from the bed to close it before the water did damage to the hardwood floor, then hurried to the kitchen to shut that window, too. Somewhere outside, a loose shutter banged. A quick inspection of the rest of the house satisfied me the noise emanated from the Wallaces'.

I dared opening the deck door a ways to peek outside. Through the slanting rain, I caught only a glimpse of my neighbor's back deck. Several lilac bushes planted years ago by Constance Wallace had grown, further obscuring the view. The banging noise continued.

Lightning flashed, illuminating the yards long enough for me to see the figure on Amy's deck peering in the window. Startled, I drew back. Who the hell would be out in a storm? Crime, while not unheard of in Vermillion, was also not rampant. People tended to leave their houses unlocked when in residence. Even boat keys were often stored in dock boxes.

With my heart beating faster than usual I reached for my cell phone on the counter with shaky hand. I peered out again. The rain had lessened and my view was clearer. The figure was gone. A moment later, the

Wallace kitchen light flashed on. The errant shutter no longer banged. Of course, how silly of me. I'd seen Amy fixing the problem.

With no hope of sleeping further, I made coffee, and flipped on the small TV on the baker's rack in the corner. A severe thunderstorm warning had been issued for Vermillion and Post Counties. That's what had passed over me. Already, the rain had reduced itself to a soft patter and the thunder and lightning had moved toward the northeast.

I poured a cup of coffee, sat at the kitchen table, and set up my laptop. It occurred to me that keeping a diary of daily activities sounded like a good idea. I spent the next couple of hours chronicling the events and conversations from when I first met Mark Bridges to my last discussion with Amy at lunch yesterday. As I worked it dawned on me that I liked Amy as much as I disliked her uncle.

I also Googled the Wallace family, but information was scarce. I then tried to find something on the accident, but came up with zilch. After ten years, the incident was no longer newsworthy.

By ten o'clock, the storm was a thing of the past. Sun broke through the clouds promising a good day. I decided to drive into town to see what had changed over the years.

As I walked to my car, a movement from the Wallace front porch caught my eye. Amy sat in one of the Adirondack chairs, staring out over the lawn toward the rolling hills. She glanced toward me. I waved.

"Hi, I'm going into town. Would you like to come along? We can have lunch at Victoria's Tea Room—if it's still there."

Amy laughed. "It's there. So is Victoria, and I'd love to come. I haven't been there in ages. Let me change into something more appropriate."

She rose and went inside while I inspected the lawn and trees for storm damage. Other than a few broken stems on some bushes and a couple of displaced twigs, the wind and rain hadn't wreaked havoc with Mom's landscaping.

Then I saw it—a footprint in the flowerbed. The tread was clearly visible in the mud oozing through the thinning mulch and looked to have been made by a work boot. The print was just under one of the living room windows, and I wondered now if the figure I'd seen during the storm was responsible. I drew back in alarm and inspected the rest of the landscaping. No other footprints appeared. *Perhaps it wasn't Amy on the deck peering in the window after all. Is there a prowler on the loose? Or a Peeping Tom?*

Uneasy, I walked back to the driveway and gazed toward Brad's. The house was closed and his car gone. I'd ask if he'd seen or heard anything unusual when I next saw him.

Amy, wearing navy blue slacks, a light blue v-necked top, and white sneakers, crossed the yards to join me. In the car, I maneuvered around the potholes again trying not to create a shower of muddy water. I hesitated telling her about my find, but at the same time needed to know if she'd been outside on her deck.

"That was some storm this morning."

"It sure was. Woke me out of a sound sleep."

"What was the banging noise?" I asked, turning onto the road into town.

"I'd left the back door open a bit for air. The wind

caught the screened door. Guess I hadn't latched it well enough."

"Hope you didn't get too wet closing it."

"Why would I get wet? I simply reached out and closed it."

I shifted my gaze from the road to look at her. She stared straight ahead, a slight smile on her lips.

"I thought I saw you on the deck."

Now, she whipped her head toward me, her eyes wide. "Me? Good heavens, no. I'm scared to death of storms. I would never be outside during one."

That answered my question. "How odd. I was sure I saw someone."

"In that rain? You probably saw the table umbrella." She caught her lower lip between her teeth and transferred her gaze back through the windshield.

I didn't answer, but drove on into town. I knew I hadn't seen any damned umbrella. It must have been a prowler. But who would be skulking around on a stormy night?

****

"When you said Victoria's Tea Room hadn't changed, I didn't know you meant it literally," I said after we'd been seated near the large bay window in the front.

Amy laughed. "There are some things about Vermillion that will always be the same."

"The traffic sure is different. Can't believe I had to pay to park."

My gaze traveled to the street thirty feet beyond the window. I'd been forced to park in a lot two blocks away. Being Saturday, shoppers strolled up and down the sidewalk, and the automobiles alternated between congestion due to stop lights and clear intervals with little activity.

"Weekends have been a pain ever since they opened up the east end of the lake for development. Houses sprang up like mushrooms."

"I suppose that had to happen sooner or later."

"It's a doubled-edged sword," she said with a sigh. "More money for the town, but more cars and people clogging the roads and sidewalks."

A waitress stopped by the table. Both of us ordered a glass of Pinot Grigio.

"By the way, I met my neighbor on the other side, Brad Forrester, yesterday," I commented when the woman had left.

"Is that who's there? I should go over and say hello. Mrs. Forrester died some time ago, and nobody kept the property up. I guess someone provided lawn mowing services, but the house took a beating. Glad to see he's back."

"I remember him from when I was a teenager. I didn't see him often, but when I did…" I placed my hand over my heart and sighed.

Amy laughed. "You sound just like Abby. She thought he was a hunk, too."

"Good grief, how old was she?"

"Eleven, I guess, maybe twelve. She was always wise beyond her years when it came to boys. I, on the other hand, am a stammering idiot around men. Guess that's why I'm an old maid."

"I'd hardly classify you as that. You're still young. And I am a firm believer that we all have a soul mate out there."

Our wine arrived and we ordered lunch, a turkey

wrap for Amy, while I indulged my craving for seafood with the Shrimp Newberg in puff pastry.

"Thank you, ladies. Your order will be out in a few minutes," the waitress said, gathering the menus before heading back to the kitchen.

We both sipped our wine and stared out at the crowded sidewalk. A man walked past, a bag marked with the logo, Bridges Sporting Goods clutched in his hand.

Bridges Sporting Goods? As in Mark Bridges? He didn't mention anything about owning property in the area when we met.

"What are you looking at?" Amy asked.

"Oh, nothing in particular."

"You suddenly frowned."

"I was just looking at the people and the shopping bags. I don't recall a Bridges Sporting Goods in town."

"It belonged to my Uncle Mark. Mom's brother. He opened it when the development began. Made good money, too, from what he told me. He sold it a couple of years ago. Said he was getting too old to be a shopkeeper. Did you ever meet my uncle?"

Lowering my gaze, I fiddled with the silverware. "Can't say that I did."

I didn't like lying to her—made me feel guilty—and for the life of me, couldn't figure out why I was here. Once again the thought flitted through my mind that Amy appeared normal. If she was delusional, I didn't see it.

"He's coming down tomorrow. I'll introduce you."

"How nice. Does he come here often?"

"No, not really. Hasn't been here since he sold the store. I see more of him in St. Louis. He's in charge of

Suzanne Rossi

my trust and is my investment counselor. Why don't you come over for a cocktail tomorrow night?"

"Sure, why not?" I wanted to shelve the discussion about Mark Bridges. No need for me to make a mistake and let it slip I'd met him. "Tell me more about your work. How on earth do you get a bird or an animal to pose for you?"

Amy sipped more wine and smiled, then launched into an explanation involving cameras and how fast-speed film was becoming a thing of the past. Digital was the way to go. I let my mind wander back to Brad Forrester and our dinner last night. A warm glow spread from the pit of my stomach as I remembered his lips on my cheek.

*Maybe I'll invite him over for Sunday brunch. At least I'd have a reason to talk to him again.*

Amy's voice brought me back into the present.

"I guess I'll get used to digital. It has its good points, but I hate change."

Our lunch arrived saving me from making a comment since I had no idea what she was talking about. The puff pastry steamed and I inhaled the delicious aroma of the sherry in the Newberg sauce.

Amy smiled as she unwrapped the silverware from her napkin, and glanced out of the window.

The utensils fell to her plate with a clatter. Her eyes opened wide and her hand fisted against her chest. She emitted a soft gasp.

"Amy? What is it?"

"I…what? Oh, it's nothing…I just…I mean…Will you excuse me for a minute?" She slapped her napkin on the table and rose, bolting from the room.

I twisted in my chair and leaned toward the

window. Amy burst through the doors of Victoria's and scampered down the porch steps. She turned away from me with her hand lifted as though trying to attract the attention of someone. I assumed she also called out, but people on the sidewalk didn't acknowledge her.

Then she halted, her hand dropping to her side and her shoulders slumping. She turned and walked slowly back the way she'd come, disappointment on her face.

I peered harder through the glass toward the stop light a block and a half away. It glowed yellow and my gaze was drawn to the red sports car zipping around the corner as the light changed.

"Are you all right?" I asked when Amy resumed her seat a minute later.

She blinked tears from her eyes, but smiled. "I'm fine. I just thought I saw someone I knew a long time ago drive by. Guess I was wrong."

While I broke the crust on the puff pastry, Amy picked up her turkey wrap and nibbled. Her hands trembled, and she kept glancing out the window as if hoping whomever she'd seen would reappear. The whole incident seemed out of character for such a quiet reserved woman. Her facial expressions flashed between fearful, anticipating, and frustrated.

Was this the kind of behavior Mark Bridges found so disturbing? *Maybe it's not who she saw, but who she thought she saw.*

"I envy you living here in the summer. I'm stuck in St. Louis with the heat and humidity."

Amy gulped her wine and signaled for more from the waitress. "It's a change."

Her short, almost curt reply made me blink with surprise. She had just stated she hated change. I wasn't a lawyer for nothing. I pressed the conversation.

"Webster Groves—such a lovely town. I love those old houses. Is yours old?"

She frowned and set her wrap on the plate. "What? Oh, yes, it's quite old. Built in 1920 or so."

"Upkeep must be a challenge, although I suppose you've renovated."

"My parents did. I don't see any reason to change. I like it the way it is."

Another contradiction. Her gaze darted constantly to the sidewalk and street outside.

"I love the old houses. So much character. I live in the Soulard area. The people I bought the house from did most of the renovations." I forced a laugh. "It's narrow, only about thirty feet wide, but has three stories and a great back yard." I was talking to myself. She wasn't paying attention.

The waitress brought her second glass of wine, and turned to me. "May I get you another, ma'am?"

"No, thank you. Why don't you bring the check?"

Amy snapped her head back from the window. "Oh, Jenny, I'm sorry. I didn't mean to tune you out, but I could have sworn I saw…" she hesitated "…an old high school friend."

*Named Abby?* "That's all right."

"What was it you were saying?"

I waved a dismissive hand. "Nothing important."

We finished our meal. Amy watched out the window. I watched Amy. She was distracted, but not as upset and shaky as earlier.

I paid for the lunch and drove home. Amy practically leaped out of my car before I turned off the key.

"Thanks, Jenny. It was fun. I'll be in touch."

She turned and ran toward her house. I was still on the porch when she peeled out of her driveway, turning toward town. She was obviously going back to search for whomever she thought she'd seen.

I glanced at Brad's. His car was parked off to the side. On impulse, I walked over and mounted the refurbished steps. A pair of muddy work boots stood next to the door along with a shovel and a tool belt. The footprint from this morning flashed through my mind.

*Brad? Oh, don't be silly. Why would Brad Forrester peek in anybody's window?*

On the other hand, I didn't really know the guy.

He answered my knock within seconds. "Hi, neighbor, what's up?" he asked, motioning me inside.

I hesitated before accepting the invitation, and then deciding I was being overly suspicious, walked in. After all, he was doing work on the premises.

"Not much. That was some storm this morning."

"Never heard a thing. Guess all the physical activity along with a great meal was better than a sleeping pill. Have you had lunch?"

"Yes, thank you." I perched on a stool at the breakfast bar, wondering how to approach the subject of Amy. "Amy Wallace and I went into town for a bite at Victoria's Tea Room."

"You're kidding? I can't believe it's still around. My mother loved it. She and her summer friends held court there every Wednesday at noon. My father used to call it the Wednesday Luncheon and Gossip Society."

I laughed. I recalled the Forresters had attended a few of Mom and Dad's get-togethers along with the Wallaces.

"Do you remember the twins?"

He poured two glasses of iced tea, setting one in front of me.

"Not much. Why?"

"Oh, no reason. I always thought Abby's death was so tragic, especially for Amy."

His brow furrowed. "Didn't she die in an automobile accident?"

"Boating. Amy was at the helm."

"Yeah, I kind of remember. Stole a neighbor's boat, didn't they? And then there was an explosion and the sister died."

"The boat belonged to the Howards."

"Seems odd that it would explode like that."

"According to Mr. Howard, the gas tanks were full."

"I'm surprised Amy would be part of a boat heist," he commented taking a long drink of tea.

I did the same. My throat was suddenly parched.

"Joy ride is a better term from what I understand."

"It's still stealing."

In spite of what Amy had told me earlier, I wondered if he'd had a chance to talk with her. "How long have you been here?"

"A couple of weeks. Why?"

"Have you talked to Amy?"

"I've seen her a couple of times, but that's all." He set his glass on the countertop and stared.

"So you haven't been in the house?"

"No. Jenny, what's this all about?"

I took another drink and sucked on an ice cube. I had no intention of telling him about Mark Bridges's fears that Amy was having a breakdown.

"I was inside yesterday. There's this huge portrait over the fireplace of Abby and Amy. She told me she'd had it done from a picture taken just before the accident. Creeped me out."

Brad shrugged and finished his tea. "Why should it? It's just a portrait. A tribute to her sister. Now if she had the walls papered with photos of Abby, then you could be creeped out."

I sighed. "I guess so, but it was such a large picture and so life-like. I had to comment on it, but at the same time felt funny talking about someone who died violently."

"Did Amy talk about her sister?"

"Sure. Very naturally, too."

"Then why worry?"

"I guess you're right. Just because I was uncomfortable, doesn't mean she is."

I set my glass on the counter next to his not willing to bring up Amy's mad dash out of the restaurant. Besides, for all I knew, she *had* seen an old friend. Still, the whole thing was so odd.

"I'd better be going. I have a couple of things to do. Would you like to come over for brunch tomorrow?"

"I thought it was my turn to host," he said with a smile.

"Ah, but I make killer French toast."

"Sold. What time?"

"Ten-thirty all right?"

"See you at ten-thirty."

He walked me to the door and as I left, I commented on the muddy boots and shovel.

"Looks like you've had a busy morning."

"Yeah, I started to repair the tie wall out back, but it was too muddy. It'll have to wait for another day."

Okay, work boots explained. But the footprint wasn't.

At home, I added Amy's odd behavior at Victoria's to my electronic journal, the storm, the possible prowler, and the footprint under my living room window along with my discussion with Brad. I had a feeling I'd need to reference this diary often.

When finished, I drove to the grocery store. Amy's car was still gone, and I wondered how long she'd search. Maybe I should have followed her discreetly. Then I shook my head. That wasn't part of the job description. All Bridges wanted me to do was talk to her. I pushed the absent Amy from my mind. Besides, if French toast was on the menu for tomorrow, I needed to buy French bread.

Amy's car was in the drive when I returned, but Brad's was gone. Too bad. The evening stretched in front of me. I didn't look forward to being alone. I'd had six years of long, boring evenings. It was time to shake off the guilt and rejoin the world of men again. Brad Forrester wasn't a bad choice. In fact, he was damned good.

Chapter Seven

*Diary of Amy Margaret Wallace*

I saw Abby again today. I was having lunch at Victoria's with Jenny when a little red convertible, Abby at the wheel, drove by. I tried to follow and get her attention, but by the time I made it out the door, she was almost a block away. I waved and called, but she didn't hear me over the traffic noise or the growl of the engine. I did note, however, that she was in the left turn lane heading south onto Elm Street.

I wanted to tell Jenny about Abby, but decided against it. She'd think me odd or delusional. Even Uncle Mark had suggested I was imagining things. I know I'm not. I suppose that's why he's coming down tomorrow—to check on me and make sure I haven't made up her old room just in case she knocks on the door.

I returned to town cruising Elm Street and the surrounding area. Some of the townies rented rooms on a weekly basis. Perhaps she was staying in one of them. I searched for over two hours, but found no sign of the red sports car.

I'm dejected and depressed. Why won't Abby talk to me?

I have to find her.

I have to tell her how sorry I am for everything and

how much I miss her. I've been lonely for too long.
Abby, come home.

Chapter Eight

Since Brad didn't have an aversion to protein, I slapped a full pound of bacon into the pan, and then assembled the makings for French toast. I'd set the inside table instead of the one on the deck. Summer heat and humidity had caught up with Lake Wildwood. The air conditioner hummed.

A knock on the door followed by its opening, told me my guest has arrived.

"Good morning," Brad said.

"Good morning yourself. Ready for a brunch to die for?"

"Sure am." He strolled to the breakfast bar and sat on a stool. "Why is it we always meet over food?"

I laughed. "I have no idea, but food is a great socializing tool. The downside is I tend to gain weight."

He craned his neck for a better view and eyed my figure. "I don't see any love handles or bulges anywhere except where they should be."

A flush of warmth radiated from my stomach to my fingers and toes. He liked what he saw. I was both exhilarated and scared. I swallowed and tried to keep the conversation light.

"I'm a perfect size eight and have been for years. Does that mean I don't have a social life?"

"My waistband's been at thirty-four forever. Guess we're both in the same boat." He made a motion toward the stove with his chin. "Anything I can do to help?"

"Not really. Pour yourself a cup of coffee and relax. What did you do last night?"

He picked up a mug from the countertop and reached for the coffee pot at the end of the bar. "Hunkered down with some discipline and wrote a scene in my newest work in progress."

"How thrilling. Is it another Joe Archer story? What's it about?"

Brad filled me in on the basic plot while I turned the bacon and readied the ingredients. Once the bacon was out of the pan, I slid the egg and spice soaked bread in. The aromas of bacon, fresh coffee, and the toast blended into a delicious scent that set my stomach to grumbling. Not a bad way to start the day.

Brad wasn't a bad start either. His blond hair was still damp from a shower and this morning he wore a pair of khaki shorts with a rich plum-colored, form-fitting T-shirt. Only a man firmly secure in his own masculinity would wear that color. I found him incredibly attractive and oozing sex appeal. It had been a long time since I'd noticed—six years to be exact. Once again I found my interest disconcerting.

"Orange juice?" I asked, moving to the fridge.

"Thanks."

"Brunch is almost ready. Have a seat at the table."

I poured his juice, and then filled a plate. As I served, another aroma assaulted my senses. He smelled of something fresh and outdoorsy with a hint of citrus. I had the most absurd urge to bury my nose in his hair or neck.

Luckily, I refrained, filled my plate, and sat opposite him. He added syrup on his toast, cut several pieces and ate. I didn't do anything silly like holding my breath. I knew he'd like it. My French toast was dynamite.

He rolled his eyes in confirmation. "Damn, this is wonderful. Where'd you learn how to make this?"

"Believe it or not, my ex-mother-in-law. She was a fabulous cook. Before my divorce, she shared a lot of her recipes. If I'm around long enough, I'll make lasagna for you."

"Lady, you got a deal."

We ate in silence for a few moments. The kitchen aromas lived up to expectations in taste. I cleaned my plate as did Brad, then rose to fill both with a second helping.

"What's on your agenda for today?" he asked as I poured him another cup of coffee.

"I hadn't really thought about it." Mark Bridges was due sometime, but I had no idea of when and refused to set my schedule to his.

"When I first arrived I had the family boat towed to the marina across the lake for repairs. Years of being on a lift and no maintenance took its toll. They called yesterday to say it was ready. Care to drive over with me and get it? I need someone to drive the car back. Afterward, we can tour the lake."

"Sounds like fun. When do you want to go?"

"Any time is fine. I have some errands to run, but they aren't important."

I shrugged. "The sooner the better. Clean up here won't take but a minute or two."

I put the dishes and silverware into the dishwasher while Brad took over the sink to wash and dry the pans. I gave the countertop one final swipe with a disinfectant wipe.

"Give me a minute and I'll be ready," I said just as someone knocked on the front door.

I hurried to the living room and opened the door to find Amy staring back at me, a smile on her face. The tense, frantic look of yesterday was gone. I motioned her inside.

She entered and sniffed. "Smells good in here. All cinnamon and nutmeg."

I laughed. "French toast. What's up?"

Brad strolled in from the kitchen.

Amy looked at him with a surprised expression. "Oh, I'm sorry. I didn't know you had company."

"No problem. This is Brad Forrester. Do you remember him? He and his family lived on the other side of us. Brad, this is Amy Wallace."

Brad stepped forward, his hand outstretched. Amy took it and smiled. "Of course I remember you. Are you staying long?"

"Through the summer, I think. I needed some peace and quiet."

"Oh, that's right. You're an author. I've read your books. Very thrilling."

"Thank you."

I couldn't tell if she was sincere or merely being polite.

Amy turned to me. "My uncle is due to arrive this afternoon. Would the two of you like to come over for cocktails later?"

So, this was how Mark intended to meet me—a neighborly get together over drinks.

"I'd love to. How about you, Brad?" I answered, sending him a glance.

Brad nodded and smiled at Amy. "Same here. Thanks for inviting me."

"Wonderful. Uncle Mark hasn't been to Lake Wildwood since he sold the business. I think he's looking forward to meeting his old friends and making new ones. I was just on my way into town when I thought I'd drop by here."

"What time do the festivities begin?" I asked.

"Five-thirty? A few drinks and some canapés is all I'm serving. I'm too nervous to do much more."

"Is your uncle staying with you?" Brad said.

"No. This is a bit inconvenient for him. He likes to slip out to restaurants and such whenever he wants without benefit of having to drive." She glanced at her watch. "I'd better be going. I'll see you tonight."

Brad's gaze followed her down the porch steps. "So, that's Amy Wallace. I remember her now. She was the quiet one, right?"

"Yes. Abby was the live wire. Let me get my purse, lock up the house, and I'm ready to go."

"Lock the house?" Brad's voice held a questioning tone.

I didn't know why I said it. The footprint under my living room window and the figure I thought I'd seen on Amy's deck flashed through my mind again. An uneasiness I'd never associated with the area once again crept up my spine.

I laughed to cover my confusion. "Guess I can't get city living out of my mind. An unlocked door in St. Louis is an invitation to thieves."

Brad smiled. "Probably isn't a bad idea down here either. I haven't heard of any crime around the lake or even in Vermillion, but why take a chance?" He cast a glance toward his place. "Think I'll do the same."

I locked up, wandered across the lawn, and settled into the passenger seat of his black Infinity while he secured his house.

"What does Amy do? Does she live here year round?" he asked, turning out of the drive and onto the road.

"She illustrates books and lives here in the summer."

"And you do literary contracts? This must be your lucky vacation. Both neighbors are in the literary business. Couldn't have done that any better if it was planned."

I shifted in my seat, not liking the tone. It held a hint of suspicion and a dart of guilt speared me. I *was* here to promote business for myself—or at least, the firm. Mark Bridges had all but promised Grayson oversight of the Wallace family trust, and me Amy's contract.

"Oh, I'm sure neither Amy nor you needs my services. I'm just a little peon in a large law firm. They keep me busy. I don't need to drum up business."

"Sorry, didn't mean to insinuate you were."

Feeling guilty as hell, I changed the subject. "So you live in Los Angeles. Where exactly?"

"I have a condo not far from the beach in Venice."

"Do you like it?"

"It's not bad, but expensive. I like the two bedroom, two bath concept. I'm considering selling and moving to a quieter community with cheaper housing. I think I told you one of my ex-wives is still sucking alimony from me."

"With two exes in the picture, I'm surprised you

aren't living in a cardboard box, especially in Southern California."

He grinned. "I had the good fortune to buy the condo before I married wife number one. I never got around to putting her name on the deed. Pissed her off. She really wanted that condo."

"Is she the one still damaging your bank account?"

"Yep. Wife number two remarried six months ago."

"Seems a shame to sell."

"The settlements were brutal. I can turn a nice profit, even in this economy. I need to replenish the coffers."

"Yet you're still on friendly terms with wife number one you said?"

He shrugged. "Never burn your bridges."

Luckily, my divorce, while bitter and angry, didn't involve much in the line of money. I walked with what I brought to the marriage, which was almost nothing.

"What about the lake house?"

"I spent what little was left to buy out my brothers when Mom died. I thought about moving here permanently, but I'm not sure I can take the isolation in the winter."

"And it still costs money even if you winterize it."

"If I sell this and the condo, I could buy a nice place in Glendale or even Pasadena. I haven't thought much about it. I have a business deal that's due to close soon. I'll think about it then."

I had no idea what real estate was selling for in either Los Angeles or here in Central Missouri, but surmised the combined total would be a welcome addition to his check book. *Everybody's hard up these days.*

"What kind of boat do you have?"

"It's a 25-foot Winn. The cockpit was covered, but several years of winters and summer sun really faded the paint. Plus a few storms had damaged the gelcoat and fiberglass. Flying debris from the wind, I guess. I had the marina do repairs and a new paint job."

Brad parked at the marina and was greeted by a man in grease stained jeans and a T-shirt.

"Mr. Forrester, good to see you. Boat's all ready."

I waited in front of the office gazing at the marina while Brad settled the bill. The business had expanded over the years. A small marina type restaurant and bar was still next door, but now the area around it was solid dock space. A sign on the one of the pilings read, *Rentals, Inquire Within.*

Brad and the man emerged. "Thanks a lot, Brad."

"No, thank you. How's business?"

"Not bad considering." He walked over to a lock box attached to the wall, opened it, and removed a set of keys.

"You're in slip number fifteen," he said handing them over.

Brad thanked the man again, and I followed him through a gate in a chain link fence. A wide seawall stretched along the lake edge. Individual floating docks accommodating eight boats per side teed off of it. Narrow walkways allowed access to each boat. Slip number fifteen was on the end.

I paused to admire the spiffy boat. Elegant navy blue and white paint gave the hull a jaunty look and the white vinyl upholstery gleamed brilliant under the blazing sun.

"What a pretty boat," I said as he handed me the car keys and jumped into it.

"I always liked it. Good for skiing and just motoring around."

Brad took the helm and inserted the key. The engine turned over immediately.

"Sam Watson is a mechanical genius," Brad declared with a grin. "She had to be towed in. Engine was a complete mess."

I cast off fore and aft. Putting the boat in gear, he slowly backed out of the space. Sharing the boat slip was a green sailboat, its sails furled, but not covered. With a good two feet between them, he had no problem clearing it.

"I want to take it out for a little trial. I'll meet you back at the house and we'll take a ride."

"No problem." I waved as he shifted the throttle forward and moved out of the marina.

I walked back down the seawall admiring the boats as I passed. A dark-haired man with a woman had just cast off. She wore a scarlet bikini that matched the boat's color and left little to the imagination. An enormous white hat with a wide, floppy brim protected her head. A pair of huge sunglasses covered half her face. I only had a momentary glance before she turned away, but stopped to look again shielding my eyes from the glare off the water. The man had maneuvered the boat and all I saw from seventy feet away were their backs. He jammed the gearshift forward and roared away, the woman laughing as she held the hat in place with both hands.

I walked slowly back to the car. The woman had looked vaguely familiar, but I didn't know why. I hadn't seen enough of her face to come to that conclusion. Oddly enough, I had the feeling I'd also seen the man. I just couldn't put my finger on it.

*Oh well, maybe they were in the grocery store the other day, or having lunch at Victoria's. And what does it matter anyway?* I started the car and drove home.

I parked and made my way down to the dock, the woman and her companion gone from my mind. I kicked off my sandals, sat in the shade of an oak tree, and dangled my feet in the lukewarm water. Off in the distance, a sailboat bobbed along hugging the far shore. Other boats zipped past towing skiers and tubers. I laughed as one participant hit the wake and flew through the air, the tube, now free of human cargo, bouncing behind the boat as if pleased with itself.

I peeked at my watch. Brad had left the marina over thirty minutes ago. *What kind of trial is he conducting? Did he have trouble?*

My questions were answered a few minutes later when the blue and white hull approached. Brad expertly sidled the boat up to the dock.

"Everything go all right?" I asked.

"Like it was brand new. Ready for that lake tour?"

I rose, tossed my sandals into the cockpit, and prepared to board. Brad held her steady while I made the transition from solid dock to bouncing boat with ease.

Some memories never die and I automatically took a wide stance to counteract the rocking motion. I waited for the boat to settle down before sitting in the left hand seat. Brad pushed away from the piling and we drifted out a few feet. Then he shoved the gear lever forward.

The sudden burst of speed pinned me to the back of

the seat. The wind ripped through my hair. Just like the woman in the red boat, I couldn't contain the laugh that burst from my throat.

Brad slowed and drove along the shoreline. Things had changed over the years I'd been away. Fishing cabins had been torn down and replaced with palatial homes, the windows and decks overlooking the water. Some owners had clear cut the trees, while others had left the terrain in its natural state.

We motored toward the dam. I remembered Dad and my brothers anchoring in this area to fish amid the shallows dotted with old stumps and weeds near the bank. They'd often brought home bass and catfish for dinner.

"Want to take the helm?" Brad asked.

I was familiar with boats this size. We'd owned a twenty-four-foot Chris Craft and I'd learned at a young age how to maneuver and dock. But it had been years, and since this was Sunday, the lake crowded.

"Not today. Maybe tomorrow when there are less boats and skiers around."

"I'd forgotten how much fun I had here as a kid."

"I was on a trip down memory lane, too. Most of the old cabins are gone. Kind of a shame. They gave the place character. Now it looks very—I don't know—cookie cutter."

Brad sighed. "I guess it's to be expected." He frowned and wrinkled his forehead. "God, I just got a terrific idea. Suppose one of the homeowners gave a party and a guest was murdered?"

"You often get ideas like this?"

He didn't reply, but tapped his fingers on the wheel, a strange half-smile on his lips.

"I can see it now. The partygoers are on the deck, the patio, around the pool. When they all go in for dinner, one is missing. He or she is found floating under the dock, an ice pick embedded in their back."

"Gruesome. And this was done in full view of a lot of people, none of whom saw or heard a thing?"

Brad grinned. "Details. I'll expand. Look, do you mind if we go in? I'm serious about this plot and want to get it down on paper while it's fresh in my mind."

"Not at all."

He thrust the gear lever forward and we skimmed across the lake dodging skiers and other boats with fluid ease. As we approached the dock, the red boat from the marina sat some thirty yards offshore. The man paddled around in the water with a flotation device. The woman lounged on the bow, her back supported by the windshield, the hat covering her face. I hoped she had lots of sunscreen. Her skin had a light tan, but the sun could still burn.

Brad docked and secured the boat. We climbed the steps to an upper viewing deck where I paused to catch my breath.

"Mom rarely went down to the dock. Claimed it was too much trouble coming and going. Said she'd consider more outings if Dad would install an elevator," I said.

Brad, who didn't appear to be even winded, laughed. "I know. My mother used to say much the same. That's why Dad built this deck. She could sit up here and see forever."

He spoke the truth. While the trees hid the dock and a portion of the shore, the view of the middle of the lake was spectacular. Beautiful blue water lapping against the green foliage of the distant bank with the boats dotting the surface was the stuff of postcards. From this vantage point, I didn't see the red boat.

"Do you mind if I'm totally rude and go inside? I have the body. Now I need the means, motive, and opportunity."

I turned from the railing and followed him across the back lawn. "Go write the next New York Times bestseller. Don't forget Amy's party."

He halted at the back door. "What time is it again?"

"Five-thirty."

"Right. I'll walk over with you." He waved and disappeared inside.

I shook my head. I knew enough writers to understand this was not unusual. *Authors. What a strange breed.*

I skirted the edge of an old tie wall. One of the upper supports had either rotted or given way. Mud from Friday's rain still congealed in smooth puddles in what once had been neat flower beds. Brad had his work cut out for him. I wondered how he managed his time between writing and the house repairs. I imagined authors wrote obsessively, not leaving the keyboard for hours on end.

I climbed my front porch steps and fished the key from my purse to unlock the door. A quick glance toward Amy's showed her car still gone. I looked at my watch—almost two. She must have had some heavy duty errands.

I was about to go inside when a movement from the woods between the Wallace home and the cabin next door caught my eye. I squinted, but saw nothing unusual. The figure in the storm came to mind. I still wasn't sure what I'd seen in the downpour. I almost walked over for a closer look, and then shrugged. *Don't be silly. It was probably just a rabbit.*

I entered the cool house and turned to close the door when a motorcycle, its throaty engine growl unmistakable, fired up from the road. I looked, but the trees blocked my view. A second later, the engine revved. I listened to it grow fainter until the only sounds remaining were the chirping of birds and the hum of insects.

A chill ran up my spine. For some reason, the woman in the red boat popped into my head.

Chapter Nine

Cars jammed the Wallace driveway and the babble of conversation drifted across the lawn to my front porch where I waited for Brad, now ten minutes late. I glanced at my watch deciding to give him until five forty-five. If he didn't show, I'd go on my own. A few seconds later, a door slammed and Brad hurried over.

"Sorry I'm late. Got all caught up in things."

"So, who's the killer?"

He laughed. "Haven't decided yet. Might be the jilted lover or the wife of the jilted lover. Could even be the family dog."

I chuckled along with him. He looked good tonight with his hair still damp from a shower and that fresh clean scent that always clung to him was magnified by his aftershave. His attire was casual. The navy shorts and red polo shirt along with the white sneakers gave him a nautical look.

I'd also gone casual with white slacks, a sunny yellow tank top, and a pair of bronze-colored sandals.

On the walk over to Amy's Brad touched one of my earrings.

"This is different. I've never seen feathers on jewelry."

"It's not my usual style, but I bought them a few weeks ago. They're called dreamcatchers. Too dramatic for a cocktail party?"

"Not at all. I like them. They give you a saucy look, like you're all fun and flirtatious."

I'd never considered myself in those terms, but a warm sensation crept over me at Brad bringing it up. I laughed and tossed my head, the feathers tickling my shoulders.

The doors to the Wallace home stood wide open and we walked in. Amy immediately stepped forward, a tense, harassed look on her face.

"Brad, Jenny, I'm so glad you could make it. The liquor is set up on the breakfast bar and the canapés are on the dining room table. Help yourselves. I'll introduce you around in a few minutes." She hurried off to greet another couple just entering.

"What would you like?" Brad asked.

"Bloody Mary is fine."

While he mixed the drinks, I wandered over to the table and sampled hors d'oeuvres. Amy flitted around like an uncomfortable butterfly. Her hands waved and her head jerked from side to side as she gazed about the room. She didn't look to be enjoying her role as hostess. Clearly, she was out of her element and why she'd chosen to throw a cocktail party was beyond me.

*Because Mark Bridges asked her to do it?* A dart of anger pricked me. Why would he want to put his niece through something like this when it was obvious she wasn't suited to play the part? As an excuse to meet me? He had my cell number. All he had to do was call. I'd have met him in town. All this cloak and dagger stuff was ridiculous.

My old friend, guilt, jabbed my stomach. I was partially to blame for Amy's unease. I resented that her uncle was the cause of my problem. For the first time, I realized my semi-workaholic existence of the past few years, had not only isolated me, but had also made me passive. I needed to become more involved. And not just in *Amy's* life.

Brad handed me my drink and whispered, "Why the scowl? Is the food that bad?"

"No, not at all. I didn't realize I was scowling." I popped the cracker with smoked salmon into my mouth.

Most of the guests had congregated on the deck. We stepped outside, and came face-to-face with Mark Bridges.

"Hello, I'm Amy's uncle, Mark Bridges."

He and Brad shook hands. "Brad Forrester. This is Jenny Devlin."

"I seem to remember those names from years ago. You were neighbors, right?"

"That's right. I live next door. Brad lives next to me."

I sipped my drink, the resentment deepening. Pretending not to know him and engaging in cocktail party chit-chat seemed silly, not to mention duplicitous. The dirty feeling from when we'd first met returned. Instinct told me this whole business was unnecessary.

"Oh, yes, of course, I remember now." Bridges smiled but shot me a pointed glance.

I glanced at Brad who must have caught Mark's action. He lifted an eyebrow and his eyes had a questioning look.

Amy's uncle smiled back, asking, "Will you be staying long in Vermillion?"

"A few weeks. It's always nice to get out of St. Louis for a while in the summer."

"What is it you do, Mr. Bridges?" Brad gulped a good portion of his drink.

"I'm semi-retired. I'm a lawyer—trusts, wills, deeds. That sort of thing. I also had a sporting goods store here in Vermillion. Finally sold that a few years ago, too."

I'd forgotten he was also a lawyer. I should have Googled him, too. That same old uneasy feeling crawled up my spine. Something about this just didn't ring true.

"Brad? Brad Forrester, is that you?" Brad turned as a man approached. "Hell, you probably don't remember me. My name is…"

When Brad turned to answer the man, Mark leaned over and said in a low voice, "We have to talk. Alone. Meet me on the front porch in five minutes."

"Mr. Bridges, don't you think that will look a little strange? Besides, this is a party. Someone is likely to overhear us."

"But I have to know what you've discovered. You've had three days."

I sighed and sipped my Bloody Mary. "And I have to go about this slowly. I can't just walk up and ask Amy if she's seen her dead sister lately."

"But I want to know your impressions, your reactions." He paused and frowned. "Okay, meet me tomorrow morning for a cup of coffee at the Jesse James Café. It's on Main just down from Oakwood. Nine o'clock."

I didn't like him giving me orders or the intensity of his demands. "I know it. I *did* live here during the summers."

He ran his hand through his white hair, and tugged

at his earlobe. "Yes, of course you did. Sorry. I'll see you tomorrow."

He moved off abruptly to speak to someone else. I drained my glass. The animosity I'd felt toward him in St. Louis rose again. I didn't like Mark Bridges and what was worse, didn't trust him either.

Brad rejoined me. "What were the two of you discussing? Looked pretty intense."

I shrugged. "Not really. We chatted about my folks, that's all."

He eyed my empty glass. "Refill?"

"Sure."

I handed the glass over and decided to have a few more canapés, since they would probably constitute dinner. Before I could enter, a woman touched my arm.

"You're Jenny Devlin, aren't you? Goodness, it's been a long time. I'm Raelene Goodwin. My late husband and I lived down the road. Your mother and I were great friends."

I remembered the lady. She'd been a member of that summer clique of women who shopped, gossiped, and played bridge every Tuesday afternoon. We chatted for a while about the old days, Mom, and how Lake Wildwood had changed before she moved on to someone else.

Brad brought my drink and a Styrofoam plate of food. "Thought you could use this."

"Boy, can I ever. I'm starved." We moved toward the railing where I set the plate and my drink down. I picked up an artichoke stuffed mushroom popping it into my mouth. "This is good. I don't see Amy having had time to make them, and they taste too good to be frozen."

"Maybe there's a place in town that does catering." He also ate a morsel. "Not bad at all, but then I've been to so many cocktail parties with bad food I'm not the best judge."

As another partygoer claimed Brad's attention, I finished the food and went back inside for more. The crowd suggested either Mark Bridges had a lot of friends in Vermillion or Amy had handed out invitations like confetti. I glanced around the room. All the seats in the living room were taken, and I realized that other than when we'd arrived, I hadn't seen Amy.

Curious, I made my way downstairs. Several guests played pool while others tossed darts at a dartboard. Still others sat at the bar chatting. A quick glance at the outside patio revealed a few older people sitting in lawn chairs around an empty fire pit. Amy was not among them.

I ventured down the hallway and peeked into the two bedrooms. No one. Ditto with the bathroom.

*Where could she have gone?* I wasn't worried, just curious.

I climbed back up the steps to the main floor and turned left toward the two bedrooms and another bath. One of the bedroom doors was closed. I leaned my ear against it and heard what sounded like sobbing. Without bothering to knock, I opened the door and entered.

The trees shading the house along with the closed curtains had sent the room into premature semi-darkness. Amy sat on the foot of the bed crying.

"Amy? Are you all right?" I closed the door and sat next to her, my arm automatically finding its way around her shoulders.

She sniffed and wiped her cheeks with her fingers. "I hate this. I'm a lousy hostess. I never know what to say to people."

"So why did you do it?"

"Uncle Mark asked me. I never could say no to him."

Guilt at my small role in her unhappiness hammered at me, and was then replaced with the resentment and sheer dislike I felt for Mark Bridges.

"Well, you're not a lousy hostess. You greeted us when we came in. I felt welcomed. And I saw you talking to other people. Don't be so hard on yourself."

She sniffed again. "Thank you. You're very kind. Sometimes I think Uncle Mark forgets I'm not Abby."

"What?" Her words shocked me.

"This would be so her thing. She'd greet people with a drink in hand, laugh, and talk about whatever interested them. She'd be the life of the party. Me? I'm the one who sits in the corner smiling and watching the parade pass by."

"I remember you and your sister being polar opposites."

She'd stopped crying and now stared straight ahead at a series of family photos, including some of Abby, on the wall.

"Abby was vivacious and fun-loving, always ready to try something new—everything I wasn't. She attracted vivacious, fun-loving people like the devoted to an Elvis vigil. It didn't surprise me that when we turned eighteen she headed out on her own with no more than a wave and a duffle bag. A part of me always wanted to be like her, but I could never call up the courage to do the things she did. I could never just catch the first bus or train out of town with no clear idea of where I was going." She turned to gaze at me. "Does that make sense?"

"Of course. I wouldn't do it either."

"But neither would you sit in a corner all night too afraid of butting into a conversation for fear of having someone think you're rude."

"Amy, the people you invited here tonight aren't strangers. You've known them for years. Going up and asking, 'Hi, are you having a good time? Do you like the canapés?' won't constitute anything except a polite response. No one will think you're rude."

She smiled. "I guess not. I'm just a worry-wart. Always was. Abby used to tease me when we were kids. 'Amy, why worry about something that may not happen? So what if it rains? We'll get a little wet. Don't borrow trouble.'"

From what I remembered of Abby, she'd borrowed more than her fair share of trouble.

Amy sighed and shook her head. "God, I miss her."

I wanted to ask about the accident, but thought I might come off as pushy. Besides, a cocktail party wasn't the right time or place. Instead, I rose pulling her up with me.

"Why don't we go show the rest of your guests what a good hostess you are?"

"How?"

"We can start by you showing me your garden. Remember? I complimented you on it the other day. I'm a total idiot when it comes to landscaping. Maybe I can pick up some tips."

Amy smiled and we exited the bedroom, taking the stairs to the lower level, then out through the sliding glass doors to the patio.

I decided I liked Amy Wallace very much. Her uncle could go to hell. I'd tell him so tomorrow, too. *If he thinks she's delusional then let him bring in a doctor. Don't use me.*

Amy kept up a lively commentary on the different flowers, bushes, and ground covers along with the water and light requirements as we eased our way down the terraces. Most went over my head. I'd never been keen on gardening. Some people had green thumbs, mine was black. I'd once killed a cactus.

"I even tried to spruce up around the dock this year. Would you like to see before the light completely fails?" she asked in an eager tone.

I didn't really, but agreed anyway not wanting to disappoint her. About halfway down the steps I had a feeling of being watched. I glanced up over my shoulder. Mark Bridges stood at the deck railing above staring at us. He nodded, and then turned away.

The Wallace dock was large, perhaps twelve feet square. Along the bank Amy had planted several flowering bushes and containers on the dock held the only flowers, other than roses, that I recognized— geraniums. The scarlet, pink, and white blossoms looked lovely against the gray of the wood. Even the dock pilings had hanging baskets. They swayed in the gentle breeze from decorative hangers. She explained what each variety was and how to care for it.

"Amy, this is beautiful. Is the dock new?"

"Yes. I had the old one replaced last year. It was rotting. This is a new kind of composite material. Supposed to last longer."

I glanced out over the water. Dusk would be

settling in soon. Already the lake traffic had thinned to an occasional skier taking that one last run, and the fisherman casting his line for yet another fish. I turned for the stairs.

"Well, I guess we should be heading back. You've done a remarkable job. Wish I had your talent."

I started my climb. From above, the chatter of the party slid down the hill. I paused at the first landing about a third of the way up and looked back. Amy had not followed. Trees blocked my view of the water, but not far away a boat moved at a fast clip.

"Amy?"

I retraced my way to the bottom. Amy stood on the furthest edge of the dock, one hand clutching a plant hanger on the piling, the other shielding her eyes from the glare of the setting sun off the water.

"Amy? Are you all right?"

Her head whipped around and she stared with wide eyes. "What?"

"I said, are you all right?"

She looked out over the water again, then released her hold on the hanger and relaxed.

"Yes, I'm fine. Just enjoying the last of the day."

I didn't believe her. Her expression had been tense, almost frightened, not like she enjoyed anything. In the distance, a red boat moved off at a fast clip. The distance and waning light prevented me from seeing the occupants.

We commenced climbing, neither of us saying a word until reaching the top where Brad met us. I stopped while Amy continued on across the lawn to the patio.

"Admiring the view?" he asked.

"More or less. Amy was showing me the garden and the new dock."

"I don't know about you, but I'm about to call it a night. I've got some things to do and want to get back to my story. You ready to go or do you want to stay longer?"

"I'm ready."

We found Amy on the patio talking to an older woman and said our goodbyes, thanking her. Rather than wind our way through the house, we crossed to the terraced walk leading to the front of the house. As we passed the porch, Mark Bridges stood talking with another couple. I didn't have to turn my head to know he stared.

Brad walked me to my door, and then dropped a light kiss on my forehead.

"I'm glad I went. Saw some folks I hadn't seen in years. It got me out of the house."

"And away from murder and mayhem?" I teased.

"Only for a short time. I spent most of the afternoon plotting out the first five chapters. Now, I'll see if I can produce."

He paused, ran a knuckle down my cheek, and then leaned over to kiss me again—on the lips this time and harder. He backed away and smiled.

"I'll see you tomorrow."

The touch and kiss awakened sensations I'd almost forgotten I had, but before I could formulate a reply, he turned and walked toward his place. Inside, I sat in the darkening living room thinking about the last couple of hours—and Brad.

We'd gone our own ways at the party, but boy, oh, boy, the goodnight was a doozy. My lips still felt the imprint of his. I wouldn't mind getting to know him better—a lot better. Just his simple touch made my stomach quiver.

And I wanted him to touch me. I wanted his lips caressing my skin sending me to a fever pitch. A throb deep in my soul reverberated to the very tips of my fingers and toes. I hugged a sofa pillow hard to my chest. Even the short affair that had destroyed my marriage hadn't affected me so...so...vibrantly. Was that the right word? I was both scared and exhilarated.

As much as I wanted to keep my thoughts on Brad, Mark Bridges intruded on all things pleasant. He'd been pushy and demanding. I didn't like him and *would* tell him to take his literary contracts and put them where the sun refused to shine. Unfortunately, if I did, I'd probably be out of a job. Grayson, Banks & Wilkes stood to make a sizable chunk of money from the Wallace estate. *And even lawyers have to eat.* No matter. I was sure I could land another job with a smaller firm.

And so what if his remaining niece had a few odd moments? *All of us do at one time or another.*

Amy had opened up to me some, but it didn't seem right to ask about her belief that Abby was alive yet. I felt sorry for her. She wasn't crazy, merely insecure—a sad, lonely lady who would no doubt make a wonderful wife and mother. I wondered if I could introduce her to a couple of the law clerks at the office before I got fired.

Eventually, I rose and wandered into the bedroom where I turned on the bedside lamp. Throwing myself on the bed, I picked up the book I'd started weeks ago. Maybe I'd finish it by the time I went home.

I didn't remember dozing off, but jerked awake and glanced at the clock next to me—almost midnight. More than a doze. I'd racked out for close to four hours. I yawned, sat up, and swung my legs over the edge of the bed. If I tried to sleep now, I'd be up before dawn.

In the kitchen, I made a ham and Swiss sandwich, uncorked a bottle of white wine, poured a glass, and took them onto the deck. The moon was full—a hunter's moon. The light dappled through the trees in splotches of gray and black.

Amy's house was dark, the party long over. At Brad's a light gleamed from a back window. For a moment, I considered going over, but dismissed the idea. He was probably working and wouldn't appreciate the interruption.

Finished eating, I picked up my glass and strolled toward the dock steps. As kids, my brothers and I thought it great fun to sit on the dock in the dark and tell ghost stories. To be on the safe side Dad had installed low wattage lights to illuminate the way down the stairs.

I followed them now and sat on a built-in bench pulling my feet up and hugging my knees. The lake was calm and the moon cut a brilliant swath across the water. From the other side of the lake, lights shone or winked off as people retired reminding me of a string of blinking Christmas tree lights. The air smelled of damp, vegetation, and a hint of fish. To an outdoors person, it was heaven on earth. I was a city type, but didn't mind the aroma. It beat the hell out of St. Louis on a hot summer night. City smells and heat did not mix.

I drained my wine and stretched. Maybe I could read another couple of chapters before turning in. From my left came the sound of an outboard motor. In the darkness, a boat, running lights off, slowly made its way past the Wallace dock toward mine.

I rose not liking the idea of someone tying up to a dock in the middle of the night or even cruising past one. Call it living too long in the city, but I imagined thieves, especially with the absence of running lights.

My movement and the white slacks I wore must have alerted the driver to my presence. The rpm's increased and the boat moved away toward the middle of the lake. Gradually, the sound ceased.

I waited for several minutes, but heard no more. Reluctantly, I climbed back up the steps, pausing every once in a while to gaze over the water. All was quiet.

As I crossed the yard, Brad's light still shone. I hesitated, tempted to talk about my uneasiness.

And say what? I heard a boat on the lake? What a concept. A lot of people take boat rides at night. *Yeah, but with the running lights off?*

Shaking my head, I walked into the house. *Don't be paranoid. This isn't St. Louis. It's Lake Wildwood in Vermillion, Missouri. Nothing's ever happened here.*

Chapter Ten

*Diary of Amy Margaret Wallace*

This hasn't been the best of days. I had to play hostess for my Uncle Mark, but he forgets I hate social things like parties. However, since he hasn't been back to Vermillion in a while, I agreed.

I stopped by Jenny's and met another old neighbor, Brad Forrester. I invited him to the party, too. He's an author—mysteries, I think. He seemed nice.

I went into town and bought liquor along with a bunch of hors d'oeuvres at Katie's Catering, keeping an eye out for the red sports car. Didn't see it, but I'll search again tomorrow. Sooner or later, I'll find Abby.

Uncle Mark arrived all excited about the party and seeing his old friends again. Naturally, I failed. I finally broke down and cried.

Jenny brought me out of my funk. She asked about the garden, and while I know she didn't have any real interest, she listened anyway. I think I could like her. Maybe even as a friend.

We went down to the dock for a few minutes. Jenny had already started back when the throb of an outboard caught my attention. It was Abby in the little red boat. This time she waved.

I froze, unable to think, to move, to wave back. Then she laughed and roared away.

Is she playing a game? Why didn't she pull up to the dock? Does she want to torment me?

I don't know what to do. I'm confused, bewildered, and—scared.

Chapter Eleven

Stifling yet another yawn, I focused my attention on the road into town and my meeting with Mark Bridges. I had no idea what to tell him. The role of spy didn't sit well with me, and Amy, whatever her problems, deserved privacy.

I didn't sleep worth a damn last night. Dreams of skulking thieves tiptoeing up the dock steps had me awake and peering out the windows into the darkness on more than one occasion. As a result, I'd overslept. I pressed my foot on the accelerator. Bridges didn't strike me as the kind who tolerated tardiness. *And do I care?* Well, yes. I don't like being late. Luck was with me. I found a parking space near the café.

The Jesse James Café hadn't changed since it was built, sometime in the late 1950s. The Formica table tops were so old they were in style again, and the wooden chairs and bench seats in the booths shined from over a half a century of rear ends sliding over them. The place was half-full, and I finally spotted Mark Bridges at a back booth. He waved and I threaded my way past several tables to him.

"Good morning, Miss Devlin." His voice held a hint of frost. An almost empty coffee cup sat in front of him. I'd been right. He was unhappy at having to wait for his information.

I slid onto the bench with a murmured greeting and

vague apology for being ten minutes late. A waitress stopped by with the coffee pot and large mug for me. The aroma reminded me I hadn't indulged in this eye opening luxury yet. I ordered a cheese omelet. Bridges ordered pancakes, bacon, and eggs.

When the waitress left, he fastened his gaze on me. "Well, Miss Devlin, is this private enough for you?"

I wanted to smack him. "I didn't think a social setting was the appropriate venue for a spy debriefing."

His took a deep breath. "I apologize. I didn't mean to snap and be nasty, but I'm so worried about Amy. I noticed you walking with her in the garden area."

"Yes, she found hostess duties overwhelming and offered to show me around. Did she do all the landscaping herself?" I knew the answer, but asked anyway. Let him come up with information for a change.

"I have no idea about the plants and such. My sister was the guru of that sort of thing."

I reached for the small cream pitcher. "Well, the garden was lovely and Amy obviously takes great pride in it."

He unwrapped his silverware from the rolled up paper napkin. "Yes, I suppose so. What have you observed?"

I added cream to my coffee and stirred. His impatient tone pissed me off. "I can't see that Amy is delusional. She never mentioned anything to me about Abby being alive and well. She talks about her, but always in the past tense and matter of factly."

"What about her behavior?"

"Not knowing her personality, I can't judge."

His brows drew together in a scowl. "I hope you

realize the consequences of not cooperating. Your law firm stands to gain a significant account."

I should have told him to cram it. Instead, I bit my tongue and counted to ten. Something told me I needed to hear more.

"I assure you I'm not deliberately putting up barriers. But odd behavior to me might be perfectly normal to another person. Perhaps you can tell me more about her personality."

I sipped my perfectly brewed coffee while mentally patting myself on the back for throwing the ball into his court.

He sighed heavily and gulped from his cup. "Abby couldn't help being the center of attention. Some people are like that. I remember my sister, Connie, saying that as a baby, Abby always cried the loudest until she got fed first."

"So, she learned at an early age how to get what she wanted."

He nodded. "By the time she was three, she had it down pat."

"And Amy?"

"With Abby around, it was easy to overlook Amy. As they grew older, the personality gulf widened. Abby indulged in cutting classes in high school, smoking, drinking, and generally having a good time. She barely graduated. She wasn't stupid, just disinterested. Amy always had her nose in a book or an artist's sketchpad in her hand and was valedictorian of her class. I often wondered how two sisters, twins, could look so much alike, yet be so opposite in behavior."

So far, he hadn't told me anything I hadn't already seen for myself.

"What were they like as kids? Any sibling rivalry?"

Our food arrived and we spent the next couple of minutes eating. My omelet was light and fluffy and the cheddar cheese added just the right amount of sharp, piquant taste. I bit into a slice of toast, the melted butter perfect on my tongue.

"How's the food?" he asked. He ate like a man condemned. Almost half of his pancakes had disappeared.

"As good as I remember."

"Now, what was it you asked?"

"Sibling rivalry. Any of it between the twins?"

"Some, I suppose. Abby was the dominant one and usually got her own way. I don't recall any fights or bad blood." He paused and chuckled. "Although Connie told me Abby talked Amy into switching places once to take a history test."

I couldn't see Amy in the role of Abby. "I've heard of twins doing that. What happened?"

"They got caught. Amy just couldn't pull it off. She aced the test—out of character for Abby—and the teacher immediately suspected the switch. When confronted by the principal, Amy caved and confessed."

"So, Abby flunked?"

"Big time. And it was a final to boot. Funny, it's the only time I ever heard of Abby getting mad at her sister. I believe she called her a wuss with an overabundance of brains, but no guts."

"Polar opposites," I murmured.

Bridges finished his eggs and sent me a sharp look. "Abby was smart—damned smart. She just had different priorities."

*But obviously not the right ones.*

"What about after high school? Did Amy go to college?"

"The St. Louis Academy for the Arts. She did well and graduated with honors."

"And Abby?"

"Took off to experience life."

"How did Amy feel about that? I understand they had opposing personalities, but were they close?"

He frowned and pursed his lips. "I wouldn't say so."

"Amy strikes me as being a very solitary person. Did she ever hold a job outside the home?"

He drank the last of his coffee and frowned. "I think she worked for an advertising agency for a while, but after the accident, she quit and worked freelance from home."

"What more can you tell me about the accident?"

"Not much, I'm afraid," he replied setting his cup down and pushing his empty plate away. "I was out of the country when it happened. My sister and brother-in-law had their hands full with Amy and the aftermath. They only told me the bare bones of it—the girls had taken a joy ride in a neighbor's boat, had an accident, and Abby died." His gaze fastened on mine. "Now, Miss Devlin, you have some of the background. What have you observed?"

The waitress refilled our cups and removed the dirty dishes. It gave me a chance to marshal my thoughts. I suspected he withheld information about the accident. Surely, Constance Wallace would give him the facts. So far, the only odd behavior Amy had exhibited had been during lunch on Saturday. I decided to tell him.

Bridges listened, and then rubbed a hand over his chin. "An old friend or Abby? And she actually ran out of the restaurant in pursuit?"

I nodded. "I watched her run part way down the street before returning."

"How did she act afterwards?"

"Distracted. She constantly watched out the window. When we got home, she took off immediately in her car. I assume to look for whoever she saw."

He frowned. "I don't like this. She's chasing a ghost—or someone who looks like Abby."

"You'd think someone in town would notice a stranger who is a dead ringer for Amy."

"My point exactly. She's imagining things. I didn't see much of her at the party last night. You seemed to spend some time with her. How was she?"

I hesitated, not wanting to reveal the depth of Amy's anguish. I only gave him a part of what I'd observed.

"She felt overwhelmed and inadequate. Said she wasn't much of a hostess."

Bridges waved a hand. "She was fine. Amy always overanalyzes and worries unnecessarily."

"She also said she thought you sometimes forget she's not Abby."

"What nonsense. There's no way anyone would ever confuse the two."

I drank most of the cooling coffee, and then stared into the light tan contents. I didn't like his inference—that Amy was forgettable. "It sounds as though you liked Abby better than Amy."

He drew a deep breath. "It's true. Abby was always on stage, so to speak. If you'll pardon the cliché, she could charm the birds from the trees. The girl could manipulate and wheedle with the best of them. She made me laugh at the world, at myself." He paused and smiled as if remembering some long ago event. "It was hard *not* to compare the twins. Abby was just so much more—alive."

"Only she isn't, is she?"

He stared straight into my eyes. "No. She isn't."

"Tell me, Mr. Bridges, do you see much of Amy in St. Louis?"

"Not too much. We go over the trust and her investments three or four times a year, but she has little social life. Rarely leaves the Webster Groves house except to come here. I wish she'd sell this place. Get rid of the unpleasant memories."

"She seems to deal with it well. And for all we know, she *did* see an old friend out the window."

He shifted on the bench and shook his head. "You don't really believe that, do you?"

I didn't answer and drank more coffee. I didn't know what to believe, but in spite of what I'd observed, feared Mark Bridges *could* be right about his niece. And according to him, Amy didn't have much in the line of friends.

"I can see from the look on your face, you don't. Once the trust is in good hands, I plan to travel for extended periods. That's why this insistence on Abby being alive is so disturbing. I can't leave the country with Amy so...so delusional."

The waitress stopped next to the table. "Anything else I can get for you?"

"No thanks, just the check," Bridges said with a frown.

She nodded, pulled a pad from her pink uniform skirt pocket, flipped through it, detached a page, and set it on the table. He glanced at it before turning his attention back to me.

"Thank you, Miss Devlin. I appreciate your time and effort with this. I'll try to get Amy to elaborate on things. In the meantime, please keep your eyes and ears open. If she talked to you yesterday about the party, she might again about Abby."

He slid from the booth and walked toward the register while I sat sipping the last of my now lukewarm coffee. Should I have told him about Amy's strange behavior on the dock? Tell him what? That she looked odd and tense staring out over the lake at dusk? For all I knew she did this every night.

I shook my head and glanced at my watch. Ten o'clock. I wasn't ready to go home. It had been a long time since I'd strolled the streets of Vermillion. Now seemed like a good time to do it.

I rose and left the café still perplexed as to why Mark Bridges had enlisted my aid. For the first time, I wondered how he'd known *where* I worked. That strange shiver of uneasiness skittered up my spine again. I needed to investigate Mark Bridges.

****

Vermillion was one of those small Midwestern towns with a split personality. Permanent residents kept the population at around four thousand during the winter months. But come summer, the number grew threefold. Once the getaway for numerous families from St. Louis and Kansas City, the area now attracted visitors from places like Arkansas, Oklahoma, and other distant states.

Resorts catering to family fun and fishing had blossomed over the last ten years. They dotted the shoreline with dock space and beaches made with tons of sand trucked in from nearby gravel pits. Some locals resented the intrusion and building boom calling it intrusive to the peace and quiet, while others welcomed it as an economic opportunity.

I could see both sides of the argument. The recession had hit the tourist industry hard, but Vermillion looked to be doing fine. Only a couple of empty store fronts stared silently along the four-block main thoroughfare. I guessed that instead of spending a fortune going to Disney World, families decided Lake Wildwood would do.

And the area had its attractions. A small amusement park was just south of town and two nearby state parks with hiking trails were available. The Vermillion Country Club, which in spite of its snooty name was open to the public, provided golf and tennis. My family had used it frequently.

I wandered down the street window shopping until stopping at Willard's Five and Dime. Nostalgia washed over me. How often had I dashed in for a magazine, a book, or new tube of lipstick lo those many summers ago? For old time's sake, I entered and walked the aisles reliving part of my childhood.

The town square hadn't changed either. The First Bank of Commerce, its clock tower proudly proclaiming the correct time, still stood on the northeast corner of Main and Vermillion. Baxter's Drug Store remained across the street. Sadly, the Vermillion Movie

House was gone, replaced by a three-story office building most of which seemed to be occupied with a law firm. At least the architecture blended in with the older buildings. The entrance to City Park was also where I remembered it, completing the four corners.

The roundabout in the center of the square was adorned with the statue of Horace Bedford Vermillion, accomplishment unknown. It was nice to see some things hadn't changed.

A hand touched my shoulder. "Jenny, what a surprise."

I turned to face Amy. This morning, her voice was calm and she smiled.

"Good morning. Recovered from last night yet?"

She laughed. "More or less. I slept like the dead. Went to bed as soon as I cleaned up after everyone left."

"No one stayed to help?" Guilt nagged. I'd never offered either.

"It was no big deal. Most of the food was gone and the plates and glasses were all plastic. A few minutes, a trash bag, and problem solved."

"Well, I enjoyed myself."

"That's what everyone said. I don't know why I let myself get all uptight and nervous like that." She glanced up at the statue. "Contemplating Horace Bedford Vermillion?"

"He's always been there. I never did know exactly why he's so honored to be standing in the town square."

Amy laughed. "Horace Bedford Vermillion was a pioneer in the 1800s. Vermillion existed then under another name. He arrived, opened a store, became the first mayor, and managed to get the town name changed to honor him."

"And grateful citizens erected a statue so they'd never forget."

"Something like that." She glanced at her watch. "I'm having lunch with Uncle Mark and one of his friends later. Would you care to join us? I'm sure he wouldn't mind."

Two meals in one day with Mark Bridges? *I don't think so.*

"Thanks for the invitation, but I can't. I may be on a short vacation; however, I did bring a few files from the office with me."

"Oh, I see." She looked dejected as though lunch with her uncle wasn't high on her list of things to do either.

"But I'm free for a while to walk through town with you if you'd like."

She perked up immediately. "That sounds like fun."

We turned from the square and strolled down the street.

"I'm surprised to see Willard's and the drug store in business what with the discount stores north of town."

"Baxter's still has the lunch counter. Remember it?"

"Ten stools and the best root beer float ever made."

"It remains popular with the locals for lunch. And there's a certain charm about Willard's. The original wood floor is intact. Do you find Vermillion has changed much?"

"Oh, little things here and there. The boutiques have new names, but stand in the same places." I commented on how the town seemed to have survived the recession.

"I guess we're centrally located enough to draw people in from surrounding counties. Most of the businesses stayed afloat. The summer crowd this year is bigger than last, so that's a blessing."

"The Fourth of July is coming up soon. Do they still have fireworks in the field east of town?"

"Oh yes. People bring blankets, coolers, and lawn chairs. It's a tremendous social occasion."

"Maybe I'll go. Brad might like to attend, too. How about you? Would you like to join us?"

A shadow danced across her face. "No, thank you. Fireworks remind me of war. I wouldn't have made a very good soldier. I don't like loud noises. Thunderstorms make me run and hide."

I remembered Mark Bridges telling me Abby's death had occurred around the July 4th weekend. No wonder Amy didn't celebrate.

*So why does she come here every July 4th?* I could see her uncle's concern. It was like a morbid fascination with a wreck on the turnpike and a habit Amy should break.

We continued our walk by crossing the street, stopping occasionally to comment on clothing in the shop windows.

"Amy, look at that sundress. It would look wonderful on you."

"Oh no, I never wear red. I don't look good in it. Now, Abby can pull that off," she said, using the present tense.

The comment sent a dart of concern through me. Was it a simple slip of the tongue or something more…delusional?

"But Amy, you and Abby were twins. You look exactly alike. If red looked good on her, it's logical to assume it would on you, too."

"Abby was flamboyant and loved the color. I just never felt comfortable in it."

Now that she was talking about Abby, I probed. "Did you and Abby ever indulge in the whim to change places?"

Amy turned from the window and continued walking. "Just once. I took a test for her. We got caught and Abby was furious. Said I shouldn't have answered all the questions correctly. It just wasn't in my nature to give a wrong answer when I knew the right one. It was shortly afterward that she cut her hair real short. She said she didn't want to look the same ever again." She chuckled. "Abby stayed true to her word. She went through a blonde and a redhead phase before high school was over."

Her answer coincided with what Mark Bridges had told me. I pushed the envelope by asking another touchy question.

"Did you and Abby also have that psychic connection?"

"You mean where I wake up in the middle of the night knowing Abby was in trouble or something?" She frowned and shook her head. "No. We were too different for that. Abby was mercurial. She blew with the wind. I was always steeped in routine."

So far, everything I'd learned suggested Abby and Amy weren't close. Still, being responsible for your sister's death must have weighed heavily.

Amy stopped in front of a store window. The sign

surprised me.

"A pawn shop? In Vermillion? Didn't this used to be a dry cleaners?"

"Hudson's. Mrs. Hudson sold it when Mr. Hudson died several years ago. Turned the town on its ear when Luke Granger opened the shop. Many of the old guard thought a pawn shop was seedy."

"Luke Granger. Wasn't he like the local bad boy?"

She laughed. "That's him. Some thought a business like this a bad image for Vermillion. I heard he made good money during the past couple of years. He sold the place last winter. Guess he wanted to move on to greener pastures."

"Recessions do that. People sell off what they don't need to make ends meet."

"I know. I feel so sorry for..." Amy broke off abruptly and stared into the window. Her hand clutched my arm and she drew in a sharp breath.

"Amy, what's wrong?"

"That ring!"

"Which ring?" The store window was full of them along with other jewelry.

"The square cut ruby surrounded by diamonds." Her voice had a breathy, almost strangled tone.

I followed her pointing finger. The ring in question was beautiful. I estimated it at five carats and the filigree setting suggested vintage.

"It's lovely."

"It's also Abby's!"

"What?"

"Our grandmother Wallace gave it to her on our sixteenth birthday. I got the bracelet. They were family heirlooms. That ring never left Abby's finger. She was wearing it the night of the accident. Come on!"

Amy tugged at my arm and pulled me into the shop. The man at the counter looked up as we approached.

"Please, that ring in the window. The ruby-and-diamond with the old-fashioned setting. Can I see it closer? Where did you get it?"

The man raised his eyebrows at her question, and then walked to the window and removed the ring bringing it to us.

"You have a good eye. This is the real thing."

Amy snatched the ring from the box and slipped it on her finger. It was a perfect fit.

"I know it's the real thing. It belonged to my sister."

"Whoa there, lady. I bought this fair and square from a woman two weeks ago."

"I'm not saying you didn't."

"Amy, are you sure this is Abby's ring? Maybe it's just similar."

"No, I'm sure."

A sliver of doubt sliced through my mind. Could Amy be right about Abby after all?

She turned back to the man. "Can you describe this woman? Did she look like me?"

His eyebrows rose again. "Not a bit. She was about your height, but had long blonde hair. Couldn't see her eyes. She wore big, dark sunglasses. Said she was staying in the area for a while and needed some ready cash. The ring's worth a lot, so I gave her a thousand bucks and she left."

"That's all?" I questioned.

He shrugged. "It was an out and out sale. I lowballed her and she didn't even argue. Just said, 'Give me the cash.' I did and she walked out."

"How...how much for the ring?" Amy asked.

"Five thousand ought to do it."

I gasped. "Amy, you can't be serious. That's a lot of money for something that might not be what you think it is."

"I'm serious, and it's Abby's. I'll have to go to the bank and move some funds around. Maybe Uncle Mark can give me an advance on my trust dividend. I'll ask." She slipped the ring off. "Can you hold this for a day or two? That's all the time I need."

He replaced it in the box, saying, "Sure, no problem. What's your name?"

"Amy Wallace." She pulled out a checkbook, flipped it open, and wrote. "Here's a five-hundred-dollar deposit. I'll have the rest by Thursday."

I was appalled at her impulsive gesture. "Amy, don't you think you should wait?"

"Why? It's a family heirloom and I want it back. I'd also like to ask this blonde a few questions about where and how she got it."

Whirling, she stalked out the door leaving me no choice but to follow. The shy, timid woman had transformed into someone determined to get answers. Confused, I hurried after her.

Standing on the sidewalk, Amy chewed on a fingernail and muttered, "It's true. I wasn't wrong and I'm not seeing things."

"What's true?" I asked.

She didn't answer, but stood with her forehead wrinkled in thought. "What? Oh, nothing important." She looked at her watch. "Jenny, will you excuse me? I have to get to the bank, and then meet Uncle Mark. I'll talk to you later."

Without bothering to say goodbye, she turned and walked away.

I retraced my steps back to the window of the pawn shop, eyeing the now empty space where the ring had sat. Amy's behavior concerned me. It was like a whole different person emerged in the store. She was decisive, forceful, and determined. Qualities I hadn't as yet seen in her.

Then something the shop assistant said brought me down to earth with a thump. *She wore big, dark sunglasses...*

The woman in the red boat! I had no idea of her hair color. The big floppy hat had hidden it. And she had looked vaguely familiar. *Because she looked like Amy?*

Amy's voice also echoed in my mind. *She went through a blonde and a redhead phase...*

My breath caught in my throat and my heart thudded. In front of me the sidewalk seemed to rise and dip. I placed my hand on the building to steady myself—the rough bricks already hot from the morning sun—closed my eyes, and took a deep breath before opening them again. My equilibrium had returned, but apprehension still clogged my throat.

*Oh my God! Is Abby Wallace alive and back in town?*

## Chapter Twelve

I managed to gather my scattered thoughts on the drive home. Doubt assailed me. Could Amy be right? Had Abby returned? And for what purpose? If she was on the up and up, why not just contact Amy?

I pulled into my driveway still concerned about my neighbor. Was the ring Abby's? Or was it a similar ring? Amy, so quiet and reserved, had been animated to the point of hysteria. I couldn't wait to get inside to my computer. I needed a deeper search into the accident.

A note was pinned to the front door. I removed the thumbtack and read.

*Dear Jenny, if you're free tonight, how about dinner in town? There's a seafood place called the Half Shell I've heard is pretty good. My treat. I'll pick you up at 6:00. If you can't make it, give me a shout on my cell.*

He left the number, but I could see no reason not to accept. Amy and her problems, and Mark Bridges and his spy games, not to mention the drama of this morning, had put me in a tense mood.

I walked inside pulling my tank top from my sweaty back. Already the heat and humidity felt like August. Even the breeze off the lake had given up. I cranked the air-conditioning up another notch and poured a glass of iced tea, then plunked my fanny down at the kitchen table. Time to Google. But first, I recorded this morning's strange events in the electronic journal.

Using an advanced search, my Google inquiry was once again disappointing. Very little I didn't already know came to light—the boat hit an object in the water, exploded, and no trace of Abby Wallace was found. I had no idea how to infiltrate the local police reports, and if I did, would the reports still be there? After ten years even those could have been sent to that great electronic storage locker in cyberspace.

I switched my focus from the accident to Amy. Her Google profile was brief and dealt with her career. No mention was made anywhere of the accident and Abby's assumed death.

I then typed in Abigail Wallace. It wasn't an unusual name, and over a million hits popped up, so I refined the search. Still nothing. I was either doing something wrong or there simply wasn't any information available for a woman who'd "died" ten years ago.

At two o'clock my cell rang. I wasn't surprised to find Mark Bridges on the other end. Without so much as a, "hello, how are you," he launched into his speech.

"What the hell happened at the pawn shop and why didn't you call me immediately? Amy met me for lunch demanding an advance on her trust dividend so she could buy a ring that supposedly belonged to Abby."

"I didn't call because I didn't know what to say. She seemed so sure and for the first time since I've been here, Amy was enthused about something."

"Well, she was enthused about the wrong damned thing. For crissakes, why would a ring belonging to Abby suddenly show up in a pawn shop in Vermillion,

Missouri? I've got the answer—it wouldn't. And why didn't you stop her from putting a deposit down to hold the damned thing?"

"Stop her how? It's her money. If she wants to buy the ring, that's her business. What's the harm?"

"The harm is she thinks it belonged to her dead sister!"

I'd had it with Mark Bridges. He could go stuff it. Grayson would fire me, but I was ready to tell him the same.

"Even if it doesn't, she's happy to think it does. And if Amy's happy, that's what counts. Why are you so gung-ho on insisting she's disturbed?"

"Because she is. She thinks she sees Abby around every corner, which is impossible. She's either hallucinating or mistaking every brunette in a red sports car for her sister. It's not normal. Amy needs help—preferably away from that house. All it has are bad memories."

*He's constantly harping on Amy leaving the house and bad memories. Who's he trying to convince? Amy? Me? Himself?*

"Amy seems comfortable and I haven't heard a word about her seeing dead people." I paused. "Are you going to give her the advance?"

"No. She then informed me she wanted to sell some stocks to cover the cost. I had no choice in that. I'm her broker. I buy and sell on her behalf—and on her instructions. She demanded I put the sell order in before the close of business today. She didn't want to wait. You should have talked her out of it."

His tone was more than testy. It was downright furious, but I was damned if I'd take the blame for this.

"I'm sorry things aren't going as you had hoped, Mr. Bridges. Perhaps it would be best if we terminated this deal. I don't see any reason to spy on the woman just because she has a few quirks regarding her deceased sister. If you want to slap her in a rest home, find a concurring doctor and a judge. I don't know why you roped me into this in the first place. Which reminds me, how did you find me?"

"What? Oh, I talked to your parents when I was here to see Amy one time. They bragged about how proud they were of your accomplishments. Now, back to my niece…"

I interrupted. "I am not going to spy anymore. That's it. Done. Finito. Got it?"

Bridges was silent for a second, and then sighed. "Please forgive me. I'm upset. This has been escalating for over a month, and I'm worried about my niece. If she needs help, then I want her to have it as soon as possible. Please continue to be her friend. She likes you. Maybe she'll talk on the ninth."

"The ninth?"

"July ninth. That's the ten-year anniversary of the accident. I just have the feeling something is brewing."

"I will continue to be Amy's friend because I like her. But my spying days are over. You can call my boss if you like; I don't care. And neither do I care what you think. This whole idea was silly to begin with."

Heavy breathing from his end followed my speech. I thought of Amy. Today, her eyes had sparkled and she'd seemed alive, hoping to track down the mysterious blonde who might hold the key to Abby's— what? Demise? Disappearance? *Reappearance?*

"Mr. Bridges, why would Amy insist Abby was

alive?"

"Because no body was ever found. The assumption was the explosion had…well…"

I could understand why he didn't finish. It wasn't a pretty thought—a woman being literally blown apart. On the other hand…

"Has it occurred to you Amy could be right?"

"What do you mean?"

"If there was no body, then is it possible Abby *could* be alive?"

A sharp intake of breath on the other end conveyed his shock.

"Certainly not! The lake was dragged for weeks and if she'd survived why didn't she come forward. And I don't want to hear about amnesia. That was what Amy insisted from the beginning. No, Miss Devlin. Abigail Marie Wallace died a gruesome death. No body was ever found, because one no longer existed." He paused. "Will you continue to help Amy? I don't mean spy, but if you see or she says anything…well, strange or delusional will you call me?"

"I'll think about it. Now, if you'll excuse me, I have work to do."

I didn't say goodbye or give him a chance to answer. I simply hung up and sat cupping my chin in my hand.

I strongly suspected Amy's uncle wasn't telling me the whole story, and that pissed me off. I was being used, but didn't know how. And that bit about him having talked to my parents made me curious. Mom hadn't mentioned anything to me about it. On a hunch I called her.

"Jenny, how nice to hear from you. How are things

at the lake?"

"Great. Just like old times." I brought her up to date on Brad and Amy. "I also met Amy's uncle, Mark Bridges yesterday. He says you told him all about my brilliant mind."

Mom laughed. "I suppose that's possible, but it must have been a long time ago. I haven't seen him in years. How is he?"

"Oh, fine." So, it had been a while. But what had brought my name to his mind for this project? He must have one hell of a memory.

"And how's Amy?"

"She's good."

"Such a quiet girl. She came over to say hi the last time we were there. Is everything all right with the house?"

I assured her the house was in good shape before ending the conversation. I supposed Bridges could have tucked that snippet of information about me into the corner of his mind. On impulse, I called my boss.

"Ah, Miss Devlin, how are things going with our prospective client's request?" Grayson asked.

"Uh, fine, just fine. I was wondering; how did he come to pick our law firm for this?"

"As I recall, he showed up saying he had heard good things about us, and since you had known the family in question, asked for you specifically. Why? Is there a problem," my boss said in a sharper tone.

"Oh, no, I was just curious, that's all." I was sure Mark Bridges would give Grayson the bad news I had refused to do any more of his bidding soon. Better him than me.

"I see. Well, let me know when this assignment is

over. I envision some great things for you with the firm."

I thanked him on what likely would never occur now and hung up. Something just didn't add up. My dislike of Amy's uncle had deepened, and I didn't trust him one iota. He had another agenda. What I wasn't sure.

Then a thought occurred to me that sent goosebumps up and down my arms.

*What the hell happens to the trust if Amy is institutionalized again—or dies?*

****

I slipped the sterling silver hoop into my ear, and then stepped back to check the effect in the mirror. Not bad. I adjusted the hem of my royal purple tank top and smoothed it over the gauzy white skirt. The simple silver thong sandals completed the ensemble. I added a silver cuff bracelet. I looked pretty good. Sometimes, it's just fun to get dressed up.

I needed this night out. After my discussion with Mark Bridges along with my chilling question regarding the trust, I Googled him. Nothing untoward jumped out at me. I then tried to put everything out of my mind and concentrate on work, but failed to make any headway with even a simple contract.

*What's wrong with me? I haven't done one ounce of real work since coming here. Maybe I'm more involved with Amy and her problems than I thought.*

A soak in the tub helped my mood somewhat. Anticipation of dinner with Brad brought it the rest of the way home.

A knock on the door told me my date had arrived. I opened up and stared in surprise. His navy blue slacks and bright green polo shirt was the perfect combination of casual yet elegant. Or maybe it was the way he wore them—with a confident attitude. Most men shied away from strong, vibrant colors. On him, they looked good—damned good, not to mention sexy as hell. Together, we displayed an interesting color palette.

"Hi. You look great. I'm glad you could make it," he said, entering the living room. "I should have called, but had to go to Jefferson City. I needed to do some research that wasn't online."

My gaze snaked up and down his body. "Thank you. You look pretty good yourself."

He grinned. "Are you ready? I hear the Half Shell has the best clam chowder outside of Boston."

I laughed. "Let me change my purse and we're outta here."

I transferred my driver's license, a credit card, compact, lipstick, and cell phone to a tiny white clutch with silver trim.

"I'm ready."

He cupped my elbow with his hand and steered me through the door. "I'll never understand women and accessories. What is the allure of shoes and purses? My first wife had an entire closet devoted to both."

"What is the allure of big screen TVs, HD everything, and fifty sports channels for men?" I countered.

"Touché." He opened the car door for me and I slid in.

As we drove away, I glanced toward Amy's. Her car was in the drive. I still had no idea how to broach the subject of Abby with her. Maybe Brad could help.

"So, how goes the writing?"

"Not bad. After the party last night, I wrote for four or five hours. Tonight, I'll have to edit three thousand words down to half or less."

"Why?"

"When I'm in the creative mode, I just write. It's like stream of consciousness. I don't bother with good grammar, punctuation, spelling, or anything. My main objective is getting the idea down on paper. Over the next day or so, I let the editor in me make revisions."

"Do you always work at night?"

"Not always. By the way, sorry if I left you standing on the doorstep. But last night I was in the mood and did it."

"What? Writing or the kiss?"

He sputtered with laughter. "Both, although I referred to writing. That's not to say I didn't enjoy the kiss. What did you do the rest of the evening?"

"Oh, I read a little, had a late dinner, walked down to the dock, and then went to bed." There was no reason to tell him about the boat that sped away. "I saw your light and almost came over, then thought better of it."

"Good idea. When I'm down and dirty with a story, I hate interruptions."

The drive to the restaurant didn't take long, and soon we were escorted to a table by the hostess.

The Half Shell is one of those places in a strip mall that has to make do with the space available. The owners had designed the long, narrow space with a bar up front, dining in the middle, and the kitchen toward the back. The décor was what I expected to find in a resort oriented town—low-key and tasteful, but nothing spectacular. The room was half full and the noise level not yet intrusive.

A waiter stopped by and took our drink order. Brad had a martini and I decided on a Bloody Mary. We took a few minutes to look over the menu, which for the location of the place, was extensive.

When our drinks arrived, Brad waved the waiter away. "Give us ten minutes or so to enjoy our cocktails, then we'll order." The man nodded and left. Brad turned his gaze on me. "So, what did you do today? I can tell you mine was pretty boring. Nothing like a library to put me to sleep."

I stirred my drink with the garnish celery stick in it and stared into the tomatoey depths. I felt guilty at my participation in this spy business, and even though I knew Mark Bridges wouldn't be pleased, I decided to come clean to Brad. Besides, he might have some insight.

"It was upsetting to a certain extent."

His eyebrows rose as he sipped his martini. "Upsetting? How?"

"My being here isn't a case of wanting to, but of had to."

"I don't understand."

I heaved a sigh, withdrew the celery stalk from the drink and laid it on the cocktail napkin, then took a long healthy swallow.

For the next several minutes I filled him in on my James Bond role and the reasoning behind it. When I finished, we both drained our glasses. Like magic, the waiter arrived.

"Another round, sir, madam?"

Brad looked at me. I shook my head. "I'll have wine with dinner."

"I'll have another. We'll order when you bring it."

As soon as we were alone, he frowned. "I don't get why he brought you into the equation. All he had to do was call her doctor and explain the situation. I'm sure Amy must have had a psychiatrist for many years, perhaps still does."

"I know. It doesn't make sense. And I feel like a rat for having spied on a perfectly nice woman, who may or may not have problems."

"I don't like this. Why didn't you tell Mark Bridges to kiss off?"

"I did this afternoon. Earlier, he dangled the carrot of a lucrative deal in front of my boss's nose. Grayson, Banks, & Wilkes stands to collect a lot of billing hours from this. The trust alone will buy one of the partners a new BMW every year. Even I benefit with the literary contract. Now, of course I fully expect him to withdraw the trust supervision from the firm and I'll be on the street out of a job."

His drink arrived and we ordered—New England clam chowder, salad, Chilean sea bass with cilantro sauce for me and the same for him with the exception of Lobster Newberg. I also added a glass of Pinot Grigio.

"Make it two," Brad said. The waiter left and we resumed our conversation. "What is the point of any of this? I mean, what's her uncle's bottom line? What's the agenda? Does he want to put her on the funny farm for a while, have her supervised at home by a companion? What?"

"I don't know. He didn't say."

"Have you observed any odd behavior?"

"Define odd."

He leaned back in his chair. "Good point. You

might find my writing at two in the morning odd, but to me it's perfectly normal."

"There have been a couple of things." I told him about the lunch at Victoria's, my finding her in tears yesterday, the incident on the dock, and finally today's display at the pawn shop. I also voiced my suspicions about someone being in the woods next to Amy's along with the sound of the motorcycle. I didn't bring up the nocturnal motor boat. I had no evidence it was involved in this.

"All right, that's odd, but not odd enough to call in a shrink."

"There's something else. It might or might not be relevant." I told him about my first night at the house and thinking I saw someone on Amy's deck and the footprint under my living room window.

"And Amy dismissed this?"

"Said I must have seen the umbrella moving in the storm."

"Could you have?"

"It's possible, but explain the footprint."

"I can't, unless it was an old one that didn't get washed away."

"No way. It rained like a sonofabitch."

"Maybe it was some homeless guy seeking shelter, who then split when he realized the house was occupied."

"A homeless guy?"

He shrugged. "You said you thought someone was lurking in the woods, and the woods are pretty thick next to Amy's."

The idea of someone camping out in those woods didn't sit well. Maybe tomorrow I'd go for a walk and

Suzanne Rossi

see what I could find. I didn't feel in danger, just not at ease with the thought.

Our chowder arrived and wine was served, and for the next several minutes I concentrated on the creamy taste. It was as good as any in St. Louis—or New England. The salad came next followed by the entrée.

I didn't need a knife. Fork tender, the fish flaked easily and I popped a bite into my mouth. The cilantro sauce was perfect, not too strong, but just enough flavor to give it taste. The herb infused rice and steamed green beans complimented the fish.

We spoke little during the meal. I didn't bring up the subject of Amy until we had coffee.

"So, did I do the right thing?"

"I think so, especially telling Bridges to kiss off. If you want my opinion, it doesn't sound as though Amy Wallace is any more delusional than I am when I plot a book. Let her believe what she wants as long as it gives her comfort. When she begins preparing meals for a non-existent sister, then it's time to be concerned."

"And I can't help speculating that Amy could be right and her sister is alive."

"So far, there's no proof of that. Other than Amy's observations."

"Brad, there's something else." I told him of my thoughts concerning the trust if Amy were to die.

His eyebrows rose. "That sounds like something I'd write. You think he's setting her up?"

I bit my lip. "I don't know. It seems kind of far-fetched."

"Also dangerous. Why bother? All he has to do is have her declared incompetent, institutionalized, and get power of attorney. Then he'd have no one to answer to on how the money was spent or invested."

"I Googled him this afternoon. All seems to be on the up and up. He had his own law firm with two partners. He did trusts and wills, while the other two concentrated on divorce and criminal law. He semi-retired twelve years ago. Sold his portion of the firm to his partners and from what I could see did little things on the side."

"Like his niece's trust?"

"I don't think she had the trust then. Her parents were still alive—but perhaps he dealt with their investments or something."

He sat back with a thoughtful look. "You suspect he's playing fast and loose with Amy's trust? Is that what you think this is all about?"

"I honestly don't know. It worries me, but who the hell do I ask? Any inquiry from me would look odd and might get back to him."

"I see your point. I could always call his former partners saying I was thinking of him as an investment counselor. In the meantime, maybe we both should get to know Amy better."

Brad paid the check and we drove home in silence. I was thinking about Amy and assumed Brad was outlining his next chapter. As he pulled into my driveway, I spotted Amy sitting on her porch swing.

"I guess now wouldn't be a bad time to say hello and ask about the ring," I said.

"I'd like to see her reaction, too."

We strolled over hand in hand. "Hi, Amy. Did you buy the ring?"

She rose and frowned. "More or less. Uncle Mark refused my request for an advance on my trust, so I sold some stock. I'll be able to write a check on Thursday."

I turned to Brad and pretended to tell him about the ring for Amy's benefit. "Amy believes she found a ring belonging to her late sister in a pawn shop here."

"Really? What a coincidence. Are you sure?"

"Oh, yes."

"I wonder how it got here," he said with a smile.

Amy started to speak, closed her mouth, and shifted from foot to foot.

"I went back to the store and asked the man more questions about the blonde. He didn't have much to add. I can't imagine Abby parting with that ring. I want to find the woman and ask her where and how she got it."

I rubbed the back of my neck, confused by something she said. "Funny. From what I've heard, Abby didn't sound like much of a sentimentalist. Perhaps, she gave or sold the ring to this woman."

Amy caught her lower lip between her teeth before speaking. "That's entirely possible."

"Was Abby wearing it when she died?" Brad questioned.

"I think so. I really don't remember."

Odd, at the pawn shop she'd been adamant her sister had worn it the night of the accident.

Brad gave her a gentle look. "Perhaps then, you made a mistake. The ring isn't Abby's, but a similar one."

A sheen of tears filmed her eyes. "No, it was Abby's." She paused, frowned again, and then spoke softly as if talking to herself. "She couldn't take a chance of being seen in town even though she's been driving through it and boating on the lake. She had the blonde do it."

I cast a glance at Brad. He returned the look with a raised eyebrow.

"Amy, who's been in town and boating? I'm confused," I said.

She blinked the tears away. "Please, don't think I'm crazy, but I think Abby is alive."

The admission stunned me. She stood calm as can be on her front porch and made a statement that didn't make sense.

"Amy, how is that possible?" I asked in a soothing tone. Was this the breakthrough we'd been anticipating?

She rose and paced back and forth a few steps. "I don't know. But it's the only explanation I can think of for the ring. Maybe she's spent all these years with amnesia and is just now beginning to remember. *Maybe* she finds Lake Wildwood familiar. *Maybe* she doesn't yet remember *me*."

Brad took a step forward and gently clasped his hands on her shoulders.

"Amy, I understand your guilt and anguish over the accident, but face facts. You survived. Your sister didn't. And as much as you loved her, she isn't alive."

Amy twisted out of his grasp with a sob.

"Oh God, you're just like Uncle Mark. You think I'm crazy. And I know Mom and Dad blamed me for what happened. I was the sensible one. I was the one who should have said no to stealing the boat. I was the one who should never have been at the controls."

"Amy, my God, it was an accident," I said disturbed by her outburst.

"No, no! It wasn't! I saw whatever it was in the

water. I did nothing to avoid it."

"You were an inexperienced boater! You wouldn't do something like that deliberately. You didn't mean for Abby to die. We know you loved her."

She stared with wide, wet eyes, and then cried, "No, you don't understand at all! Nobody ever did. I didn't love her. I hated her!"

Chapter Thirteen

Amy clapped her hand over her mouth, turned, and ran through the doorway into the house. I moved to follow, but Brad stopped me.

"No, let her be for now."

"But she's upset!"

"And probably embarrassed."

"But she needs someone!"

"I agree, but not now."

He tugged on my arm and led me across the lawn. I tossed a glance over my shoulder, worried about Amy. Her words shocked and disturbed me. I wanted to comfort the poor woman. I unlocked my front door and entered. Brad followed.

I plopped onto the sofa while he sat in a chair.

"Do you believe what she said?" he asked.

I heaved a sigh. "No. If she hated her sister, she wouldn't have a portrait hanging on the wall."

"And she wouldn't feel such awful guilt."

"I feel guilty for not going after her."

Brad shook his head. "Don't. She said something in anger and frustration. Plus she said it around people she doesn't know all that well. Wait until tomorrow."

"I guess having people question her…stability is stretching her nerves." I paused and remembered what Mark Bridges had said about sibling rivalry. "There must have been times when Amy resented the flamboyant Abby."

"There were times when I thought I hated my brothers. The older one was smarter, and the younger one cuter. It's natural."

I sat back and rubbed my hands over my upper arms. "Suppose Abby is alive and in a state of semi-remembering?"

He ran a hand through his hair. "Are you going to call Bridges with this?"

"No."

"Good. From what you told me tonight, he's doing more harm than anything else."

"And she said nothing about actually seeing Abby."

"I have no idea how amnesia victims act or react, but walking around for ten years not remembering, and then suddenly getting glimmers doesn't sound logical."

"It doesn't sound logical to you or me, but we aren't experts. The only thing I know about amnesia is what I've seen in movies or read in books."

Brad wrinkled his forehead with a frown. "Maybe tomorrow you can invite her for dinner at my place. Get her mind off her dead sister."

"That's a good idea. Maybe later she'll talk to me about Abby."

"Could be. She came close tonight. I could throw a barbeque on the Fourth. You don't have plans, do you?"

"No, I hadn't thought much about it," I confessed. "I assumed I'd go into town, watch the parade, eat the usual food, and then catch the fireworks."

"That's better than my idea. First thing in the morning, why don't you ask Amy to join us in town and for dinner afterward? I'll fire up the grill for the three of us. Maybe take a ride on the lake before the fireworks."

I shook my head. "I'm not sure about the lake thing or the fireworks. Amy doesn't like loud noises. Bridges said the anniversary of the accident is July ninth."

"She still has to eat, and a parade is festive."

"That's assuming she'll even talk to us. We weren't overly supportive of her theory about Abby." I paused for a moment to think. "Brad, why don't you investigate amnesia, while I see what I can do to help Amy?"

"Makes sense. I'll also think about how to approach Bridges' former partners. Try asking the police about the accident. They might let you see the report, if it's still around."

"Won't they think it odd for an outsider to ask after all this time? And what if they go to Bridges or Amy and tell them?"

"Then ask at the newspaper. Could be someone there was around then. Between the two of us, we should come up with a few answers." He glanced at his watch and rose. "I'd better be heading home."

I didn't want him to go. Sharing my real mission in Vermillion tonight had made me realize how much I liked the guy. I had a friend, a partner of sorts, who didn't judge or ask too many questions about the last few years. Brad gave me hope the future might be something to anticipate.

I leaned back and rested my arms along the back of the sofa, staring at him through my eyelashes. "Do you have to go? How about a nightcap?"

He paused, gave me a slow, sexy smile, then sat next to me and entwined his hands in my hair. His lips caressed my temple. "Did I tell you how stunning you look tonight?"

"I believe you mentioned it briefly." I snaked my arms around his neck.

He rose, pulled me to my feet, and then lowered his head until his lips were just inches from mine.

"Allow me to further show my appreciation." Those fabulous lips curled into a half smile teasing me with promises.

"Talk, talk, talk. That's all you author types know how to do. I like action."

The smile widened, then his lips claimed mine in a kiss that sent searing heat radiating from the pit of my stomach to the tips of my toes. It washed over me in waves. My legs trembled as I kissed him back.

His hands roamed up and down my spine, then slipped to cradle my derriere. He pulled me closer. His erection nestled comfortably in just the right place on my body. I wiggled my hips slightly and groaned.

Brad stopped kneading my rear end. One hand strayed up to my hair where he gently clenched a fistful and tilted my head back. His lips left mine and traveled down the side of my throat to that ultra-sensitive pulse point above my collarbone.

I gasped at the lightning licking my nerves. With desire building like a tidal wave, I pulled his shirt from the waistband of his slacks, and ran my hands up his chest. Smooth, sculpted muscles greeted my touch, the skin hot.

His hands slid under my tank top. Nimble fingers made fast work of my bra fastening. He cupped my breast and pinched the erect centers into diamond hard points.

"Where's the bedroom?" He spoke in a hoarse growl.

"Down the hall, first door on the left." How I managed to speak coherently was a mystery.

Brad didn't hesitate. He picked me up as though I weighed nothing and carried me to my bedroom before setting me gently on my feet next to the bed.

I stared into those blue eyes and slowly removed my top and bra, then unzipped and pushed my skirt to the floor. He undressed with that sexy, half-smile on his lips. My gaze ran up and down his naked body in appreciation. He was lean, but I had no problem discerning his muscles. Not quite six-pack abs, but damned close. He looked magnificent.

He moved closer and encased me in his arms again. His lips caressed my temple, moved to my cheek, and then my neck. He bent me back over his arm and kissed the globe of my breast before taking the erect center into his mouth where he laved and sucked.

My legs wobbled. I clutched his shoulders and moaned. How long had it been since I'd felt a man's touch? Too long. Guilt and self-disgust had kept me celibate for years. But now, it was as though I'd been rescued from a deserted island and let loose in a candy shop. Okay, so I was mixing my metaphors or similes or whatever. I knew what I meant. Brad had awakened the need stored inside me. I wanted him. A fire roared deep in my being.

He knelt as his lips traveled further down my body. With his tongue exploring my navel, my legs threatened to collapse. And when his teeth tugged at my thong pulling it down my thighs, I came close to dying.

His hands finished removing my panties, and then

his lips found my hot, slick core. Unable to help myself, I cried out. My hands transferred to his hair and clutched. I moved his head to the rhythm of my undulating hips. The coiling spring deep inside my core tightened to the point of pain, the kind I wanted to keep forever.

Then, the spring snapped. Spasm after spasm ripped through me. My hips moved at a frenzied pace. My hands tugged his hair. I cried out again and again. Over much too soon, my orgasm finally died. My legs went limp and I fell back onto the bed.

Brad, a smile on his lips, followed me. He pushed my thighs apart and knelt between them. I reached out a trembling hand and encircled his erection. It burned and throbbed against my palm. He paused, leaned down and fumbled in his slacks pocket before removing his wallet and extracting a foil packet. He ripped it open with his teeth and sheathed himself. Without a word, he nestled between my legs, and then lunged deep inside.

He moved slowly at first gradually building speed. The coil retightening told me I would come again. With every thrust, our breaths increased. Finally, he leaned forward and buried his lips in my neck. I wrapped my legs around his waist and matched his ever increasing movements. The heat built, and then erupted in another series of contractions that had me gasping and demanding God to let it go on forever. With a hoarse cry, Brad lunged deep. I felt the throb of his release as I milked the last of my orgasm.

With a groan, he collapsed and rolled to the side. We both lay gasping for breath. My heart pounded and the blood roared in my ears.

Several minutes later, he picked up my hand and

raised it to his lips.

"That was fabulous," he murmured. "You are terrific."

"You're not so bad yourself. It's been a long time."

He was silent for a second. "Yeah, me too."

I digested this information before admitting, "I kind of swore off men and sex after my divorce."

"I didn't swear off women and sex, but I sure am more discriminating than I once was. Now, I have to really like the lady." He squeezed my hand.

I squeezed back. "I take that as a compliment."

"It is. And I'm flattered you chose me to help you rejoin the world. Was your divorce that bad?"

I hesitated, not wanting to spoil the moment with memories I'd rather stayed buried. A vision of my last confrontation with Jim flashed in front of my eyes.

"Bad enough."

Brad rolled onto his side, his still hard erection pressing against my thigh. He slid his hand over my breasts then leaned over and flicked his tongue at my nipple several times until it was pointing erect again.

I knew we weren't finished with this. The desire pooled in my belly once more time and my breaths quickened along with my heartbeats.

"Oh, God, Jenny, I want you again," he said with a moan.

"I know. I want you, too." I pushed him onto his back and slung a leg across his hips. "My turn."

I started with his chin and worked my way down his hard, sinewy body, stopping for a few moments to let my tongue and teeth play with his nipples. His hands fisted in the bedspread and he couldn't contain the groan that emerged from his throat.

I moved on to his navel while my fingers cupped and caressed the softness beneath his still sheathed erection.

He gasped and thrust upwards. "Jenny, oh Jesus, Jenny, I can't hold it."

I moved back up his body kissing and caressing his overheated skin before straddling his hips. Without hesitation, I lowered my body taking him all the way inside.

He cried out, and I laughed. The night was just beginning.

\*\*\*\*

I awoke to sunlight streaming in the window and Brad snoring softly beside me. I had no idea of the time and didn't care. I was also clueless as to how many times we'd made love. Self-imposed celibacy has a way of catching up and demanding release. And oh, boy, did I release. We'd snatched brief naps to recharge our sexual batteries before tackling pleasure again.

I rolled onto my back and stretched like a satiated cat. The movement woke Brad who turned to me and smiled.

"Good morning, sunshine. Do you feel as good as I do?"

"Better," I replied in a purring tone.

He gathered me to him and kissed me on the tip of the nose. "Can't possibly feel better than me."

"Wanna bet?"

He laughed. "What time is it?"

"I have no idea."

Propping himself up on his elbow, he gazed across my body to the clock on the nightstand, and then flopped back onto the pillows.

"Nine-fifteen. Should we consider getting up?"

"Hmm, maybe.

He sat up and threw back the sheet. At some point in time during the night, we'd taken time to pull down the bedspread. Rising, he padded around to my side of the bed and gathered his clothing.

His body was as finely sculpted during the day as it had been at night. As he dressed, I toyed with the thought of another round of toe-curling sex, but shelved the idea. I'm not sure I could have lived through it.

Finished, Brad turned, sat on the edge of the bed, and kissed me.

"I've got to shower, shave, and check my e-mail. Give me an hour."

"Good idea."

"How about we spend the day on the boat? Tomorrow's the Fourth and the lake will be crowded."

"What about Mark Bridges, amnesia and the accident?"

He nuzzled my neck. "We can work on that later. Not likely to get much info that's offline for a few days. I'm in a totally selfish mood right now. How about it? Sun and water, the boat?"

I should have been thinking about Amy and her problems, but great sex and Brad trumped neighborly concern. Sunning and swimming sounded like a great idea. "We can have lunch at the marina. I noticed a new restaurant nearby when we were there."

"Deal. Why not ask Amy to join us for the parade?"

"All right." I liked that idea. It didn't seem as callous as just forgetting about the outburst the night before.

He kissed me again and left the room. I dawdled longer in bed, rolling over to sniff the residual scent of Brad Forrester on my pillows.

I finally rose, entered the kitchen to put the coffee on, and hoped no one peeked in the windows. I was buck naked.

I showered and dressed in a yellow bikini, and then tossed a filmy cover-up over it. The forecast yesterday had promised hot and humid conditions. As a precaution, I twisted my hair into a knot on top of my head and secured it with a large combed clip. All day in a boat didn't call for wearing my shoulder length hair loose. I packed a tote bag with suntan lotion and a towel, and then filled a small cooler with ice and bottled water.

Two cups of coffee, four sausage links, a couple of scrambled eggs, and a slice of toast hit the spot. Sex is good for the appetite. Later, I wandered onto the front porch and shielding my eyes from the glare of the sun, gazed toward Amy's. Her car was gone from the driveway. It hadn't occurred to either Brad or me that she might already have holiday plans. I guessed with Mark Bridges in town, she was still playing hostess in some form.

Turning, I walked across the lawn to Brad's. The front door was open slightly. I pushed it further and heard him talking.

"I know we had a deal, and I'm telling you it's off...I don't care. I'll return the money tomorrow...I don't like this. The woman deserves better, and I don't enjoy intruding into people's lives...Look, find yourself another author...This isn't for me. I feel sleazy." His voice faded as he must have left the room.

I backed away. I had no idea what the conversation was about, but his words mirrored my feelings about the relationship I had with Mark Bridges.

*He's probably talking about some book deal or maybe he hired a private investigator to dig up dirt on his ex-wife—the one still collecting alimony.* In either case, it was none of my business.

I waited a few seconds, and then knocked on the door. A moment later, he answered with a smile.

"Hi, you ready to go? Did you talk to Amy?"

I shrugged. "She's not home. Probably with her uncle."

"In that case, shall we journey onto the high seas?"

I laughed, handed him the cooler and tote bag, and followed him through the house to the deck and back yard. On the dock he jumped into the boat first, and then helped me in. The motor started with an easy purr. He cast off and we motored onto the lake. Moving at a fast pace, the wind tugged at my hair and I released the clip holding it in place. The breeze felt good against the heat.

We anchored in a cove large enough to accommodate several boats and still retain some breathing space, yet small enough not to attract water skiers or tubers.

Brad tossed two inner tubes out of the back of the boat into the water.

"I don't know about you, but that water looks damned inviting," he said, stripping off his T-shirt and shorts. He picked up a bottle of suntan lotion from the back bench and rubbed it into his skin.

My gaze wandered up and down his body. Much to my disappointment, the swim trunks were modest, but I took solace in his muscled legs and good-looking abs.

I rose, slowly pulled my cover-up over my head and dropped it onto the seat. Brad's gaze echoed mine of a moment ago only he grinned—with appreciation, I hoped. He entered the water in a shallow dive, resurfacing a few feet from a tube.

Suntan lotion hit my skin, too. SPF30 was a minimum. As a blue-eyed redhead, the sun could turn me into a lobster within minutes. Whatever tan I accrued was always light.

Tossing my sunglasses on the dashboard, I followed. The cool water enveloped my overheated body bringing instant relief from the sun.

Man-made lakes were often murky with visibility no more than three feet down. Lake Wildwood was no exception, but this little cove proved different. I looked straight to the mud-covered bottom eight feet away. Fish darted between the stumps and leftover branches of what had once been a small ravine.

I paddled over to join Brad, hoisted myself into one of the tubes and closed my eyes against the glare of light off the water. The splashing a few feet away told me he had done the same.

"You ever been to this cove?" he asked.

"I don't think so. Whenever we swam, it was generally off the dock. All boating activities came complete with skis, tube rafts, or fishing gear."

"That's right. I seem to remember your brothers as being intensely athletic."

"Are you kidding? My parents' garage always looked like a sporting goods store had expanded into new territory."

"Are they still sports oriented?"

"James is a marine biologist down in Miami, which means boats, fishing, scuba, and snorkeling. If he was in the water any more often he'd grow gills. John spends his free time at triathlons. Jared will slap on a pair of skis—water or snow—in a moment's notice. So, yeah, I guess you could say they're still intensely athletic."

"And not to mention competitive, right?"

"From the tops of their heads to the tips of their toes." Heating up again, I dipped my hand into the water and flicked droplets onto my skin.

"And how about you? Are you into sports?"

"Not so much anymore. No time. I did, however, play my fair share of soccer, softball, tennis, and golf while growing up. If nothing else, having three older brothers endlessly teasing me about playing like a girl gave me incentive to keep up with them."

"And kick their butts?"

I laughed. "On occasion. How about you? Were you into sports?"

"I did the usual things, but now all I play is golf or tennis once in a while. My interests were more toward books. Thrillers, suspense, and mysteries satisfied my urge for adventure."

"So, who inspired you down the road to becoming an author?" I asked trailing my fingertips in the cool water.

"Can't say there was any one author, but I had a freshman English professor at the University of Nebraska who encouraged me to send articles into magazines. I was hooked with my first acceptance and check."

"Ah, you became rich and famous overnight."

Brad chuckled. "To the mighty tune of twenty-five dollars. Why are you a lawyer?"

"I know a lot of people consider my profession one step above that of politician and one below used car salesman, but the law fascinated me. I was always arguing with my brothers." Brad laughed at my statement. "I stumbled into contract law by accident when a friend asked me to review a contract for a condo she was buying. I found a lot of questionable clauses. She refused to sign and I realized I'd found my niche. I occasionally find my way into a court room for a breach of contract issue, but I'm content."

*At least I was until Mark Bridges entered my life.* I tried to push him from my mind. Why let him spoil a perfectly lovely day on the lake?

We talked and swam until the heat and the suntan lotion wearing thin forced us back into the boat. Brad pulled up the Bimini top for protection while I uncapped a couple of bottles of water.

"What say we head for the marina and some lunch?" he said.

"I've about had all the sun I can take for a day. Besides, I'm starving."

We pulled the tubes onboard, weighed anchor, and sped across the lake to the marina. I expected the restaurant to be a wing and burger haven. I was surprised to find an eclectic menu serving everything from burgers to fried chicken to salads. Dress requirement were posted: ladies' swimming attire must be covered, men must wear shirts, and shoes or sandals were a must. The patrons were a mix of older people and families. The lack of walls on the lakeside guaranteed a good view.

Brad ordered beer and a small pizza, while I stuck with a diet soft drink and a chicken salad sandwich. The service was quick and we polished off a good meal in less than an hour.

Back home, Brad helped me from the boat onto the dock and gathered up most of our gear.

"What's on your agenda the rest of the day?" he asked.

"I'm not sure, but I think it involves a nap."

"I think I'll head into town and grocery store for some burgers, hot dogs, potato salad and whatever for tomorrow. Why don't you see if Amy'd like to join us?"

I slid the tote bag over my shoulder. "Sounds good. Do you have plans for tonight?"

He hesitated. "Actually, yes. I have some calls to make and wanted to get more done on my new story. Tomorrow's going to be a washout as far as work is concerned."

"Oh, I see." I wondered if this was his way of saying, thanks for a good time, but let's not get emotional about it. And then, I wondered if he thought I was pushy. "Come to think of it, I have a few things to do, too. My laundry is piling up."

He picked up the cooler and headed for the stairs. "Okay. I'll come over early tomorrow morning." He grinned over his shoulder. "I have a yen for sausage and eggs."

"Well, if you're going to the store, you'd better include them on your list. I'm out."

He laughed and started the long climb to the top. I dropped my sandals to the dock and slipped them on. Casting a final glance out over the lake, a red hulled boat towing a skier flashed by a hundred yards away. A woman wearing a scarlet bikini, the big floppy hat, and sunglasses sat at the helm. The skier, a man, clutched the rope and hunched over, clearly not enjoying himself. Suddenly, the woman turned sharply to the right. The skier's momentum sent him over the wake and tumbling. She cut the engine to idle, but I heard her laughter. From the water I heard several curse words.

*Abby?*

The man retrieved the skis, hauled himself onboard, and then pulled in the rope. He pushed the woman out of the way before taking over the controls. Within seconds, they sped off.

Why did these two always seem to pop up? And was the woman a blonde?

Chapter Fourteen

July 4<sup>th</sup> dawned hot with soaring humidity, and I wondered if the cloudless blue sky would remain that way.

The rest of yesterday had proven a colossal bore without Brad. I was put out he had chosen writing over spending time with me.

*No wonder he's got two ex-wives floating around.*

I was immediately ashamed of my thoughts. My attitude surprised me. Just because I was smitten for the first time in years, didn't mean he felt the same. He didn't owe me anything, and his actions hadn't suggested otherwise.

To keep busy, I did two loads of laundry, some light housekeeping, and tried to find more on the accident in the local newspaper's online archives, but struck out—again. After a mediocre microwave dinner, I knocked off another five chapters in the book I was reading before calling it a night.

This morning I awoke late, showered, and was slipping into my sandals when someone knocked on my door.

I opened up to a smiling Brad carrying a plastic grocery bag.

"Here you go. Eggs, microwavable link sausages, and some cantaloupe as a surprise."

My unjustified pique over his writing vanished as

he handed me the bag. "Have a seat. This shouldn't take long. How goes the writing?"

"Not bad. I managed to plot out the next three chapters and wrote about three thousand words."

"Wow, that sounds like a whole book," I said, ripping open the sausage box and placing the frozen links on a plate.

He laughed. "It's about fifteen pages, give or take. When I'm in the zone, I'm in the zone. I write like a crazed author."

I grabbed a frying pan, slapped some butter in, and turning on the heat, set it on a burner. I dropped two slices of bread into the toaster, and then cracked four eggs into a bowl.

"Maybe that's another plot line," he mused.

"What? Author commits murder to obtain firsthand knowledge of the forensics?"

"Something like that."

Breakfast didn't take long to either make or consume. While eating, Brad kept me informed on his progress with both the plot and the characters on his current work. I had to admit, I found the birth of a novel from a small seed of an idea to full-blown reality interesting.

"Sounds pretty intense. Do you actually become your hero?" I asked, regretting my thoughts of yesterday and ex-wives.

"I try to think like him, and yes, the process can get intense. I need to concentrate on internal conflicts, goals, and motivations as well as dialogue. Can't just slap words on a page. The dialogue should also be true to character. And of course, the hero has to have an inner self he doesn't like to share with people around him."

"You mean like with Joe Archer?" I asked, naming his detective hero. "I get a kick out of how hard-boiled he is on the outside, yet when no one's looking, he feeds the feral cats running around his neighborhood."

"You got it. Joe has a soft side, but tries to hide it." He glanced at his watch. "What time is that parade?"

"Starts at eleven. Do you want to go?"

"Sure, why not? Sounds like fun."

He helped me clean up before we wandered onto the front porch. I secured my hair on the top of my head, shielded my eyes from the sun's glare, and looked toward Amy's. Her car was still or perhaps again, gone.

"I hope Amy's all right. She either came back late last night and left early this morning, or she didn't come home at all."

"Maybe she stayed in town with her uncle."

"Could be. We might see her at the parade."

I volunteered to drive. The ride into Vermillion was slow. Everybody seemed to be heading in the same direction. If memory served, the town went all out for the celebration with floats, bands, cars full of dignitaries, and war veterans marching like in their active military days.

I finally found a parking spot at the elementary school, a good six blocks from the main parade route. I slapped my sunglasses on against the glare of the hot sun. Within minutes, sweat trickled between my shoulder blades as we walked down the sidewalk. We wedged our way into the crowd near the starting point. The sounds of bands tuning up drifted to us on the light breeze.

"Hope this starts on time," Brad said. "It's hotter

than hell out here." He glanced around. "Hold my spot, I'll be right back."

He turned and walked away. I craned my neck to watch, but soon lost him in the crowd. The sun beat down on my head and the asphalt of Main Street. In the distance, shimmers of heat rose from its surface. The thought of a dip in the cool lake off the dock sounded like a good idea. I didn't envy the band members in those heavy uniforms. And for the older vets marching, I hoped they stayed hydrated. A quick glance up the street showed the red cross of a first aid station. The city had no doubt learned from past mistakes.

Someone tapped on my shoulder. I turned to face Amy.

"Hi," I said in a bright tone hoping to convey I wasn't thinking about her behavior of the other night. Even though curious, I resisted asking where she'd been on the theory it was none of my business.

A tiny smile broke through her solemn expression. "Hi, Jenny. I thought I spotted you in the crowd. I...I wanted to apologize for the other night. I was upset with Uncle Mark, and then when you and Brad made the same comments he did, I guess I kind of lost control."

"Think nothing of it. We should apologize to you. We had no right saying anything."

"I didn't mean what I said, of course. I adored Abby, even when she tried my patience. This time of year always gets to me a little."

I wanted to ask why she subjected herself to the holiday at the very lake where the accident occurred, but held my tongue. In a mob waiting for a parade to begin was not the right place to bring up the subject. I wondered if her outburst had been accurate after all.

"Brad and I are going to grill a couple of burgers or hot dogs later. Would you like to join us?"

"Oh, thanks, but one of Uncle Mark's friends invited us over for a barbeque. I'll be home before dark though. If you aren't going to the fireworks, would you come over and keep me company?" She hesitated. "I feel funny asking just you, but I don't know Brad very well, and I count you as a friend. I'd like to talk to a friend—if that's all right with you. I mean, if you and Brad have plans, please don't change them on my account. I just thought…"

Her pathetic rambling trailed off. Instant compassion flooded through me. I'd been here almost a week and this was the breakthrough I'd been hoping for. Her tone had sounded, not desperate, but more yearning. I couldn't say no.

"Brad and I don't have any plans into the night. I'll be glad to spend some time with you. Just honk your horn when you get home and I'll run over."

A smile lit her anxious face. "Oh, thank you, Jenny. I have a bottle of wine in the fridge. We can have a drink and just talk."

"Sounds good to me."

"Well, I'd better get back to Uncle Mark and his friends. I'll see you later." She turned and melted into the crowd.

I turned my attention back to the street elated Amy thought of me as a friend. Maybe all those years ago, she'd remembered the teenager who always had time to say hi to her younger next door neighbor.

Up ahead several bandsmen stretched a banner across the front of the lead band. From behind them, a drum roll signaled the beginning of the parade. An old-fashioned thrill ran along my nerves as the notes of *America the Beautiful* sounded. That song had always given me goosebumps.

"Here," Brad said in my ear.

I turned and he handed me a baseball cap. I crammed it over my topknot.

"Thanks, that helps."

"Willard's is doing booming business in hats, sunglasses, and suntan lotion. Stick out your hand."

He uncapped a bottle of lotion and squirted some in my palm. The scents of banana and coconut drifted up my nostrils.

"You think of everything. I forgot all about hats and possible sunburn," I said, spreading the cool white cream on my arms and face certain I smelled like a fruit salad.

"When this is over, why don't we head for home and swim off the dock?"

"Good idea. I saw Amy. She stopped to say hi and apologize." I gave him the lowdown on our brief conversation.

He refrained from answering until the band passed by.

"That's a good idea. Maybe she'll say something about the accident. While you keep her company, I'll do research on amnesia. We can compare notes tomorrow."

We spent the next hour waving at parade participants, and then headed home. Since I didn't have a boat at my dock, we used it for our midday swim. Brad had hauled one of those huge inflatable round floats over. He tied it to the dock and we sunned until the heat forced us into the water. We called it quits around four, and wandered back to his place for dinner.

The burgers were great, and while it certainly wasn't a feast, it tasted like haute cuisine with Brad. We chatted on the deck until the shadows lengthened into twilight.

I sighed and rose. "I guess I should go home. Amy will be getting back soon." I stared into his blue eyes. "I can't think of when I had a nicer day than this."

He smiled. "Me, neither. Sometimes, I think we lose sight of the simple things in life. I'd forgotten how much fun I used to have here with my family. Lately, my life has been one event after another. If it's not a book signing tour, it's a conference where I present a workshop."

"I know what you mean. Do you know I even brought a couple of contracts with me? I guess I'm so used to working, I don't know when to quit. How insane is that?" I shook my head. "I'm so glad I found you here."

"I'm glad you did, too." He pulled me into his arms and kissed the life out of me, then stepped back. "I'll see you tomorrow. Have a good time with Amy."

I walked across the yard and settled in a rocking chair on my front porch. Brad Forrester was becoming important to me, and that was something I hadn't expected to happen. Or was I once again confusing great sex with love? I'd been there, done that, and screwed it up royally. Was there such a thing as second chances? And if there was, did I want—and was I ready—to take another chance? God knows, I'd learned my lesson the hard way with my ex-husband, Jim. I'd betrayed him. I hadn't talked to him since we'd signed the divorce papers six years ago. I'd heard through friends he'd left St. Louis, but had no idea where he lived now.

"Jim, I hope you're happy and I'm sorry for everything," I said out loud into the rapidly darkening night.

Headlights swept up Amy's driveway just as a boom in the distance signaled the beginning of the fireworks. I rose and walked over to the car.

She opened the door and jumped out. "Wow, got here just in time."

Even as she spoke someone nearby from down on the lake exploded an illicit M-80. Several bottle rockets soon followed. Amy flinched.

"Come on, let's get inside," I said taking her arm. "I don't know about you, but I'm looking forward to a glass or two of wine."

She laughed with a nervous twitter, but followed, opened the unlocked door, and flipped on the living room lights.

"Have a seat, Jenny. I'll get the glasses."

I wandered over to the sofa and sat. She soon joined me with the wine, and took a seat in one of the overstuffed chairs. With a smile, she saluted the portrait of her and Abby. I found it a bit bizarre, but said nothing.

In the distance, fireworks boomed. Closer, more bottle rockets and firecrackers snapped off. Amy didn't appear to be frightened or even to notice. I waited for her to speak, but she continued staring at the painting. Finally, I broke the silence.

"I'm glad you suggested this. I like a nice quiet evening with a friend."

She shifted her gaze to me, smiled, and sipped some wine.

"This is always such a hard holiday for me. If I was alone, I'd just cry or go to bed early hoping sleep would make me forget."

"So, why come?"

She shrugged. "I don't know. Sometimes, I remember all the fun we used to have, especially when we were little. I learned to swim off the dock. I was never very good at it, but Abby could swim like a porpoise. She always did everything better than me."

"Could she draw or paint wildlife?"

"No. Art and reading were too sedate for her." She smiled and sipped more wine. "Thank you for keeping me company."

"I'm glad I can be here for you." I had no idea where she was going with this.

"Jenny, if you don't mind, I'd like to talk about Abby."

Chapter Fifteen

My hand clenched around the stem of the wine glass. She wanted to talk about her sister. I swallowed. This could be the resolution of why I'd come to Lake Wildwood.

"Of course, Amy. Talk about whatever you want. I'll listen."

She inhaled and deep breath, held it for a moment, and then exhaled with a loud sigh.

"I suppose you know all about the accident."

I took a sip of wine. "No, not really. I was in law school at the time, and all Mother said was that Abby had died in a boating accident."

"I can remember that weekend like it was yesterday. We were all sitting on the porch when this little red Miata roared up the drive. It was Abby. We hadn't seen her in two years. I can still hear her laughter when we rushed to greet her. It was so Abby. Just show up and surprise everyone. She loved the spontaneity of surprises. I always considered just dropping in unannounced on people rude, but then that was just one of the differences between us."

"It is rude, but as you said, some people do it all the time," I said.

She nodded. "Exactly. And that was Abby's way. She looked fabulous—slim and fit. Her tank top matched the car color and she'd cut her hair in a very hip, edgy style, all angles and spikes. It took me years to finally get up the courage to cut my hair shorter. I'm such a stick in the mud."

"Why change a classic hairstyle when it works for you?"

Amy smiled and sipped more of the wine. "You're being kind, although I did whack it off every once in a while. Tried it real short once. Didn't like it. Now, where was I? Oh, yes, Abby drove up full of life and energy. Outgoing—introverted. Bright—dull. Abby—Amy. It didn't matter. I loved her and wished I had her courage to do something other than exist.

"For the next three days, Abby kept us entertained with stories of her exploits. I marveled at her ability to throw caution to the wind. But as the weekend wound down, I had doubts.

"We may not have shared the same zest for life or the same manner in showing that zest, but we were still twins. Absence strengthened that special bond.

"Abby laughed a little too much—was a little too gay and carefree, as if her attitude would prevent us from asking for details of the places she'd been and the people she'd seen." She paused to gulp the rest of her wine, and then rose to refresh the glass.

I could easily see Abby in some kind of trouble and using the family cottage on the lake as a bolt hole.

I sipped and shook my head when she raised the bottle as a question for a refill to me. She returned to her seat.

"I remember that last night so vividly. We sat on the dock around midnight, passing a bottle of Chianti between us. In the distance, lightning flashed and thunder rumbled. Abby's never-ending stream of conversation had finally ceased. She gazed out over the water, a thoughtful expression on her face, and handed me the bottle. I took a sip and passed it back.

"I asked her what was wrong. She denied any kind of problem and questioned me asking. Abby always did that—answered a question with a question in order to buy time to think up a lie. I pressed her, but she still evaded the truth."

From what I'd heard, Abby Wallace had possessed the ability to see black as white. Denial was her middle name, not responsibility. But I couldn't very well say that to Amy.

"Maybe that was the truth. Maybe she just missed her family," I said.

Amy shook her head. "No, there was something. I felt it."

"How did you end up on the lake?"

"Abby noticed the Howards had a new boat and wanted to take a closer look. I knew we were in trouble the instant she grabbed the keys from the dock box."

"Did you say something?"

"I tried to stop her, but she brushed my objections away. 'We aren't stealing, we're borrowing. Besides, the Howards aren't here, so how would they know?' The next thing I knew, we were aboard."

"But it was stealing."

She sighed. "I know. Don't you think I've gone over this a million times in my head? It was wrong, I knew it was wrong, but did it anyway. Abby was like that. She could convince anybody to do anything she wanted."

From what Bridges had told me, the Howards hadn't pressed charges. They should have, but I guessed they felt a death resulting from stupidity was punishment enough.

"So, you went for a joy ride."

Amy gulped half the wine in the glass and nodded. "I wanted to go back. A storm was coming." She closed her eyes. "Lightning flashed and thunder boomed. Abby ignored it all and pushed the throttles to full speed. The boat had big engines and skimmed the surface of the water at a terrifying speed. I was scared and begged her to turn around."

"Did she?" I asked knowing that at some point in time Amy had taken the controls.

"She throttled back to idle in the middle of the widest part of the lake. She laughed and told me if I wanted to go in, I'd have to do it myself. The wind was rising fast and the water churned, bouncing the boat from side to side."

Her eyes widened as she relived those last few minutes of her sister's life. I had no problem seeing the fear and revulsion.

I sipped more wine to calm my nerves and wondered if Amy had ever told anyone else the story, other than her psychiatrist—and the police.

"So, that's why you were at the controls?"

"I'm not very good with boats and took it slow, but the storm was faster. It broke a few minutes later. Abby sat on the back bench. She…she teased me for being a slowpoke and a…scaredy cat. I…I got angry and pushed the lever all the way forward. Visibility was just a few feet. The rain was pounding, almost blotting out the sound of the engines. The all of a sudden, this thing appeared in front of the bow."

"What thing?"

She gulped air and let it lose in a gasp. "I don't know. It was big. Maybe a fallen tree or a log dislodged from the bottom of the lake. I couldn't move. We hit it at full speed. I was thrown overboard and hit the water. Then, there was this blinding flash and the explosion almost deafened me. I remember screaming Abby's name over and over. I grabbed a floatation cushion drifting by. Then everything goes blank.

"I suppose people heard the explosion and called marine rescue and the police. I seem to remember debris floating by and…and the smell of gasoline. It clung everywhere—on my clothes, my skin, in my hair, in the water. It was there, stinking. I think I recall fire, too. I…I must have swum out of the flames. I don't remember.

"I slipped in and out of consciousness. And then someone found me. I woke up in the bottom of a police boat. They kept asking me questions, but all I could say was, 'Find Abby. Find my sister.'"

"I was in the hospital the next day when a policeman came in and said there was no trace of Abby. They'd found a rubber sandal, one of those flip-flops she always wore at the lake, floating about a mile away. I think Mom or Dad may have identified it as hers, but I'm not sure.

"The days turned into weeks and still no sign of Abby. I begged the police to search the area, convinced she'd survived and was in need of help. I suggested amnesia, but no one paid much attention to me. Not even Mom and Dad. At the memorial service I half expected her to walk through the doors full of laughter at attending her own funeral."

She ceased talking and finished her wine, her gaze

riveted on the portrait above the fireplace. Her stream of consciousness ramblings made me wonder if she'd forgotten I was even here. I waited for her to continue. Instead, she rose and poured another glass, drinking a large portion. She resumed her seat and her story.

"They never found her, but that didn't stop me from hoping." She finally turned to look at me. "Do you know I even hired a private investigator? He must have knocked on every cabin door on Lake Wildwood. Nobody had seen Abby and no unidentified females had presented themselves at local hospitals. In the end I gave him the information Abby had told me about her life the past two years. I have his report. Would you like to see it?"

Without waiting for an answer, she leaped from the chair and ran into the hallway. A minute later, she returned with an aged envelope and handed it to me. Little rips and tears in the paper told me she'd pulled the contents out hundreds of times. I didn't want to read it. Not now.

"May I read it later?"

"Of course, take it with you. I cared about finding her. I had to find her. Tell her how sorry I was. It was an accident. Honest. An accident."

I wanted to cry for her—this poor lonely woman who still felt the guilt after all these years.

"Of course, it was an accident, Amy. No one ever said otherwise. In a way, Abby brought it on herself. She should never have handed over the controls to you with a storm brewing."

"Sometimes, I wonder if she didn't do it deliberately," she said in a low tone.

"Do what?" I asked, confused. Die?

"Make me take over knowing I'd make mistakes. When we were teenagers, she used to call me challenged on doing the easy things. It was her way of saying I was incompetent."

*The strong preying on the weak. Survival of the fittest.* Only Abby had miscalculated and not been the survivor.

"You were inexperienced, not incompetent. Don't think that way. Abby showed an unfortunate lack of judgment. If she'd shown some sense, she'd have kept control."

I didn't add that if Abby Wallace had had any sense of judgment at all, she'd have never taken the boat in the first place.

"Perhaps." Her gaze drifted back to the painting. "To this day, I can still hear her laughter as we pulled away from the dock. I can still smell the lake. I hate that smell. All rotting vegetation, gasoline, diesel, and dead fish. It rose as if to suffocate me. And the wind from a full speed dash across the water pulled my hair loose from the bun I'd had it in. It streamed out behind me like a wild curtain. And the engines—they throbbed and vibrated beneath my feet. I was both terrified and exhilarated.

"When Dad found out I'd spent over three grand on a private investigator, he said I needed help. I had to face the fact Abby was dead. What could I do? The police thought she was dead. Mom and Dad said it was so. All my relatives believed it. I was the only one holding out hope.

"I had a breakdown. I couldn't stop crying. I felt alone, abandoned. Six months after the accident, my parents committed me to a sanitarium. A psychiatrist helped me understand it wasn't my fault, but to this day, I only partially believe that. I was released six months later. A year of my life was gone, but Abby's was finished forever. I tried to pick up the pieces. A friend of Uncle Mark's suggested I send my wildlife sketches to a publisher he knew. Within two years, I had enough work to keep me occupied. I still think about Abby every day. Daddy died of a heart attack several years ago. Mom died in an automobile accident not long after that. I'd give anything to have things the way they used to be."

She drained her wine and leaned back in the chair, her head resting on the top of the cushion as though exhausted. She'd had a miserable time, but had seemed to get on with things. What had brought on this sudden concern that Abby was still alive? Loneliness? The desire to have what can no longer be? I realized with a psychic jolt that I could empathize.

"Amy, do you still believe Abby is alive?"

She looked me in the eye and smiled. "I know she is."

"Because a ring you saw in a pawn shop window resembles one she owned?"

She hesitated, as though weighing her answer. "Not only that, but…"

The sentence trailed off and she caught her lower lip between her teeth.

"But?" I prompted sitting forward in anticipation.

"She's alive. I've seen her."

I sat back again. Here was the confirmation Mark Bridges sought. Given what she'd just told me, I wasn't surprised. I was, however, intrigued.

"You've seen her? Where?"

"About a month ago, I was on the dock watching the sunset. Suddenly, this little boat whipped by not a hundred feet from shore. Abby was at the helm. Then a few days later, I was walking in the woods and heard her laughter. I'd never forget Abby's laugh. I tried to find her, but couldn't."

"And the day we had lunch at Victoria's?" I asked slowly.

She nodded. "She drove by in a little red sports car."

I remembered seeing a red sports car at the intersection up the street. Oh my God, it sounded so plausible. "And on the dock the other night?"

"She came past again in the boat."

"But, Amy, why would Abby not just come forward and say something? Why do this?"

"I told you. Maybe her amnesia is lifting bit by bit. I have to find her."

I didn't know what to say. Was Amy Wallace having massive hallucinations, or telling the truth? Both had disturbing consequences. I could see how Mark Bridges would find her admission alarming. But then, I had had questions only the other day, too.

"I can see by the look on your face, you think I'm around the bend like Uncle Mark does," she said, her tone challenging. "He wants me to sell this place, return to St. Louis, and put myself under Dr. Carlson's care."

"Dr. Carlson?"

"The psychiatrist from the Valley View Sanitarium. I'm not crazy. I did see Abby. And the ring was hers. I have no idea how the blonde woman got a hold of it."

The blonde. I'd forgotten about the blonde. The

blonde could have known Abby. Perhaps Abby had told her about Lake Wildwood. She could have even sold or given the ring to the woman. But why would this mystery blonde suddenly show up now, ten years almost to the day after the accident? I didn't have an answer, and that bothered me. And the thought that *maybe* the blonde was Abby added another dimension to the plot. Amy's voice brought me out of my thoughts.

"The funny thing is I'd decided to sell this house come fall. It's too much trouble maintaining two houses a hundred and fifty miles apart. Now, of course, I have to keep it. It's Abby's one link to the real world again. If she remembers and comes here, what would she do if a new owner opened the door?"

"Amy, has it occurred to you that your uncle could be right? He only wants what's best for you."

"Yes, I know, but he's not right. I am. I'd stake my life on it. Jenny, please help me. I've looked in every motel, bed and breakfast, and rooming house in town. I can't find her. Help me search. She might be staying out of town. Take her picture to motels and such in Stone City, Lakeview, and Watertown. I can go to towns south of here. Maybe Brad will help, too."

She rose and walked into the kitchen, refilling her glass again, gulping half of it down before coming up for air. She gazed at the empty bottle before opening another.

"I know what I ask sounds bizarre, but I can't do it alone and for some reason, I not only like, but trust you. Don't take this the wrong way, but sometimes I think of you as a substitute Abby. Even though we were chalk and cheese, we could and did talk to each other. I miss that the most."

She asked for help. She needed me, and at the moment *I* needed that. My suspicions of the last day or so about Abby being alive grew stronger, even though Amy was the only one to admit having seen her sister. All I'd seen were two people in a boat. At least, she hadn't claimed conversations with Abby yet—just sightings. And then there was that damned ring. I had to find out the truth.

"All right, count me in. I'll talk to Brad tomorrow, but I can't guarantee he'll come. He's busy on a new book."

"Thank you, Jenny. You don't know what this means to me." She polished off the wine, and then set the glass on the counter. "Whew, that's a load off my mind." She brushed a hand over her forehead, then shook her head and clutched at the edge of the counter.

I set my glass on the coffee table, rose, and hurried to join her. "Are you all right?"

"I'm sorry, but I've had a little too much to drink."

"Would you like me to help you into bed?"

"No, that's not necessary. I'm glad we had this talk. Thank you for listening." She turned and walked, swaying slightly, down the hallway.

A glance at my watch showed she'd talked for close to three hours. I returned to my wine glass. The envelope with the private investigator's report was next to it. What possible use could it have now? I admitted to a strong curiosity as to what it said. I stuffed it into my pocket, re-corked the wine, put it in the fridge, rinsed the glass at the sink, and left.

As I walked across the lawn, the occasional putt-putt of outboard engines signaling late returning revelers drifted across the water. Here and there, a stray firecracker along with a bottle rocket popped and fizzled in the night air. I paused on my front steps. No lights showed from Brad's. I'd have liked to share tonight's revelations with him. Tomorrow would have to do.

Inside, I pulled the report from my pocket, sat in a chair by the fireplace, and turned on a lamp.

I withdrew the six page report. Six pages covering two years. Abby must have been a busy girl. I skimmed the first four pages. They dealt with her life and misadventures in Los Angeles, Las Vegas, San Francisco, and San Diego. Nightclubs, a couple of DUIs, an arrest or two for disorderly conduct fueled by her vivacious and sometimes out of control personality. She ran with a pretty wild crowd, but never stayed in one place long enough to get into real trouble. Until she hit Dallas.

I read the last two pages with an uneasy feeling creeping over my skin. It prickled like the warning just before lightning struck. I wondered what Amy had thought of her twin's activities.

No wonder she'd returned to Lake Wildwood ten years ago. Abigail Marie Wallace had an outstanding warrant for drug trafficking.

## Chapter Sixteen

*Diary of Amy Margaret Wallace*

I know I told Jenny I was going straight to bed, but I'm too excited to sleep. My head is swimming from all the wine I drank. Nevertheless, I want to get this down while I can. Tomorrow will be a busy day.

Tonight I did it. I told Jenny all about the accident and having seen Abby in town and on the lake. I must say, she didn't seem too surprised by the news. Or perhaps she was being polite.

I feel so liberated. Jenny is kind and sympathetic. She didn't laugh or get that look in her eyes that said I must be hallucinating. That came from Uncle Mark. I know what he has in mind for me. Imagine how surprised he'll be when I produce Abby. I can see it now. His eyes will bug out and his jaw will drop.

And Abby will have a good laugh. It'll be the ultimate surprise.

But the best news is Jenny agreed to help me find Abby. I even suggested Brad Forrester might like to assist, but I'm not sure I completely trust him. I sometimes have the feeling he's watching me, measuring what I say and do. Of course, I've only seen and spoken with him a few times. Still, when Abby returns to her full memory, he could write about it. A bestseller for sure.

As I said, tomorrow will be a full day. Jenny, God bless her, said she'd go to Stone City, Lakeview, and Watertown to the north in search of Abby.

Oh, I'm yawning. Guess that wine is kicking in. Time to go to bed. I'll need all the rest I can get.

Who knows? By this time tomorrow, I may have my sister back.

Chapter Seventeen

Dawn was breaking. I stood at the railing of my deck, a cup of coffee in my hand, staring over the yard and down the hillside toward the lake. Tendrils of mist threaded their way through the trees only to disappear in the lightening sky.

To say I had a lousy night's sleep was an understatement. Tossing and turning, I couldn't get Amy's narrative or the report out of my mind. Had the Dallas police come knocking on the Wallace's door? Was the warrant even still valid? As an attorney, I should have known, but I didn't deal with the criminal side of the profession. I was a contract lawyer for crying out loud. What did I know about warrants? I knew they varied from state to state.

Amy's story and the private investigator's report now had me firmly in her corner. Abby was alive and I strongly suspected had faked her death—or at least taken advantage of the situation. It was clear in my mind. Abby swims to safety. Not an impossible feat since Amy said her twin could swim like a fish. Then Abby walks down the highway and into a new life— sans arrest warrant. Never mind that her family is devastated by her so-called death. As long as Abby was safe, then nothing else mattered.

I gulped my coffee and banged the cup down on the wooden railing, angry at the actions of a self-absorbed woman. How could she do this—and why? I knew the why. The trust had to be at the bottom of this cat-and-mouse sighting game. Somehow, Abby had heard of her parents' deaths. She now wanted her share and she didn't care how she got it.

The eastern sky glowed a glorious pink as the sun crept higher into the sky. A faint whisper of a breeze swirled the mist shredding its concealing blanket. In an hour all would be clear.

I turned, walked back inside, and poured another cup of coffee before heading into the living room. Setting the cup on the table, I stretched out on the sofa and tried to make sense of this whole mess. I'd been doing that most of the night.

My biggest question was did Amy, after having read the investigator's report, also believe her sister had deliberately disappeared? Forget the amnesia angle. Did Amy believe it? And if she did, what did she think? Was she angry? Afraid? Confused? And would she reach out to help?

Amy didn't appear angry or afraid. Confused was closer to the truth. I also believed she didn't give a damn about the money. She just wanted her sister back. Abby was the only immediate family she had left. The problem was I didn't think Abby cared about Amy nearly as much as Amy did about her.

The lost sleep caught up with me. I fell asleep and didn't awake until after ten. I showered and dashed onto the front porch ready to share my knowledge and suspicions with Brad, but stopped short. His car was gone. A quick glance to my right showed Amy's parked where she'd left it. The house, however, was closed tight. I assumed she was still in bed. After her catharsis last night, I could understand. It must have been exhausting reliving the accident and telling me about it.

I wandered back inside and hit a bowl with some cereal and milk. Not wanting to take time to make more coffee, I had orange juice instead. As I ate, I pondered my next move.

Mark Bridges was no longer in the equation. My desire to protect a fragile Amy said he didn't need to know about any of what had transpired. Let her have her privacy.

I tried to look at the situation in a logical manner.

Abby was in a boating accident. She was presumed dead even though no body had ever been found. Still, Amy's theory of amnesia gradually wearing off could be valid. It wasn't outside the realm of logic to think she could have returned with partial memories.

I shook my head. It's hard to be logical when you don't believe it. I had no idea where Brad had gone, but wondered if he'd done any research into amnesia like he'd said. If he was still gone by this afternoon, I'd Google it myself. A lot hinged on the subject.

I finished breakfast and was putting the bowl into the dishwasher when someone knocked on the door. I opened to find a smiling Amy.

"Hi, Jenny, how are you this morning." Her voice was chipper and upbeat.

I stepped back. "Fine. Come on in. The question is how are *you* this morning?"

She entered and laughed. "I feel liberated! I am so glad to finally be able to tell someone the truth and not be accused of seeing things." She rummaged in her purse before pulling out a small manila envelope. "Here are a couple of pictures of Abby. One was our high school graduation. I know it's kind of old, but here's one taken her last weekend home."

I took the envelope, opened it, and slid the photos out. The person staring back at me was so like Amy, I couldn't resist lifting my gaze to the woman before me.

She laughed again. "Two peas in a pod, right?"

"Sure is. Even as kids."

In the graduation photo, Abby's hair was not the spiky do of the portrait above the fireplace, but long, the shining black tresses falling over her shoulders like a smooth curtain. Her smile was pure mischief waiting to happen.

The second picture was a snapshot taken on the dock and the inspiration for the painting.

"When can you get started?" Amy asked. She looked up with eager eyes. "I'm heading south to a few towns now. Last night you said you'd go north." A frown marred her forehead. "You are going to help, aren't you?"

"Sure. I haven't had a chance to talk to Brad. He's gone, but I said I'd help and I will."

Her smile beamed. "Oh thanks, Jenny. I'll be home later. Let me know if you find out anything."

She waved and left with a jaunty step. I wished Brad was around. His input would be helpful. I took a deep breath. This could be a very interesting day.

I grabbed my purse and headed outside. Brad still wasn't home. I hesitated, fingering my car keys. I knew the towns Amy had suggested I visit. The furthest away, Stone City, was less than a forty minute drive.

Casting another glance toward the Forrester house, I slowly descended the porch steps. I really needed to talk with Brad, but had no idea where he'd gone or

155

when he'd return.

*The least he could have done was leave me a note.*

On the other hand, I had no claim on his time or knowing his agenda. He was an author and probably had a deadline. I knew enough about writers to understand research was essential to their work.

With a shrug, I opened my car door and slid behind the wheel. Depending on traffic, the trip should only take a couple of hours.

I put the car in gear and drove off.

****

Lakeview was the first town on my route. It was located six miles from Lake Wildwood. It did not have a lake view. On a good day, the population was no more than a thousand people. During the drive, it dawned on me that I had no way to contact Amy if I did find something. I hadn't thought to ask and she didn't volunteer a cell phone number.

I slowed as I entered the town. The Shady Inn motel was close enough to Vermillion and cheap enough to lure budget conscious families to the area.

I showed the clerk the photos of Abby along with a story about how she was a missing person.

He stared for a moment before shaking his head. "Nope, ain't seen her."

"She might be driving a red sports car. Seen anything like that?"

"Maybe. People come and people go. If I saw one, I don't remember."

"Are there any bed and breakfasts or boarding houses in Lakeview?"

"Nope. This is it, and business ain't been all that good what with the economy."

I thanked him and headed for Watertown, an even smaller town ten miles east on Route 14. The name came from a small stream that eventually fed into Lake Wildwood. It had one main street, no stop lights, and definitely no tourist accommodations. It did, however, have a café on the edge of town. My stomach growled reminding me that cereal was not long-lasting. I pulled in and joined the three other cars in the parking lot.

Inside, I sat at the counter and ordered a soft drink along with a burger. The place was surprisingly up to date with gleaming Formica table tops, and dark red vinyl on the seating.

The waitress brought my drink. I took a pull through the straw and once again flashed the photos of Abby, getting the same response.

"You say she's missing?" another waitress said looking at the picture over the woman's shoulder.

"Yes, she's my cousin and has a habit of just taking off every once in a while. Worries the family to death."

"Yeah, I can see how it might."

"She's been known to drive a red sports car on occasion. Have you seen one lately?"

The first woman shook her head. "No, can't say that I have."

"I did," the other waitress said.

"Where?"

"Here. Must have been a couple of days ago. A man and woman pulled up, came in, had lunch, and then left."

"But it wasn't this woman?" I asked.

"No. At least, I don't think so. I mean I didn't pay much attention. I just noticed the car. My boyfriend would have loved it. Oh yeah, she wore these really funky sunglasses shaped like hearts and a big ole hat."

My heart rate accelerated. Just like the woman in the boat. Now I was getting somewhere.

"I don't suppose you noticed if she wore a rather distinctive ruby and diamond ring?"

The first waitress furrowed her forehead as thought in thought. "You know, I served a customer wearing something like that, only she had long blonde hair. That's why I remember her. Both she and the ring were knockouts. We don't get a whole lot of jewelry conscious diners in here."

"When was this?"

"Two, three weeks ago. I'm not sure."

*Abby as the blonde again?*

The time frame fit with Amy's sightings of Abby, and the pawn shop owner's information.

"Was there a man with her?"

She shook her head. "Can't remember for sure, but I don't think so."

I turned my attention back to the second waitress. "What about the woman with the sunglasses? Was there a man with her?"

"Yeah, I remember him. He kind of flirted with me. I thought it was sleazy with his girlfriend sitting next to him and all."

"What did he look like?"

She shrugged. "He may have had dark hair, but I don't know for sure."

"Burger up!" a voice called from the window to the kitchen.

The waitress brought my food. I ate, thanked the women, tossed some bills on the counter along with a generous tip, and left.

I sat in my car for a moment tapping my fingers on the steering wheel. Something wasn't making sense, but I couldn't figure out what.

Amy had seen Abby in a red car and a boat several times. Abby had dark hair unless she'd bleached it, but if that were the case, Amy might not have recognized her. And if she did, would certainly make mention of the fact.

And a blonde had stopped for lunch in a diner in Watertown wearing a ruby ring. A blonde had also pawned a ruby ring belonging to Abby in a Vermillion hock shop.

*Abby and the blonde have to be the same person.* I started the engine. My next stop was fifteen miles away.

Stone City earned its name from a large quarry on the outskirts of town that had once employed most of the townspeople. Now it stood abandoned and, no doubt, a gathering spot as an illicit swimming hole for adventurous teenagers. Show me a teen who obeys "No Trespassing" signs.

This was the largest of the towns on my list with a population of close to six thousand. Two motels, one a mom and pop operation and the other a chain, answered the need for overnight travelers. Interstate 70 wasn't far away.

Neither of the desk clerks at the motels could identify Abby.

"Are there any bed and breakfast places in town?" I asked an older lady behind the counter at the locally owned spot.

"One up on Hill Street. It's called Greenpeace after that environmental group. The owner is big on that kind of stuff."

I thanked her after obtaining directions and finally found the place behind a jungle of bushes and shrubs screening it from the road. I parked out front and hurried up the path to the spacious front porch. All this overgrown vegetation gave me the willies. Insects buzzed and I imagined things that slithered lurked not far away.

A man answered the door, and for a moment I stared convinced the ultimate hippie had retired to central Missouri. This guy hadn't managed to leave the sixties behind either. As creepy as the foliage was, this dude was creepier.

Unfortunately, he couldn't help me. His only two guests in the last three weeks had checked out this morning, and the woman didn't look a thing like Abby Wallace.

I didn't even ask about a red car. All I wanted was out of there and rushed back down the path to my car.

I wound my way through residential streets admiring the Victorian style houses with their neatly trimmed lawns and bushes—a contrast to Greenpeace. I was half a block away from the intersection to the main drag when a red sports car flashed by. The momentary glimpse showed a dark haired woman at the wheel.

I punched the gas and arrived at the corner, then had to jam on the brakes as I waited for three cars to pass.

"Come on, come on," I muttered. Didn't anybody go the speed limit anymore? Were they practicing for a parade?

When the final car cleared, I turned left and pulled around to pass one of the slow moving drivers. Up ahead, the red car hung a left at the light. I approached the intersection just as the light went red, but turned anyway. The red car with the dark-haired driver was a block away.

Then from behind me came the all too familiar whoop-whoop of a siren. I glanced in the rearview mirror and cursed. A police car, its lights flashing was on my tail.

Frustrated, I pulled over and watched helplessly as the red car disappeared. The cop gave me a lecture on running red lights and a ticket. I spent the next twenty minutes or so cruising the side streets looking for the red car before finally admitting defeat. It and its driver were long gone.

With a sigh, I turned around and aimed for home.

****

I stomped into the house pissed as hell. Amy was still gone, as was Brad. And all I had to show for almost three hours was a traffic ticket for a hundred and twenty bucks. I needed to cool off.

Dumping my purse and keys on the kitchen counter, I headed into the bedroom, unearthed my bikini, changed, grabbed a beach towel from the linen closet, and made my way down to the dock.

I jumped into the cool water. It felt good and I floated on my back letting the slight current take my body toward the Wallace dock.

I finally rolled over and swam back. Spreading the towel on the sunny edge of the dock, I lay down and allowed the hot sun to dry me. The water had cooled my temper and I tried to organize my thoughts.

I'd come up with bupkus on Abby, but with sightings of the blonde. I assumed her companion at the diner in Watertown was still with her. A dark-haired man. I sat up with a jerk.

Of course, how stupid of me! The man and woman in the boat! The woman had worn a hat. She could have tucked her hair up underneath it—or worn a wig during her blonde sightings. If that was the case, then her presence in Vermillion took on sinister implications. Still the boat had to have been rented. Why not go to the marina and ask Brad's friend—oh, crap, what was his name?—who had rented either the boat or the slip? There had to be something on paper. It was so logical I wanted to kick myself for not having thought of it before.

*I'd never make it as a private investigator.*

I scrambled to my feet and made a dash for the steps. Winded, I paused at the top to catch my breath before hurrying inside to dress. While I combed my damp hair, another thought occurred to me.

Amy'd been looking for *Abby* in town, not the blonde. If she's renting a boat or dock space at the marina, then it's logical she and the guy she's with must be staying close by. *When I'm done at the marina, I'll have a name to inquire about at the local motels and resorts.*

Gathering my purse from the counter where I'd left it, I rushed out to my car. I opened the car door, tossed my purse inside and was about to slide behind the wheel when I glanced toward Amy's.

A shadow along the far property line caught my attention. Had I seen movement in the bushes near the woods or was it just a trick of the light? Sunlight and shadow can sometimes give the impression of movement. And then I remembered Brad's comment about a homeless person perhaps being responsible for the footprint under my living room window. And now I wasn't so sure I *hadn't* seen a prowler on Amy's deck that first night.

Without stopping to think about the possible consequences, I walked across the lawn. Amy was still gone, but if someone was skulking around the woods, the authorities needed to know. As a rule, homeless people aren't violent and while I didn't want a confrontation, I could take a quick look around.

The property next to Amy had been owned by a man and his wife who loved to fish. The house had never gone beyond the cabin stage, and their love of nature had precluded the need to thin out the trees and foliage. I had no idea if they still owned the place, but suspected the house stood empty—at least for now.

I paused at the edge of the woods. The rhododendrons were large and well-tended. I supposed Amy's mother had planted them years ago. I noticed a small gap between two bushes.

Hesitating, I peered into the woods through the foliage. Birds chirped and leaves rustled in the occasional breeze drifting up from the lake. I heard and saw nothing.

I pushed my way past the bushes. I had to check out that cabin. It probably wasn't the smartest thing to do, but then nobody had ever accused me of being Einstein.

A path of trampled vegetation led off at an angle. Had it been made by human feet or was it a well-traveled highway for possums and raccoons? Both critters along with foxes had been known to inhabit the area in heavy numbers creating havoc with gardens and garbage cans.

I moved cautiously down the narrow path keeping a close eye out for poison ivy or oak. I was highly allergic to both and didn't want to spend any time covered in calamine lotion. Insects circled and swarmed around my head. I kept busy chasing them away with impatient hand gestures.

The trail followed a fairly straight line. Would animals do this or would they tend to meander more? Not being much of a nature lover, I had no clue.

I broke out of the woods. Before me stood a dilapidated cabin and what was left of a yard. The trees shaded the plot and a thick mat of old leaves substituted for grass. A gap in the trees to my right showed the remains of the steps to the dock. I had no intention of testing them. They were probably rotting.

The cabin appeared intact although the roof had a wavy appearance as if some of the sheathing had rotted. The curled shingles reminded me of a bizarre feathery hairdo.

I slapped at a mosquito on my cheek as I made my way to the front of the place and mounted the porch steps. They creaked and groaned under my weight, but held. Dirt and grime covered the windows, so I tried the door. It opened on squeaky protesting hinges. I stepped inside.

The cabin was still furnished and stank of mold. I'd rather die than sit on either the sofa or the chairs. Apparently, someone else wasn't so discerning. A sleeping bag was rolled up on the floor next to the sofa. A glance toward the kitchen area showed several cans of food on the counter both open and unopened. Flies buzzed around the rims of the opened ones.

My arms broke out in goosebumps. Someone *was* living here, although not home at the moment. I needed to get the hell out and call the police.

I whirled and ran out the front door not bothering to even close it behind me. The thought of returning to that narrow pathway gave me the shivers. I headed straight for the neglected driveway. This was little more than an overgrown path, too. The deep ruts made walking difficult, so I moved to the side trying to avoid the roots of trees and vines that had encroached for years. A tree had fallen ages ago blocking access. Getting a car up this thing would be impossible.

I stepped over the fallen tree, and then stopped. There in the dirt were several faint tire tracks. I stooped to inspect them closer. Behind me a twig snapped and footsteps rushed toward me.

Before I could rise and turn, pain exploded in my head. I toppled over as my world went black.

Chapter Eighteen

*Diary of Amy Margaret Wallace*

I'm sitting in a café sipping coffee and ready to cry. I have to write this down or explode. I spent over three hours searching for Abby and found nothing. It's as if she doesn't exist.

Of course, that's what Uncle Mark believes, but it's not true. She's alive. I know it. Maybe Jenny had better luck. I should have gotten her cell number. Or given her mine. This not knowing is killing me.

Am I tilting at windmills? Has my mind gone south again? No! I know what and who I saw. I will not allow Uncle Mark or anyone tell me otherwise.

I need to get home. To see Jenny.

I have to find my sister. Now!

## Chapter Nineteen

I wasn't completely unconscious. More stunned than anything. In the twilight realm of reality, I heard footsteps run past me, then a motorcycle rev up and roar away.

My head throbbed, but I pushed myself to my hands and knees, then using a tree for support, rose. My vision was blurred and the scenery spun. I wrapped both arms around the trunk ignoring the bark scraping at my arms. Something trickled down my cheek. I put a shaking hand to the side of my head. Blood. Not a lot, but enough to scare me. Nausea clawed at my stomach, and I threw up.

I had to get home. If I passed out here, no one would find me. Sucking in several deep breaths, I finally released my death grip on the tree and ventured a few steps toward the road. The dizziness returned and I dropped to my knees until it cleared. Finally, I stumbled out of the driveway and onto the asphalt. A car screeched to a halt, missing me by a hair's breadth.

I cried out, fell against the driver's side fender, then to my knees, my head pounding and the world spinning again.

The car door opened and someone scrambled out.

"Jenny? Are you all right? Oh, my God, did I hit you?" Amy exclaimed.

I pulled myself upright. "No," I said in a gasping

voice. "Someone attacked me. In the woods."

Amy didn't hesitate. She grabbed my arm and guided me to the passenger door, opened it, and shoved me into the seat. She slid back behind the wheel, and fished some tissues from her purse.

"Here. It's the best I can do for now. When did this happen? Have you lost a lot of blood?"

My sense of time was skewed so I wasn't sure and judging from the amount of blood splattered on my T-shirt and shorts, I'd have to say I was running on empty. My hand strayed to the side of my head and came away sticky, but not slick as earlier. The bleeding had either stopped or slowed.

"Just get me home. I don't want to throw up in your car."

She pulled into her driveway, backed out again, and headed into town.

"Not on your sweet life. I'm taking you to the hospital. You said someone attacked you? Who?"

"I have no idea. Didn't get a chance to see. Just wham and the lights went out."

Reaction set in and I shivered like a Chihuahua in January. I clenched my teeth to stop them from chattering and closed my eyes.

"Don't you dare go to sleep," Amy commanded. "Stay conscious. Talk to me. Does your head hurt bad?"

I refocused my eyes on the road ahead. Trees and light poles flashed past. Amy was flying, taking the curves like a race car driver. I shook my head. The resulting stab of pain cleared the fog.

"Bad enough."

"What were you doing in the woods?"

"I…I thought I saw someone, and wanted to see if

there was a prowler. Oh my God, I never knew my head could hurt like this."

"Hang on. We'll be there in a few minutes."

Amy raced down the side streets of Vermillion and pulled up to the hospital emergency room entrance. I was helped by orderlies from the car onto a gurney, and then rushed back to an exam room. A nurse stuck a needle in one arm. A blood pressure cuff encircled the other while someone inspected my head. Wires were attached to my chest. Then came the questions.

"Are you hurt anywhere else?"

"How many fingers do you see me holding up?"

"Do you feel dizzy or nauseated?"

"BP's 120 over 60. Respiration is 15, pulse 104."

I answered as best I could.

"Hello, my name is Doctor Townsend. And what happened to you?" a male voice asked.

"I had a close encounter with a blunt object," I replied.

He gazed at my wound. "From the bits of bark embedded in your hair, I'd have to say a tree branch. Don't worry, you'll be fine. A couple of stitches should do the trick. Were you unconscious at all?"

"Not really. I saw stars and things went a little dark, but I could still hear."

"Any blurred vision, nausea, or dizziness?"

"A little at first, but not now. I did throw up."

He turned to one of the nurses. "Clean out the wound. Let's do a CAT scan before I sew her up."

"A CAT scan? Is that really necessary?"

"You may have a concussion. I want to make sure there's no intracranial bleeding." He smiled as though to say, don't worry, I'm the doctor.

It didn't work. His words scared the crap out of me. I swallowed hard and shuddered.

I was wheeled down a maze of corridors, placed in a weird looking cavelike machine, told not to move, and rolled through like I was on a conveyor belt. Finished, I was transported back to the exam room where I awaited the results.

After what seemed an eternity, Doctor Townsend came in with another one of those patented doctor smiles. He must have aced that med school course.

"Good news. X-rayed head; saw nothing." He laughed at the old joke. "You'll be fine. I'm going to sew you up and tomorrow morning you can go home."

"Whoa, whoa," I said struggling to sit up. "I wanna go home tonight. As soon as you're finished."

He pushed me back down. "I'd really like you to stay for observation."

"Why? You said I was going to be fine."

"You are, but I like to be on the safe side."

"And I like my own bed. Look, I'm feeling much better. No dizziness, no nausea, and no blurred vision. My head hurts like a son of a bitch, but I have a whole bottle of aspirin in the medicine cabinet."

"Why don't you think about it while I stitch you up?"

I didn't need to think about it. I'd only been in a hospital once after a car accident while in law school. The experience was enough to make me hate them like a rash on my rear end. I hated the smells and whoever suggested a quiet rest in the hospital didn't know squat. Hospitals are noisy. People talking in the halls, nurses coming and going, and ringing phones at nurses stations made sleep all but impossible. Plus, hospitals were full of sick people—really sick people. I'm not a germaphobe, but couldn't see exposing myself to some weird disease. No way.

Doctor Townsend shaved the area around the wound, and gave me four stitches. When he was done, he handed me a mirror.

I was a mess, but not as bad as expected. The shaved area looked odd, but I could always hide it with a headband. I got lucky. The cut was about two inches above and to the back of my temple.

"Are you sure you don't want to stay overnight? I highly recommend it."

"No thanks. I'll be fine. Really."

"All right, but you'll have to sign a release form. Do you have insurance?"

"Yeah, but all my IDs are in my purse back home."

"Just give the nurse your name, address, and phone number. You can come back tomorrow with the information. By the way, your friend wants to know if she can come back."

I'd forgotten about Amy. "Of course, send her in."

He left and a minute later Amy peeked around the curtain in the entryway.

"Hi, how are you?"

"Better than a couple of hours ago. Thank you so much for helping me."

"I feel just awful. For a moment there, I thought I'd hit you. You said something about a prowler?"

"I was about to get into my car when I thought I saw someone in the woods next to your house near the rhododendrons. I found a kind of a path and followed it."

"But, Jenny, that wasn't smart. Did you get a look

at him?"

"Never saw a thing. Not even when he hit me."

The curtain parted and a policeman stepped into the cubicle.

"Miss Devlin?"

"Yes?"

"I'm Officer Glen Howard of the Vermillion Police Department. I understand you were attacked."

"How did you know?"

"I called him, of course," Amy replied. "If there's someone in the woods, he has to be caught."

A woman came in asking for my personal information. I gave it to her and promised to bring in the insurance cards the next day. The woman said she'd be a few minutes longer and departed.

"Miss Devlin, why don't you tell me what happened?" Officer Howard pulled a notebook and pencil from his shirt pocket.

I gave him the facts. He listened and wrote without interrupting my narration.

"And you say there was definite evidence of someone living in the cabin?"

"Absolutely. The sleeping bag wasn't new, but not old enough to have been lying around the cabin for any length of time. And the open cans in the kitchen had flies buzzing around them."

"Any idea who owns the place?"

"No. I've been gone too long."

"It used to belong to some people by the name of Adams. He died years ago and his wife sold it," Amy said. "I'm sorry. I can't remember to whom. I think it's passed through several hands over the years. I'm sure someone must have legal title and pay the taxes, but I have no idea who."

"We can find out. Where did the attack occur in the driveway?"

"By a fallen tree. It's not a big one, but big enough to prevent a car from coming all the way up. I'm sure you can find it. I'd just stepped over it when wham, I got nailed." There was more to the story, but my fuzzy mind wasn't cooperating completely.

"Can you describe anything out of the ordinary after being hit, Miss Devlin?"

"My mind's a little foggy at the moment. I never saw a face or even a body. Just felt my head explode, and then falling over. Funny, I can remember every stick and stone on the ground, even the smell of the damp earth, but that's all."

The woman returned with a bunch of papers in a clipboard.

"Here you are, Miss Devlin. The one on top is your consent to be released against doctor's orders. Please sign on the bottom line and initial each page in the bottom left hand corner. This exonerates the hospital from any damages sought if you should become ill or die. The last two pages are statements you received care in the emergency room."

I wasn't a lawyer for nothing. In this day and age, doctors and hospitals covered their asses for every aspirin dispensed. Eager to get out of the place, I signed and initialed where indicated. My head still throbbed, but not with the intensity of earlier.

The woman thanked me and left.

"You're releasing yourself?" Amy asked.

"I'm fine. Just a little headache."

"But what if you feel ill overnight? Someone

should be with you. You can stay at my place. I have a spare room across the hall."

"Amy, that's sweet of you, but I can't put you out."

"It's no trouble at all. The bed's already made up. We'll stop by your house, get some fresh clothes, a nightie, and your toothbrush. I insist. It's the least I can do after you've been so nice to me."

I didn't feel like arguing. "All right. Thank you."

A nurse entered, unhooked me from the machines, removed the IV, then eased me into a wheelchair and pushed me down the hall. Officer Howard accompanied us.

"Give me two shakes and I'll have the car here," Amy said trotting out the doors.

True to her word, she pulled up less than two minutes later. Between the orderly, the policeman, and Amy, they got me settled into the car.

As he shut the door, Officer Howard said, "If you don't mind, I'll follow you home and check out this cabin."

That sounded like a good idea to me.

I spoke little on the ride home. Amy talked a blue streak, however.

"Hungry. You must be hungry. When did you last eat?"

"Breakfast, I think. No, I had a burger in some diner in Watertown, but that was it. By the way, no one identified Abby's picture. I drew a blank. I'm so sorry. What about you?"

She shook her head. "Nothing. Soup, I think. Chicken noodle soup and maybe a salad or would you prefer a sandwich?"

Her brief answer and change of subject confused

me for a moment. I glanced at her composed face. Maybe she was good at hiding her feelings. She'd pinned her hopes on finding Abby in one of the outlying towns.

"Just because we didn't find her, doesn't mean she isn't here," Amy said as if reading my mind. "We're just not looking in the right places. She'll turn up. She always turns up. Abby might be self-centered and thoughtless, but she isn't mean. As soon as her memory's restored, she'll knock on the door and say hi, long time, no see. You watch."

Officer Howard pulled into the cabin's driveway while Amy continued to her place.

"Now, let's get you some decent clothes. You can't get those stitches wet for a while, but maybe we can wash the rest of the blood out of your hair if we're real careful."

As she helped me across the lawn, I glanced toward Brad's. The car was parked and he sat on the porch. He rose at our approach to my house and waved. Then he must have noticed Amy supporting me and the blood on my clothing. He rushed over.

"My God, what happened to you?"

"It's a long story."

"I've got time."

Amy led me to a chair on the porch. I sank down grateful to be off my feet. Amy hovered next to me.

"Now, what happened?" He glanced at my car. "Obviously, you weren't in a car wreck."

I gave him the lowdown on my misadventure.

His eyebrows drew together in a frown. "What the hell were you thinking? You see a suspicious person in the woods and follow him?"

"I didn't see a suspicious person. I saw a movement and investigated. It might not have been the smartest thing to do, but I was curious."

"And why aren't you still at the hospital? Head injuries can cause complications after the fact."

I had to give him an explanation for that, too.

"Jenny, for the love of God, be…"

"She's staying with me tonight," Amy interrupted. "I'll take care of her. I know to wake possible concussion victims every few hours to make sure they don't slip into a coma."

Brad ran a hand through his hair. "And someone was definitely living there?"

"I don't know about living, but someone had slept and eaten in the place."

"You did talk to the police, didn't you?"

"Of course! Amy called them. An officer is over there right now checking things out."

"Jenny, you stay seated. I'll go get you some fresh clothing," Amy said.

"That's all right, I can…"

"No," she stated in a firm tone. "You rest. I'll only be a minute."

She strode into the house and I cast my gaze on Brad.

"And where have you been all day?" I didn't care if I sounded accusatory. I might not have been attacked if he'd been with me. I ignored the fact I was being unreasonable.

He looked toward the door and lowered his voice. "Doing research on amnesia. I read an article online last night that was technical enough to pique my interest. The author is a professor at the University of Missouri.

So, I tracked him down this morning and called. He agreed to meet me at noon in Columbia. I wanted to tell you, but I was running late."

"And what did you learn?"

"It was interesting to say the least. I'll tell you when we're alone. How about your chat with Amy? How did that go?"

"Beyond my wildest dreams. I feel so damned sorry for her. She needs friends and a social life."

Footsteps crossing my living room floor halted our conversation. Amy rejoined us with some clothes and my toothbrush in her hand.

"Is this all right?" she asked.

"It's fine," I sad eyeing the shorts, T-shirt, underwear and the tank top I used for sleeping. I'd tossed it on the bed this morning.

"Then let's get you back to my place. I'm making soup and a sandwich for Jenny. You're welcome to join us."

"Thanks, I may do that."

With Amy carrying the clothing, Brad placed his arm across my shoulders and walked me back across the lawns.

We were at the porch steps when crunching gravel had us turning. A police cruiser pulled into the drive. A moment later, Officer Howard emerged.

"What did you find?" Brad asked.

"And you are…?"

"Sorry, I'm Brad Forrester. I live on the other side of Miss Devlin. She told me what happened. Did you find anything useful?"

"Miss Devlin, you said you saw a sleeping bag on the floor and canned goods on the counter?"

"Yes."

He shook his head. "Not there now. Not even any trash to pick through."

"But it was there. I saw it!" I now understood how Amy must feel about her Abby sightings.

"Could be whoever attacked you got scared and cleared out."

"Did you find any footprints?" I asked.

He shook his head. "Too many leaves on the ground. Tell me again what you heard just prior to getting hit."

"I'd just stepped over the tree. I heard a twig snap, footsteps, and then nothing." Even as I said it I knew that wasn't quite true. I was missing something.

Officer Howard stared at the bandage covering my stitches. "How tall are you?"

"Five-six. Why?"

"From the location of the wound, I'd say whoever hit you must be extremely tall."

His words jogged my memory pulling another piece of the puzzle together.

"I wasn't standing," I said slowly. "I had stooped down to view something on the ground."

"Tire tracks?"

"Yes!"

He nodded. "I saw them, too."

The rest of the pieces clicked into place. "After I got hit, the guy ran off. I remember hearing his footsteps, and a minute later a motorcycle took off."

"I also found evidence of a motorcycle or scooter having been parked behind some bushes just off the drive, along with the telltales of a fast takeoff. Miss Devlin, are you sure your assailant was a man?"

The question made me blink in surprise. "No. I just assumed a man was responsible. I don't want to sound sexist, but can't believe a woman would live in that cabin. The place was disgusting."

"Jenny, did you tell him about the prowler?" Brad said.

"Prowler? What prowler?" the policeman asked.

"It was last week. A thunderstorm rolled through early in the morning. I was closing the windows when I thought I saw someone on Miss Wallace's deck. Later that morning, I saw a footprint under my living room window."

"And you didn't report this?"

I shook my head. "I forgot about it."

"I suggested it may have been a homeless person looking for shelter from the storm. It might explain why someone was in the cabin."

"It might." Officer Howard removed his Smokey hat and wiped his forehead with a handkerchief. "We haven't had any reports of vagrants lately, but what with the economy the way it is, anything is possible. I'll ask around. In the meantime, lock your doors and don't be afraid to pick up the phone if you see anything or anyone unusual."

The policeman left. I walked up Amy's steps under my own power and plunked my fanny into her porch swing. The afternoon was winding down toward twilight. It had been a hell of a day.

"You should lie down," Amy said.

"I'm fine. Really. It's quiet and peaceful out here. My head hurts, but not as badly as before. However, I am hungry as a horse."

"Oh, my goodness, of course you are. And here I

am talking."

"If Jenny doesn't mind, I'll lend a hand in the kitchen," Brad said.

"I hope soup and a sandwich is enough for you," she said flashing a smile at Brad.

"It's fine. I had a big lunch in Columbia today."

Before they could enter the house, another car came up the driveway. Mark Bridges exited and joined us. He stared at my bloody clothing.

"My God, what happened to you?"

I sighed, not wanting to go into my horror story again.

"She was attacked," Amy blurted.

"Attacked? Where? When?"

I filled him in on most of the details. "And Amy very graciously offered to let me stay with her tonight," I said, hoping to ward off any discussion he wanted with his niece.

"Who owns that place? They should be sued," he said with a frown.

"Uncle Mark, we were just going to grab a bite to eat. Would you like to join us?"

"No, thank you. I'd like to talk to you, but maybe tomorrow. I will, however, take a drink."

I hoped Bridges would keep our business deal from his niece. I liked Amy and last night had finally gained her trust. Trust and I hadn't had much of a working relationship in the past. I didn't want to lose what ground I'd gained with my neighbor.

"Come on in, Jenny. Get out of those awful clothes," Amy said.

Brad helped me out of the swing, while Amy and her uncle headed toward the front door.

Suddenly, something slammed into the side of the house a foot away from Amy's head. Simultaneously, the crack of a rifle shattered the evening air.

Chapter Twenty

Brad flung me to the porch floor. The jarring impact sent a slashing pain through my head as he covered my body with his.

Amy cried out followed a moment later by a thud. I raised my head. Amy lay face down next to her uncle. Mark Bridges crouched in the doorway to the screened portion of the porch, his face furious.

"Goddammit! Knock it off! There are people here!"

His words made it sound like an accident, but given my experience a few hours ago, I wasn't so sure.

Silence greeted his shout. We all waited a few more seconds. In the distance, a motorcycle engine revved, the sound gradually dissipating into the night. Then Brad slowly lifted his body from mine. Bent low, Bridges ran to his car, dove inside, and returned stopping at the base of the steps with a gun in his hand. He raised it toward the woods where the shot had come from.

Brad grabbed his arm. "Don't! You might hit someone."

"That's the idea."

"Uncle Mark, please," Amy said scrambling to her feet to stand in the doorway. "It was probably an accident. Kids taking pot shots at a squirrel or raccoon."

He relaxed his stance, but not his anger. "I don't

care who it is, they've got no business shooting this close to homes."

Brad helped me to my feet. "Are you all right?"

"Yeah, more or less. Did you hear it? The motorcycle?"

"I heard," he replied in a grim tone.

My voice shook and my legs wobbled. The throbbing in my head reached a crescendo. Anger at being used for target practice didn't help the situation. I'd had about all I could take for one day. My gaze swung to the side of the house. A neat round hole marred the vinyl siding. "My God, that thing just missed us."

I clenched my fists and took several deep breaths to calm the anger bubbling in my chest. I couldn't decide if I wanted to hit something or cry.

Bridges laid the gun on the top step and whipped out his phone.

"What are you doing?" Amy asked.

"Calling the cops. What's it look like I'm doing?"

"Is that really necessary? I'm sure it wasn't deliberate."

Her uncle, Brad, and I all stared. For just having a bullet miss her head by inches, she was awfully composed.

Brad looked at me, and then back to Amy. "Even if it's just kids screwing around, the police should be notified."

"And suppose it's the crazy living in the cabin next door?" Bridges demanded. He jabbed in three numbers.

My brain was ready to ooze out of my ears. All I wanted was a good jolt of something alcoholic, one of the pain pills the doctor had given me, and a good night's sleep.

"Hello, operator, I want to report shots fired…Mark Bridges. I'm at my niece, Amy Wallace's house—515 Highridge Lane…Sounded like a rifle to me. Bullet hit the side of the house right where we were standing…No, no one's hurt, but a neighbor was attacked this afternoon in the woods where the shot was fired…Jenny Devlin. I believe the police were notified…I don't know…" He looked at me. "What was the officer's name?"

"Howard, I think."

"Glen Howard," Amy supplied in a calm tone.

*How can she be so cool?* I swayed slightly. Brad caught my arm and lowered me to the porch swing.

"Officer Glen Howard took the report, operator…Yes, we'll be waiting inside."

He hung up. "They're sending someone out immediately. I don't like this one bit."

"Uncle Mark, you're making a mountain out of a molehill."

He scowled. "Amy, for the love of God, look at Jenny."

I wished they wouldn't. I was a mess of blood and dirt.

"Amy, if it's not kids it might be the person living in the cabin. Not all homeless people are non-violent," Brad said. "Some have mental problems. For all we know the man came back and decided to scare us."

"It worked," I said.

Amy's unconcerned attitude struck me as odd. Why wasn't she more outraged? The damned bullet had just missed her head. And speaking of heads…mine chose that moment to throb harder.

As we'd talked, the twilight had given way to dusk. Soon the full dark of night would be on us. Insects chirped and mosquitoes buzzed.

As if reading my mind, Brad slapped at one and said, "Let's go in before the bugs eat us alive."

Inside, Mark Bridges headed straight for the liquor cabinet, removed a bottle of Chivas and poured four glasses. Brad and I walked over to him.

"I don't want anything, Uncle Mark."

"Well, I sure as hell do." He and Brad drained the scotch in one long swallow.

"And Jenny shouldn't have any either. She has a head injury." Amy sounded like a stern headmistress— or a concerned friend.

"Don't worry. It's not that much of an injury."

Brad frowned. "Amy's right. You shouldn't drink anything alcoholic with a head injury."

He didn't wait for me to respond and proceeded to down the glass poured for me, too.

They were proven right when for an instant, the room spun. I groped my way to the sofa where I sat with a thump. Bridges drank what he'd poured for his niece, and then refilled his and Brad's glasses.

From outside, headlights illuminated the darkened screened in porch and cars crunched up the driveway. Mark hastily put the gun in the liquor cabinet and closed it. A series of car doors slammed followed by footsteps mounting the porch. Amy answered the door before anyone knocked. Officer Howard had returned along with three other policemen.

*Half the Vermillion Police Department must be here.* I wanted to giggle, but refrained. Not only would I sound like a nitwit, but a drunken one at that—and I hadn't even had anything to drink.

One of the officers stared at my clothes with a frown. "Are you all right, miss? Should we call an ambulance?"

I shook my head and waved my hand in the air. "No need. This is from an earlier incident."

A bobbing flashlight from the porch suggested one of the cops was inspecting the bullet hole. I assumed the bullet was still inside since the interior wall was undamaged.

"Miss Devlin was attacked in the woods earlier," Officer Howard offered. "I took the report. Now, what happened?"

Mark and Brad gave them the details of what had happened. All I craved was to close my eyes and go to sleep.

"And you heard nothing prior to the shot? Nobody stumbling around in the woods? No voices?" Officer Howard asked.

"Nothing," Brad replied. "Of course, we'd been talking and were just fixing to go inside and grab a bite to eat. We might not have heard them."

"Officer, I'm sure it was just kids who were probably so terrified, they took off like scalded cats. They're most likely home right now, hiding in their rooms, and crying," Amy insisted.

"Maybe," the cop replied.

"And maybe not," I answered. Her insistence on this subject was baffling. "After all, someone clonked me pretty good. And I distinctly heard the sound of a motorcycle in the distance."

Howard nodded. "We'll take a look outside just in case, not that we'll find anything at night. Hang tight.

We'll be back shortly."

He left with the other policemen.

I sagged against the sofa cushions, exhausted—too tired to so much as lift my hand.

"Jenny, are you all right?" Brad asked.

"Just tired." I struggled to stand. Brad leaped to my side and steadied me. "I need to get home and go to bed."

"But what about dinner?" Amy asked.

"Not tonight. Thank you for the invitation, but I need my own bed."

"But suppose you need help overnight?"

"I'll be there," Brad said. He cast a glance at Mark Bridges who stood next to the liquor cabinet pouring another drink. "Are you staying with Amy?"

"Of course."

"That's not necessary," she protested.

"Amy, don't argue. I'm staying. I need to talk to you about something anyhow."

*Not tonight, Bridges. Give it a rest.* I opened my mouth to voice my thoughts, but nothing came out.

Brad's arm encircled my shoulders drawing me close to his side. The warmth of his body seeped deep into mine. I was both exhausted and energized at the same time.

He guided me toward the door.

"Here, don't forget these," Amy said, handing me the clothing and toothbrush she'd taken earlier.

I leaned over to kiss her cheek. "Thank you so much for everything. If it hadn't been for you, I'd have never made it past the end of the driveway. I'd have lain on the side of the road for God knows how many hours."

She smiled and blushed, then ran her fingers over where I'd kissed her.

"I'm just so glad I could help. Have a good night, and if you need anything, don't hesitate to ask."

I stifled a yawn. "Good night, Amy, Mr. Bridges. Please let us know if the police have any developments."

Once outside, Brad hefted me into his arms and carried me across the lawn. I said nothing, just enjoyed the experience. His aftershave still clung to his skin and I breathed in the fresh scent. I'm sure I smelled of dirt, blood, and antiseptic.

I retrieved my purse and keys from the car where I'd chucked them hours ago, and entered the house.

Brad flipped on the lights. "Do you have a gun?"

"A gun! Oh, you mean here in the house. Dad used to keep one handy, but I don't know if it's still here. Look on the top shelf of the closet."

As he rummaged in the hall closet, I looked down at myself with distaste. The blood had long since dried, its texture that of cardboard on my T-shirt. Darts of pain stabbed my head. I gently fingered the bandage covering the stitches. Most of the blood had been washed from my hair at the hospital, but I still felt the stiffness in a few strands.

Brad finally found the gun and ammunition. He loaded the revolver and set it on the coffee table, then walked over to me. Folding me into his arms, he kissed my wound.

"You have no idea how scared I was when I saw all that blood."

"It looks worse than it was."

"Forgive me if I disagree. What if your assailant

had used a tire iron or wrench or something instead of a tree branch? He could have cracked your skull like an egg."

The image was disturbing to say the least. "Which leads me to believe this was a matter of being in the wrong place at the wrong time. Whoever's been staying in the cabin saw me, acted out of fear, and then scrammed."

"Only to return later with a .22 rifle?"

"How do you know it's a .22?"

He shrugged. "The report wasn't loud enough for a thirty-aught, and at that range, the bullet would have gone right through the house."

I yawned. "Maybe Amy's right and it was kids. Hell, my father gave me a .22 for my tenth birthday. My brothers and I used to plink cans and bottles in the woods behind our grandparents' house in St. Genevieve. Do you think the two incidents are connected?"

"I have no clue, but find it suspicious along with that motorcycle."

"Could have just been someone passing by on the road."

"Maybe, but I'm the suspicious sort. It's the mystery writer in me." He kissed my forehead. "Why don't you go back to St. Louis?"

I pulled away. "What?"

"You heard me. Go back home. Why continue to stay here? It doesn't make sense."

I retreated a few steps irritated at the suggestion. "What are you saying? That I'm supposed to turn tail and run?"

"Jenny, first of all you do something monumentally

189

stupid by following a prowler into the woods."

"Oh, so now I'm stupid?"

He rushed on as if I hadn't spoken, anger and frustration clearly visible on his face. "Your reward for that was a whack on the head. Now this shot. Just fucking go home!"

I fisted my hands. "In the space of a few hours, I've been knocked up alongside the head with a goddamned tree branch, and now some asshole shot at us. I'm as stubborn as a Missouri mule! I wanna know why—and who!"

"It doesn't matter!"

Both of us were shouting and if a tree branch had been available, Brad's head was in danger of looking like mine.

"Yes it does, dammit! Amy is a friend and I don't have many of those anymore!"

Brad relaxed and stared. "What do you mean?"

Tears welled in my eyes. "Do you know what it's like to be abandoned? Well, I do. I've been living like a nun for the past six years. My divorce was hideous. I strayed and when my husband found out, he was angry and bitter. He had every right to be! My family took his side, and while I expected Jim's friends to drop me, I didn't expect my friends or co-workers to do the same. Invitations to have a drink or dinner after work disappeared. No requests for my presence at dinner parties arrived. I suspected the women suddenly wondered if I had their husbands or boyfriends on my hit list."

"Jenny, I'm sorry." Brad stretched out his arms, but I waved him away.

"Five years ago, I made a change. I got a new job,

a new home, and decided work was the answer. I'm lonely, dammit! I want friends again! And Amy is a friend. *I will not abandon her!*"

The tears spilled over. This time I didn't resist when Brad took me into his arms and held me tightly. I sobbed into his chest. Six years of misery soaked his shirt. When the water stopped flowing, I pulled back.

He lightly kissed my lips. "Honey, I had no idea. My divorces were not nearly as traumatic. I guess friends see things differently when it's the guy who's in the wrong. My friends stuck around although I'm not sure I'd even call them friends anymore. Why did you stray?"

"Jim—my husband—was a sales rep for a pharmaceutical company. He traveled a lot. Sometimes he'd be gone for an entire week. I got lonely, bored. Ed, the guy in the office, was always willing to listen to my woes. His sympathy and so-called understanding wore me down. A touch led to a kiss, and the kiss to an affair. Unhappy in my marriage, I confused good sex with love. I didn't learn until after the divorce that good old Ed was a serial sympathizer. I was just another notch on his bedpost."

"I know the type. If he'd come on to you directly, you'd have probably told him to go stuff it."

I sniffed and wiped my eyes with the hem of my T-shirt. "I…I really don't know where all this came from. I haven't even thought it much less told anyone how I felt. I guess guilt can only be held in so long. I never had a sister to tell my troubles to when growing up. Even though I haven't told her anything personal, I think Amy is providing that now. Whatever, I can't just leave."

"I'm glad you told me, and of course you can't go home now. Forget I even mentioned it." He kissed me again. "Why don't you go soak in the tub while I make us dinner?"

That bath sounded like a winner. "Dinner? I'm not even sure what's in the fridge."

"I'll find something. Now scoot."

I turned, then hesitated and turned back again. "You don't really think I'm stupid, do you?"

He smiled. "For chasing a shadow into the woods? Let's just call it bad judgment. For sticking by a friend in need? No, honey, you're not stupid. Now, go get that bath."

I picked up the clothing Amy had selected for me and entered the bathroom. While the tub filled, I pulled off the filthy shorts and T-shirt, and then inspected my face and head in the mirror. A lump had formed around the stitches. I probed gently and winced when pain radiated. Damned thing hurt like a sonofagun.

In the tub I let the warm water soothe the rest of my aches and pains. Telling Brad about my life after the divorce had lifted a ton of weight and guilt from my soul. For the first time in years, I shared. And I'd shared it with a man who was rapidly becoming more than just another friend. Not one word of judgment had passed his lips. Maybe the healing had begun.

Lying back, I let my mind drift to the events of this tumultuous day. I contemplated what Officer Howard had suggested about my attacker being a woman. It could explain why my head hadn't, as Brad had so inelegantly put it, cracked like an egg. Plus, my hair was fairly thick, and if the branch used had been lying around for a while, it could have been softened by exposure. And there was no reason why a woman couldn't ride a motorcycle.

*Or maybe a scooter.* No, even in my semi-conscious state, the engine noise was more powerful than that. I didn't get a clear picture of the tire tracks. I'd been nailed too quickly, but the police would no doubt take impressions or whatever.

As the water gurgled out of the tub, I pulled on the fresh shorts and my tank top nightie. As soon as I finished eating, I'd go to bed.

I walked into the kitchen sniffing with appreciation. Bacon frying was one of those aromas that spelled home.

"Smells good. What are you making?"

"A BLT. It's quick, simple, and just enough to fill your stomach without being too much. I found some strawberries and blueberries in the fridge and sliced a banana for a fruit salad."

"Wonderful." I took a seat at the breakfast bar.

He slapped a lot of mayo on two slices of toast, assembled the sandwich, and presented it to me along with a few chips, the salad, and a bottle of water. He joined me a few minutes later.

In spite of my exhaustion, I ate like a horse. The salty bacon crunched nicely and mingled with the lettuce, tomato, and condiment in my mouth. I washed it down with the ice cold water. The fruit salad was the perfect accompaniment.

I pushed my empty plate away. "God, that hit the spot."

"Now, may I suggest you go to bed? You have had one hell of a day."

I couldn't disagree with him there. The second

wind I had gotten from being in my own house was rapidly fading.

"Let me make up one of the spare rooms first unless you want to share my room." Come sleep with me, was the best I could do.

He grinned, but shook his head. "You need sleep, and I'm not sure you'd get that with me in the same room. Just give me a pillow and a blanket. I'll camp out on the sofa."

I saw his point along with the gun on the table. A little extra security couldn't hurt. Gathering the requested items from the linen closet, I handed them to him. He tossed them onto the sofa, and then hauled me into his arms where he proceeded to kiss the breath out of me.

I was wondering if I really needed all that rest when he broke off and stepped back. Not a bad move, since my pounding heart had sent the blood rushing to my head. The resulting slash of pain cooled my ardor.

"Go to bed. We'll talk in the morning."

I kissed him on the chin. "Thanks for staying. Good night."

He drew a finger down my cheek and tapped it against my lips. "Good night."

I hesitated taking one of the pain pills the doctor had given me. After all, I did have a head injury, but then decided what the hell? He'd prescribed them and it really wasn't much of a head injury. I swallowed one, slipped the shorts off, and slid into bed. I closed my eyes waiting for the pill to take effect. It didn't take long. On the verge of sleep, my mind replayed the attack, only this time I turned my head as the branch descended and saw the blonde.

Chapter Twenty-One

I awoke with a clear head. Sunlight streamed in the window warming the room. I kicked off the covers and stretched. The pill had worked. I'd slept hard with only a faint memory of strange dreams. Not nightmares, just odd. All about woods, lakes, and boats in a weird juxtaposition with Brad, Amy, Mark Bridges, and even the mysterious blonde. Not surprising given yesterday's events. Had my mental image of a blonde woman hitting me been real or just a dream?

I rolled over and squinted against the glare from the sun at the clock on the nightstand.

Ten o'clock? You've got to be kidding. I slept for almost thirteen hours?

Tentatively, I sat up. No dizziness—always a good sign. I swung my legs out of bed and stood with the same results. Breathing a sigh of relief, I dressed, brushed my teeth, and followed the aroma of coffee into the kitchen. Brad sat at the kitchen table nursing a cup and reading the paper. An empty bowl testified that he'd already found the cereal.

"Good morning. How did you sleep?" he asked with a smile.

"For want of a better phrase, like the dead."

"You don't remember me coming in and waking you several times?"

"Not at all. Did we talk?"

"You did tell me to go to hell the last time."

I chuckled, poured a cup of fine French roast, hit a bowl with those toasted "o's," sliced a banana, covered it all with milk, and joined him.

"Are you feeling all right this morning?"

"Fit as a fiddle," I replied spooning breakfast into my mouth.

"Do you feel up to discussing what I found out about amnesia?"

"Ready when you are."

"Do you know you're talking in clichés?"

I laughed. "Only an author would notice that. I'm anxious to tell you a few things, too."

"Ladies first."

"Uh-uh, I'm going back for seconds. You start. I want to hear all about amnesia and your trip yesterday."

"My notes are at home. Give me a few minutes to freshen up and I'll be back."

Brad folded the paper, set his bowl in the sink, and left.

Shortly after, I made good my promise on seconds and was just finishing when he returned. He laid a folder in front of him on the table.

"I was online when I noticed one of the articles was written by a man at the University of Missouri in Columbia. He teaches psychology. I called him and asked if I could pick his brain. I was going to ask you to go with me, but your place was buttoned up tight. I figured you were still in bed, and I'd be home by early afternoon."

So that explained his absence. I'd have rather he pounded on the door and awakened me.

"Most amnesia is short term and comes from a

whack on the head that temporarily erases recent events."

"Like yesterday," I said. "I didn't remember everything until later."

"Exactly. It's not all that unusual. Amnesia can also be caused by toxic substances like booze or carbon monoxide. The victim may have problems recalling old information or learning new. They're often disoriented and confused. How many times have you heard someone say they were so drunk they couldn't remember a thing?"

"I've never been *that* drunk."

"Well, I have and it's true. Alcoholics can have blackouts on a regular basis, but as soon as the toxin is removed from the system the memory may return."

"Well, I don't think Abby Wallace has walked around in an alcoholic daze for ten years. There has to be another cause—if she suffers from amnesia."

Brad riffled through the papers in the file. "There's also a rarer form of the disease called psychogenic or dissociative amnesia. This can be the result of severe trauma or emotional shock."

This got my attention. "As in a boating accident and an explosion?"

He nodded. "It's possible. The victim may lose personal and autobiographical information, but usually only for a short time. However, if the brain was severely injured recovery can take years."

"Aren't there drugs or something to help?"

"Hypnosis has been used to bring out forgotten or buried memories, but it's controversial. Years ago it was associated with sex abuse cases."

"I remember that. Parents accused of abuse by their

kids when they were two or three years old, before the mind keeps cognitive records."

"Exactly."

I chewed on the tip of my fingernail. "Did you go into specifics with this guy about Abby?"

"I didn't mention any names, but asked if it was possible for an amnesia victim to spend ten years in the dark and gradually remember. I think he assumed I was gathering material for a book. I didn't enlighten him otherwise."

"What did he say?"

Brad sighed and frowned. "According to him, anything is possible when dealing with the human mind. To quote him, 'The psyche is imprecise.' That wasn't helpful."

My lawyer mind kicked into gear. "Let's assume for the moment that Amy is right. Where has Abby been all this time? Certainly not around Lake Wildwood. Someone would have seen her."

"And where was she immediately after the accident? She had to stay somewhere."

"I wonder how many cabins like the one next door to Amy dot the area. Could she have found refuge in one?"

"But how would she get out of the area?"

"I don't know. Abby was resourceful and adventurous. Maybe she hitchhiked."

Brad replaced the papers in the folder. "That's it for me. Wish I hadn't offered to buy Professor Giddon's lunch as a way of thanking him for his help. That way I would have been back here to go with you into the woods. As it was, he bored me to tears with psychological theories for close to two hours."

I laid my hand on his and squeezed. "Can't be helped and you did get answers to our questions."

"Okay, your turn. What did you find out from your night with Amy?"

I gave him the lowdown beginning with the night of the accident, the accident, and the months afterwards.

"So, Amy had a breakdown," he said. "Not surprising. Guilt can be a powerful instrument on the mind. Uh, my opinion, not the professor's."

"Ah, but here's the biggie." I told him about Amy admitting she'd seen Abby on several occasions.

His forehead furrowed. "She admitted this out of the clear blue sky? Why? You're practically a stranger."

"I like to think Amy trusted me as a friend. Or maybe she'd held it in so long she needed to tell someone other than her Uncle Mark."

"Do you think Bridges knows she unloaded the full story on you—including the sightings? Is that why he wanted to talk to her last night?"

"I have no clue and I'm sure as hell not telling him." I paused to gather my thoughts. "Throughout all of this Amy's mentioned several times that her sister was vivacious, fun-loving, a real character. But last night she gave me something that showed Abby in a whole different light."

"What's that?"

I rose. "Wait here, I'll go get it."

I found the envelope with the private investigator's report from ten years ago on an end table in the living room.

"Here, read this," I said handing it to him.

Brad read for several minutes while I poured us both a glass of iced tea.

His eyebrows rose. "Abby had an outstanding arrest warrant for drug dealing? So, Amy knows her twin was just a tad bit more than vivacious, but isn't acknowledging it. Interesting."

"Is there a statute of limitations on a warrant? I don't deal with criminal law."

"Ask someone at your law firm. I wonder if the cops came here or to St. Louis looking for Abby. If so, and discovered she'd died, the warrant could have been rescinded." He riffled through the pages. "Where's the letter?"

"What letter?"

"There should be a cover letter. All we have here is the report."

"I don't know. Maybe Amy threw it away."

He replaced the report in the envelope and tapped it on the tabletop. "Why would Amy give you this?"

"Trust? A cry for help? If you could have heard her talking, it was like a floodgate opened and the words poured out. I had the feeling this report validated her search in some way."

"That doesn't make sense."

I ran a hand through my hair, wincing when I made contact with the bandaged stitches.

"I know, but maybe it does in her mind."

"I think I'll give Trevor a call," he said to himself.

"Trevor?"

"Trevor Sloane, a friend of mine in Los Angeles. He's a private investigator. I contacted him years ago when I had questions about where my first wife spent her nights. Since then, he's become my encyclopedia whenever I need answers for my novels. In fact, Joe Archer is based on Trevor."

"How can he help?"

"I'll have him investigate the warrant. See if it's still valid, and what he can find out on Abby Wallace, especially in the last ten years. If she's alive and living under that name, she has a paper trail." Brad smiled. "Your information is more interesting than mine."

"I'm not done." I told him about my road trip to the towns up north.

"I take you found nothing or all of us would have known."

"But I did find a couple of waitresses at a greasy spoon who remember seeing a blonde wearing a ruby-and-diamond ring at their lunch counter a few weeks ago. She was with some guy."

"And you think the blonde is connected to Abby?"

"It's either a possibility or the most incredulous coincidence ever." I gave him my theory that Abby and the blonde could be the same person.

"Which makes this whole thing very premeditated. I don't like it."

"I even saw a red sports car in the last town and tried to follow. I ran a stoplight and have the ticket to prove it. I was so pissed when I got home and neither you nor Amy was back, I had to cool off in the lake."

"Sorry I wasn't there for you."

"I think I'll let Amy search for Abby for the moment. I'm more interested in the blonde, assuming she's not Abby. She must be staying close by and renting a boat or dock space. There's no evidence she's the woman in the boat I saw, but I can always ask. That's where I was headed when I got whacked on the head."

"Now, that makes sense. It's almost noon. Let's pay Sam a call and see if he can ID the woman. We should have done this days ago. After lunch, we can check out motels in the area. I'm kind of curious about that ring myself."

He rose, picking up the folder with his report in it and the envelope containing the private investigator's information.

"Give me a few minutes to contact Trevor and set the ball in motion. Meet me at the car."

He left and I took the opportunity to do something with my hair to hide the bandage before settling on a cloth headband. The elastic pressed against the lump and the stitches a bit, but not enough to cause much discomfort. I'd only be wearing it in public anyway.

I then changed into a nicer pair of shorts and slid my feet into white sandals. I stepped back to admire the effect in the mirror. Not bad. No one would ever know that yesterday I looked like something out of a horror movie. I scooped up the bloody clothing from where I'd left them on the bathroom floor and tossed them in the trash can.

Returning to the kitchen, my gaze fell on my laptop sitting on the kitchen table reminding me I hadn't updated my electronic diary in a couple of days. *And God knows the last couple of days have been eventful.*

I kept the entry short and to the point focusing on Amy's narrative, my trip north, the attack, and the shot being fired. Twenty minutes later, I flexed my fingers and stretched. I closed the lid, relieved the chore was over. A glance at the clock made me get up from the table and go outside.

*What's keeping Brad? He's been gone for almost an hour.*

My eyes strayed across the lawn toward Amy's. Mark Bridges' car was gone as was Amy's. I hoped she was okay. A chill swept down my spine. Why on earth wouldn't she be okay? I just hoped her uncle hadn't said anything to her about my James Bond role. Whatever trust I'd built up could be lost in an instant.

*And another friendship will be down the drain. Maybe Brad and I will have some luck with the blonde.* I wanted to give Amy good news for a change.

Something niggled at the back of my mind, but I couldn't pull it up. Was it something Amy had said about the blonde? Or maybe about the ring?

I shrugged and went back inside to wait for Brad. Sooner or later, I'd remember.

*If the blonde isn't Abby, she may hold the missing pieces to the puzzle.*

All I had to do was put them together.

Chapter Twenty-Two

*Diary of Amy Margaret Wallace*

My Uncle Mark is a pig! He refuses to sell the stock I need to buy Abby's ring. We argued for hours.

This morning when I got up, he was gone. A note on the table said he'd be back later.

I don't want to see him. I'm sick of him suggesting I'm crazy or having another breakdown. I'm not, damn it. I know Abby is out there and I intend to find her.

I'll ask that nice man at the pawn shop to hold the ring a while longer. Uncle Mark doesn't control all of my money. I'll use my illustrations account. It's supposed to be for charity, but this is more important.

I must have Abby's ring.

Chapter Twenty-Three

"Trevor said an arrest warrant has no statute of limitations. Once it's issued, it's in effect until served or rescinded by a judge," Brad told me on our drive into town.

"So, Dallas police are still looking for Abby Wallace? After ten years?"

"I don't know. Trevor said he'd check out the warrant and if there's anything on Abby in the last ten years."

Yeah, there were probably a lot of fugitives wandering around the country living a normal life as a hard-working father or a soccer mom. I doubted if some cop in Dallas was actively searching for Abby. Over ten years other crimes have been committed, and time has a way of moving on. While the warrant might still be active, Abby—if alive—could likely live in peace wherever she pleased without fear of arrest unless she did something that would require a background check. And would a warrant that old even show up?

Brad pulled into the marina parking lot and found a space not far from the office doors. I exited the car and fanned the cloud of gravel dust from in front of my face. The heat radiated off the light colored surface and our feet made a crunching sound on the ground stone as we walked.

Inside the marina office, Brad's friend greeted us.

"How's the boat?" he asked.

"Boat's fine. Sam, this is Jenny Devlin. She came with me last week. Jenny, this is Sam Dawson."

He smiled. "Nice to see you again."

"Sam, we have a question about a boat rental," Brad said.

"Sure. What kind of boat you need?"

I spoke up. "We don't need a boat, but we do need some information on one you may have rented, or on the dock space you may have rented to the boat's owner."

I paused and looked at Brad who nodded. He was going to let me handle this, since I was the one who'd seen the couple.

"I'll try, but with the holiday, things have been busy. What kind of boat was it?"

"I'm not good with makes and models, but it was a runabout, about twenty-two feet and had a red hull. I saw a couple in it. The man had dark hair. The woman may have had blonde hair or been a brunette and wore a red bikini along with a big hat and sunglasses. They were sitting down, so I have no idea about height or weight."

Sam frowned and wrinkled his forehead. "I don't recall any one by that description, but then I don't always handle rentals. Too busy fixing boats." He turned to the woman behind the front desk. "Hey, Patty, do you remember renting either a twenty-two foot runabout or dock space for one to anybody lately?"

"I rented several boats of that length over the holiday," she replied.

"To a dark-haired man, perhaps with a blonde woman? The boat was red," I told her.

She thought for a moment. "Yeah, I think I remember them. Came in about two or three weeks ago. Said they were on vacation and needed a boat. I don't remember much about the guy, but the woman wore these huge sunglasses and a sun hat—you know the kind—big, floppy brim. She may have had blonde hair, but don't quote me on it."

The description could have matched the woman in the pawn shop minus the hat. "Would you have a name and address? We need to find them."

Sam looked up sharply as Patty turned to the computer. "Is there a problem?"

"No, not really," Brad said. "We just need to talk to them about something. It's personal."

"I don't suppose you noticed if the woman wore a large ruby-and-diamond ring?" I asked.

"Now that you mention it, yeah, I did. A real corker of a ring, too. God, don't tell me she lost it in the lake and blames us in some way."

"No, nothing like that." So the woman I'd seen off and on was the blonde. Now all I needed was the connection.

"Here it is," Patty said. "The rental was up yesterday. According to the records, the keys were returned at noon. The boat was a twenty-two-foot StingRay, red hull, registration number MO6490RC. It should be in slip number twelve. They also rented some skis and a tow rope the other day."

"Is there a name?" Brad asked.

"Boat was rented to a guy by the name of Roger Corry. He showed a Texas driver's license."

Roger Corry? From Texas? Another coincidence? I didn't like coincidences. My suspicion level jumped.

One of these two *had* to have known Abby Wallace. *Or the woman is Abby Wallace.*

"How did they arrive? I mean, did you notice if they drove a red sports car? Or a motorcycle?" I added as an afterthought.

Patty shook her head. "I don't recall having seen them at all after the rental agreement was signed."

"Has the boat been inspected yet?" Sam asked her.

"Yes. Billy did it. He says everything was fine. Even the ski equipment was in the bottom of the boat as we requested."

"Can we take a look at it?" Brad asked Sam.

Patty turned to answer the phone.

"Sure, don't see why not. You sure there's no problem?"

"No, no, like I said, it's personal."

"Sam, Mr. Harrison's on line one. Wants you to overhaul the engine on his Winn."

Sam left for his private office. We thanked Patty for the information and left. The sun beat down on our heads as we walked toward slip twelve on the dock. I wiped the sweat from my forehead and pulled my tank top away from my damp back. A dip in the lake sounded damned inviting. Then I remembered the stitches and the admonition from the doctor about getting them wet.

"Here it is," Brad said stopping in front of the boat.

It looked like any other boat bobbing gently at its mooring. Brad stepped onboard and lifted several cushions.

"What are you looking for?"

"I have no idea." He rummaged further until finally giving up and returning to the dock. "No fuel receipts, no grocery or liquor store receipts, nothing."

"Why don't we have lunch, and then hit the motels around here? They had to stay somewhere."

"And somewhere close if they didn't have transportation to and from the marina."

With the holiday over and being mid-week, we had no problem finding a table at the marina restaurant. I swallowed an aspirin to ease the slight headache created by my headband and ordered a grilled chicken sandwich with fries and a soft drink. Brad went with his usual high protein, red meat burger and fries.

Since no crowd existed, service was quick and less than an hour later, we stood at the front desk of The Wildwood Inn. Unfortunately, no one named Roger Corry had rented a room, and none of the personnel remembered seeing a specific blonde.

We expanded our search to surrounding motels, all with the same results. Discouraged, we stopped at a fast food joint to order a couple of drinks.

"If these two stayed in Vermillion, I'll eat my hat," Brad said taking a huge gulp of his coke.

"And if they didn't stay in town, they had to have had transportation. Yet Patty said she never saw them arrive, which suggests walking."

"I don't get it. I can understand Patty or Sam not noticing. They're busy inside or in the repair yard. Parking for the docks is on the other side of the office. Damn, we should have questioned marina personnel."

"It was a busy holiday. Probably lots of cars and motorcycles coming and going. No reason to remember one in particular," I said, pulling the cold, fizzy liquid through my straw. "Didn't there used to be a campground south of town?"

"Yeah, come to think of it, there was. But that was years ago, before all the development and resorts. Would it still be in business?"

"Only one way to find out."

We finished our drinks and headed south. Sure enough, the Happy Camper Campground and RV Park was thriving. Motorized campers were to the left, and tenting campers to the right of the office.

"Excuse me," Brad said approaching the check-in desk. "But we're looking for a friend who may be staying with you. His name's Roger Corry, from Texas. Is he here by any chance?"

The man checked his registration book. "Yep, he was. Checked out ten days ago."

Ten days? "Oh, nuts, we missed him," I said to Brad who sent me a strange look. "And I wanted to see his new RV, too."

"No RV," the man said. "Used a tent."

"Maybe you misunderstood about the RV, dear," Brad said playing along. "Tell me, was his wife Elvira with him? Long blonde hair and with a penchant for huge sunglasses?"

"Not that I saw, but then he requested a campsite way in the back if I remember right. Said something about needing peace and quiet."

Brad thanked the man and we walked outside.

"So, Corry was here, but the blonde wasn't," I said.

"And where have they been since?"

"And how did they get from one place to the other?"

"Let's take a stroll among the campsites," he suggested.

We walked past several tents with cars or pick-ups

parked alongside until reaching the back of the property. I stared at the wooded area to the east no more than a hundred feet away.

"It would be convenient to leave a motorcycle parked in the woods and walk to and from your tent," Brad commented.

"Let's assume Abby is alive. What about the sports car?"

"Pay to park it in a private garage out of the sun and possible rain." He paused and wrinkled his brow. "You know, we're assuming Corry and the blonde are together. Suppose they came separately and met here?"

"Why would they do that? It's just an extra vehicle to deal with."

"No, I mean, suppose they just met here. Like ships in the night."

"But the waitress at the diner said the blonde was with a dark-haired man," I reminded him.

"True, but was it the same man?"

"Oh God, this is getting too complicated. What time is it?"

Brad glanced at this watch. "A little after three."

"Let's call it a day. My head's beginning to hurt and I'm tired. Besides, I'm a couple of days behind on my journal."

"What journal?" he asked as we walked back to the car.

"I'm keeping a journal of all that's happened. I decided it might be a good idea considering why I'm here."

I rested my aching head against the headrest and closed my eyes. At least, we had a name for the guy, but the blonde proved as elusive as smoke in the wind.

If it weren't for the ring, I'd have dismissed them both long ago. Perhaps Amy was mistaken about it having belonged to Abby. Ten years is a long time, and she so wanted her sister to be alive.

Maybe the blonde and the guy were exactly what they appeared on the surface. Two people with a chance encounter having a good time. *Good time's over, they move on.*

The car stopped and I opened my eyes. Brad had parked in front of the police station.

"Why are we here?"

"I want to see if they have any information about your attack and the gunshot. Want to come with me?"

I sure did. I sat up and forgot about my head. Opening the door, I followed Brad inside where we also found Mark Bridges.

"Well, Mr. Bridges, I see we had the same idea," I said before turning to the man beside him. Since he had a gun strapped to his hip, I assumed he was a cop. "Hello, I'm Jenny Devlin."

"Ah, yes, the woman who was attacked in the woods yesterday. I'm Chief of Police, Walter James."

"How are you feeling, Jenny," Bridges asked.

"Much better. Head only hurts a little."

"We stopped by to see if there was any progress on finding out who attacked Miss Devlin and on the shot fired at us last night," Brad told him.

"Mr. Bridges was asking the same thing. Come back to my office and I'll fill you in."

We all followed him down a narrow hallway and into a cramped room. For a chief of police, it wasn't impressive, but then what did I know of Vermillion standards? I sat in the only available chair in front of the cluttered desk.

"Regarding the attack, we have very little. We dusted for prints in the cabin, but to be honest, there are so many of them it'll take weeks to sort them all out. The place has been used by vagrants for years. So far, we've come up with eight matching former arrest records here in the state of Missouri, the latest three years ago. It's a long process. We also think we may have found the branch that was used, but forensic evidence is nil other than a small bloodstain."

"What about the tire tracks I saw?"

"When you fell and then got up again, you all but obliterated them. We took a casting, but don't hold your breath."

This was not encouraging news.

"And what about the shot last night?" Bridges asked in a sharp tone. "The bullet barely missed my niece's head."

James shook his head. "Nothing yet. We dug a .22 rifle slug out of the wall, but haven't found the casing yet."

Brad ran a hand through his hair. "Are you saying it was an accident like Miss Wallace suggests?

The chief shrugged. "Anything is possible. We're working on it."

"So, in other words, you don't have diddlely-squat," Amy's uncle replied.

"Mr. Bridges, I understand your concern, but keep in mind that accidents do happen."

"Miss Devlin's attack sure as hell wasn't an accident," Brad interjected.

The chief of police shook his head and rose indicating the interview was over. The police had less than nothing, in spite of the chief's explanations.

"Doddering idiot," Bridges muttered as we emerged from the building and stood on the sidewalk.

"He's doing the best he can," Brad answered.

"Well, you can bet I'm going to find out who owns that damned place. I'll threaten legal action if it's not cleaned up properly. Son of a bitch, I wish Amy would sell out. If she wants peace and quiet, she can buy something else far away from Lake Wildwood."

I motioned with my head to Brad to leave us alone for a minute.

"Uh, if you'll excuse me, I forgot something. Be right back." He disappeared back into the police station.

"What happened last night after we left?" I asked.

He heaved a sigh. "We argued. It's so not like Amy to give me a hard time, but she's obsessed. Still insists Abby's alive and that she's seen her. And she still is harping on that ring. Claims it was Abby's and that she has to have it. I told her I wouldn't sell any stocks for her to buy some ring in a pawn shop. I even brought up her behavior when you two had lunch."

"Oh, no!"

He waved a hand. "I didn't use your name. Just said someone had seen her and commented to me about it. I'll let her settle down for a day, and then try to make her see reality again—assuming there's any there to see."

Brad rejoined us. "Good to see you again, Mr. Bridges. Since you seem to know the chief of police, perhaps you'll keep us informed of any new developments."

"Yes, yes, of course."

I told Brad of my conversation with Bridges on the

drive home.

"I could see an argument brewing between him and Amy," he said. "Must have surprised the old man when his sweet, docile niece put up a fight. And by the way, I gave the Chief the name of Roger Corry and asked him to check fingerprints from Texas. Just a hunch. It's the mystery writer in me."

"Good idea. Although why Roger Corry would want to bop me over the head is the real mystery." I chewed on a fingernail. "You know, Bridges made a point about Amy being obsessed. I'm surprised he refused to sell the stock. It's her money, and not connected with the trust at all."

"That's the problem with having a relative in charge of your affairs, plus, we don't know how the trust is set up."

Home again Brad walked me across the lawn pausing at the foot of the steps to gaze at the woods. Amy's car was out front.

"Why don't you go talk with Amy? Thank her again for her help and reassure her you're fine. Maybe she'll tell you more about her conversation with her uncle."

"What are you going to do?" I followed his gaze and had the feeling I knew.

"I want to see this cabin for myself."

"Brad!"

"Nothing's going to happen. Whoever attacked you isn't hanging around. Same for whoever fired the shot. I'll be all right."

"But what are you looking for?"

"I'm not sure, but I've got to take a look."

We strolled over to Amy's. While I mounted the

steps, he darted around the corner of the house and disappeared. Taking a deep breath, I knocked. A teary-eyed Amy opened the door. Surely this couldn't be from her altercation with Bridges.

"Amy, what's wrong?"

"Oh, Jenny, I'm so upset."

Damn Mark Bridges. "What about?"

"The ring is gone!" She turned and walked inside.

I followed. "How can it be gone? You left a deposit."

"The woman came back yesterday and reclaimed it."

"But I thought she sold it."

"She did, but the clerk didn't check that a deposit might have been made, so when she offered cash plus a profit of five hundred he said yes."

"Well, I hope you got your money back!"

"Oh, I did. He said he had to take the money on the table rather than wait a few days for me to get things straight."

"I'm so sorry. I know you were counting on having that ring."

"It's Abby's. I don't understand how this woman got it."

*Yesterday. The boat rental was up yesterday. And Brad and I couldn't find the blonde or the guy with her.*

Amy sniffed. "I'm sorry to be such a baby. How are you feeling?"

"I'm fine. Just a tiny headache. Brad and I had lunch at the marina. Maybe the three of us can do that tomorrow."

Without asking, Amy poured us a glass of iced tea and gestured to the dining table. I sat and sipped the sweet yet tangy drink.

"Jenny, please don't think me forward, but what do you know about Brad?"

Her question took me by surprise. "He's a bestselling author who staying here to fix up his parent's old place. Why?"

"Oh, I know you like him, but have you ever gotten the idea that he's watching?"

"Watching what?"

She blushed and sipped her tea. "I don't know. Sometimes I think he's looking at me as if I'm supposed to say or do something. It kind of gives me the willies."

I sat stock still, flabbergasted. "Amy, I've gotten no sense of him watching you. I think he might be concerned about you living here on your own, but then after the last few days, he's concerned about me, too."

My mind flew back to the other day when I'd overheard his phone conversation. Could he have been referring to *Amy*? Did someone pay him to gather information on her? On my God, could he be writing a book based on the tragedy? I didn't want to believe it, but Amy's words had opened the door to doubts.

"Oh, don't mind me. It's probably my imagination."

"He *is* in the process of plotting and writing a new book. Maybe you just caught him when he was thinking."

She smiled. "That's possible. The authors I deal with zone out all the time. One minute I'm discussing an illustration and the next they're staring off into space. Forget I said anything. I feel kind of stupid now. I can be such a ninny at times."

I finished my tea in a large gulp. "Amy, if you'll forgive me, I should be going home. I'm really tired."

She jumped to her feet. "And here I am blathering on and crying on your shoulder because the ring is no longer available. And I like your idea of the three of us getting together for lunch tomorrow. It'll give me a chance to get to know Brad better."

I waved goodbye and walked slowly home. I opened the front door. The knock on the head must have addled my brains. I'd forgotten to lock it. Inside, I sat on the sofa and tried to marshal my thoughts.

In one respect Amy was right. I didn't really know Brad all that well. *But well enough to have fabulous sex with him, though.*

I ignored the voice in my head and concentrated on Brad. It was strange that we should both show up at the same time. Granted, he'd been here a week or so before me, but still it was odd.

*Another coincidence, Jenny,* the voice in my head answered.

"Oh, shut up," I said aloud.

This whole thing was silly. *If Amy claims she sees her dead sister alive and well, why shouldn't she also be a little paranoid?*

"And who's to say her uncle isn't right? Maybe she is delusional," I added to my soliloquy. I hated this waffling.

But was Brad being—what? Evasive, deceptive, cagey? Meant the same thing any way I looked at it.

Now, if I really wanted to be objective I'd have to play lawyer and ask questions.

"All right, counselor, what questions?"

*Why did Brad downplay Amy's beliefs?*

"Because on the surface, they're bizarre."

*How come whenever you or Amy sees something odd, or something happens, he's never around?*

I didn't have an answer for that. He was gone yesterday when I got whacked, and he said he'd never seen the blonde or the boat. And then there was the prowler the night of the storm.

*Maybe there's a reason.*

"That's ridiculous. Brad would have no reason to hurt me or peek in Amy's window."

*Unless he's a pervert.*

"Jennifer Lee Devlin, knock it off! He is not. A pervert wouldn't—couldn't—make love to me one day and try to bash my head in the next."

I leaped to my feet and stomped into the kitchen where I poured a glass of iced tea. Brad was Brad—end of discussion with my mind. Friend or not, Amy was paranoid, and I was listening to her. Dumb!

I took my tea and went out to the porch. Where the hell was Brad anyway? How long did it take to look at an empty cabin?

Even as I thought, he came around the corner of Amy's house. He waved and headed my way.

Suddenly, without warning, I remembered the footprint under my living room window. And the next day, I'd seen Brad's work boots, caked with mud, on his porch. Had he been working on landscaping as he claimed? Or had he been up to other, more troubling things?

A shiver of fear crept up my spine.

## Chapter Twenty-Four

I mentally cursed Amy for sowing the seed of doubt in my mind concerning Brad, and swallowed the lump in my throat. She didn't know him at all. She'd admitted that. And maybe Brad had conveyed his disbelief of Abby's being alive in his face or something, giving her the impression he was watching her. I resolved not to jump to conclusions—even though that's what I'd just done.

"Find anything?" I asked trying to keep my voice normal as he approached,

"Not a damned thing. I even looked for, but couldn't find a shell casing."

"But we don't know which direction it came from or from how far away."

Brad shook his head. "I don't think Chief James was telling all he knows. The placement of the bullet in the siding would give the police a good idea of the trajectory. I estimated from the edge of the woods by line of sight to Amy's, and then widened my search. Still came up empty. What did Amy have to say?"

"Come on in and I'll tell you."

He entered, washed his hands at the sink in the kitchen, and sat at the table while I poured us each a glass of iced tea.

I perched on a stool at the breakfast bar. "She didn't say anything about an argument with her uncle, but was damned upset about the ring."

"Why?"

"It's gone." I relayed what Amy had told me.

"Lots of people pawn stuff for quick cash, and then redeem it later, but to sell outright only to buy back is odd."

"This whole affair is odd."

He frowned and gulped his tea. "Maybe Mark Bridges is right. From an author's point of view this would make a great story, but it doesn't happen in real life. Maybe Amy *is* heading for a breakdown."

I stiffened at his words. *This would make a great story...*My doubts of earlier resurfaced—not necessarily concerning him being my attacker or a Peeping Tom, but his motives for being in Vermillion in the first place.

Before stopping to think, I blurted, "Brad, why are you here?"

"Here?"

"In Vermillion. At Lake Wildwood."

His brows drew together. "What are you getting at?"

I squirmed on my stool sorry I'd brought the subject up at all.

"I'm not a big believer in coincidences, yet here you are. Here I am. Here's Amy. You know about my motive. What gives?"

He set his glass down with a hard click on the glass table top and gave me an even harder glare.

"Exactly what are you suggesting? That I have ulterior motives for being in my own home?"

Did he? The lawyer in me took over. "Where were you when I was attacked?"

He rose and pushed back his chair. "You've got to be kidding! You think I cracked you over the head with a branch?"

I shrugged, but didn't answer.

"I can't believe this! What put this idea into your head?"

I didn't want to drag Amy into the conversation, so I shrugged again and said, "It's something that just crossed my mind, that's all."

"I don't believe you. Someone suggested it. Who?"

I didn't answer, but drained the tea in my glass.

He ran a hand through his hair. "Do you honestly believe I could make fabulous love to you one day, and the next try to brain you?"

I shrugged a third time, unable to meet his gaze. He had just asked the question I'd mulled over earlier. I didn't believe it then, and seeing his incredulous expression, didn't believe it now.

"Look, Brad, I'm sorry, but…"

"Amy," he said, some of the fire going out of his eyes. "You just got back from talking to her. She put this bug in your ear, didn't she?"

I broke down and told him of Amy's concerns, and of my suspicions regarding the footprint under my living room window.

"Okay, I can see how your mind might make that leap, but I swear it wasn't me."

"I guess the phone call started me thinking, that's all."

"What phone call?"

I admitted to having overheard part of his conversation the other day.

He gazed at the floor for a moment. "And to think I

had Amy pegged as the one with the overactive imagination. I'm hurt you'd think that badly of me, Jenny. And may I remind you I was around for one incident or have your forgotten about the rifle shot? Now, if you'll excuse me, I have things to do at home. Have a good night."

He strode toward the front door with angry steps leaving me to gaze into my empty glass. He had no explanations for my doubts, but then why should he? He'd told me he'd come here to write. He didn't ask to become involved with any of this. Now, he was pissed at me and probably at Amy, too. I was certain he viewed my suspicions as betrayal.

*Well, I botched that pretty good. Bye-bye relationship. Or almost relationship. I've done it again. Taken something that could have been wonderful and tossed it into the trash. Will I ever learn?* And could Brad ever forgive me? *Yet he didn't deny the phone call I'd overheard.*

I slid off the stool. Suddenly, the house seemed confining. Since I hadn't been to the store in a while, the cupboard was bare. Maybe dinner out and a stroll around town would help. Anything was better than sitting here and brooding.

I snatched my purse and car keys from the counter and headed for my car. A glance across the lawn showed Brad's car parked in its usual place. I bit my lip and hesitated. Maybe I should apologize.

I took two steps, and then halted. No, now was not the right time. He was angry. Leave it until tomorrow when he'd had time to simmer down.

The drive into town didn't take long and I found a parking spot not far from Victoria's. Too early to eat, I strolled down the block until coming to the pawn shop. On a whim, I entered.

A man I'd not seen before stood behind the counter.

"Hi, can I help you?"

"I'm just looking. A friend of mine was in here today, but left disappointed."

"I'm sorry to hear that. Couldn't find what she wanted?"

I shook my head. "She saw a ring in the window the other day and put a deposit down. I guess the woman who sold it came and bought it back."

"I remember. The woman bought it back yesterday. Didn't know there was a deposit on it until my boss returned from lunch. Read me the riot act for not checking, but since the woman offered more than we bought it for, he wasn't too unhappy. Cash in hand is better than a promise."

"I suppose so. Still, it's too bad. My friend really liked that ring." I paused for a moment inspecting bracelets in the display case wondering if he'd noticed how the blonde had arrived. "Uh, did you happen to notice how the blonde lady arrived?"

"What blonde lady?"

"The one who bought back the ring. Was she with a gentleman or on a motorcycle?"

"The lady who bought the ring wasn't blonde. She had dark hair."

My head snapped up. "Can you describe her?"

He shrugged. "Not really. She was medium height, had short hair, and wore this really sexy red tank top."

*Oh my God! Abby?*

I fished in my purse looking for the photos of Abby

Amy had given me before my trip north. In all the hubbub of yesterday, I'd forgotten to return it.

I finally found the snapshot of Abby and thrust it under the guy's nose.

"Is this the lady?"

He stared with a puckered forehead. "Beats me. Maybe. I don't know. Had trouble taking my eyes off the tank top. This babe did wear a pair of crazy sunglasses—red and shaped like hearts. She paid cash, slipped the ring on her finger, the box in her pocket, and left."

"Thank you. You've been very helpful."

I left and wandered down the street as I tucked the picture away again, my mind racing.

This was the first confirmation of someone other than Amy seeing her sister—if that's who the clerk saw. Could she have asked the blonde to sell the ring for her? And why on earth didn't she contact Amy? None of this made any sense.

*Or perhaps this is a woman who simply has dark hair and a penchant for the color red.*

My stomach grumbled. Food. I needed food and time to think. I couldn't go to Amy with this kind of news, and wouldn't involve Mark Bridges again at this point. At the moment, I couldn't even talk to Brad.

At Victoria's I indulged in lasagna and a salad while my mind turned over the latest development. And I'd been wrong about the pawn shop clerk being the only one to have seen Abby. I'd seen a red sports car the day of Amy's and my lunch. I'd also gotten a ticket in Stone City chasing down the same, only this time with a dark-haired woman in it. If this were brought before a judge, the case would be dismissed for lack of evidence. I had absolutely no connection between the woman I'd seen, the woman the clerk had described, or Abby Wallace.

My wound sent a pulsating throb to the rest of my head reminding me it had been a long day. I paid the check, walked back to my car, and drove home. As I exited in my driveway, I cast a glance toward Amy's. The house was dark and the car gone.

Over at Brad's the opposite was true. The car hadn't moved and light streamed from his front windows. Without stopping to think, I walked across the grass. An apology was due. Maybe he'd cooled down since our argument.

I approached the front porch, and then stopped. Through the windows, I saw Brad pacing, his cell phone clamped to his ear. The urge to eavesdrop was strong, but this time the door was closed, and with the AC on, the windows offered no chance of overhearing anything.

I retraced my steps home. I needed to work on what I'd say anyway.

I'd barely made it inside my front door when my cell rang. I sighed in irritation when caller ID confirmed Mark Bridges.

"Good evening, Mr. Bridges."

"Good evening, Miss Devlin. I'm sorry to be bothering you, but I just had a long talk with my niece. She's finally agreed that perhaps her mind has been playing tricks on her, and has promised to go back to seeing her psychiatrist again."

"Well, that's a surprise. This afternoon when I talked to her she was upset because the ring had been sold."

"I know, she told me. We had a long talk earlier this evening, and she claims she can see my point of view."

"And what about the house? Is she going to sell?"

He sighed. "I haven't been able to convince her of that yet, but at least this is a start."

"And when does all this take place?"

"The end of the week. She has a few loose ends to tie up concerning work."

"I see." Amy's sudden change of heart left me bewildered. Although saddened by the loss of the ring, she hadn't hinted at making such a decision.

"So, that's why I'm calling you, Miss Devlin. I want to thank you for all your help with this situation. And I'm sorry if I sometimes came off as being, well, abrupt," he said with a light laugh.

I didn't find anything funny about it. I'd felt like a rat spying on Amy. And why the hell was he apologizing?

"Go back to St. Louis, and your work," he finished.

"Thank you. If I helped Amy in any way, then it was worth it, but I may stay on here until Amy goes back."

"No, no, don't bother. You've disrupted your life long enough. I'll call your boss and let him know everything has been resolved to my satisfaction. I've got to go. I'm making this call from outside a restaurant in Moxley. Amy's inside. She had a yen for Chinese even though yens are Japanese." He chuckled at his joke. "Once again, many thanks."

He hung up and I slowly lowered my phone, puzzled. Why had Amy suddenly agreed to do as her uncle wished? And given our argument when I refused to continue spying for him, why had he bothered to call and literally tell me to go home? I didn't have an answer and the sudden throbbing in my head refused to allow me to think.

I swallowed an aspirin and returned to the kitchen. Something just didn't add up, but I was damned if I knew what.

I sat at the table and pulled my laptop toward me. A move of the mouse brought up the interrupted journal entry of earlier. Then I stared at the screen. When not in use, I generally closed the lid to send the machine into hibernation. Hadn't I done that before leaving for the marina this morning? I couldn't remember and shrugged. I'd finish my thoughts and go to bed.

I did just that at the outrageous hour of nine o'clock, but knowing I wouldn't sleep for a while, cracked open the book I'd been reading. I lasted all of ten pages. No way could I concentrate on a hero with a secret or a heroine with doubts. It cut too close to home.

Sighing, I slipped back into my shorts and wandered out to the kitchen. Maybe a glass of wine would help.

I uncorked a bottle of Chardonnay and carried it out to the deck. From this vantage point no lights shown from either the back of Amy's or Brad's homes. I assumed Amy was still dining with her uncle in Moxley, a town some twenty miles west, and that Brad was in his living room—hopefully not still on the phone.

I sipped my wine and wondered if I hadn't been impulsive by sleeping with a man I didn't really know and hadn't seen in years. Throw in the doubts along with all the questions, and my lack of judgment tripled.

Yet at the same time, I couldn't see Brad as even a quasi-villain in this.

I finally came to the conclusion I'd been more than an idiot. Of course Amy didn't completely trust him. She was half-paranoid, and according to Mark Bridges about to re-enter therapy. She hadn't slept with Brad. I had. Brad had every reason to feel hurt and angry. First thing in the morning, I'd march right up to his door, apologize, and see if the relationship—if any—could be salvaged.

Which brought me to another question. Did we have a relationship? One night of great sex constituted one night of great sex. Yet, there was something endearing about this man. His smile, his touch, everything about him suggested taking this further. He'd even taken the time to make me a sandwich last night. Most men would have ordered in a pizza or something. I'd loused up my marriage, but could this be a second chance at love? And was it love? And did I even want to take that second chance?

I liked Brad more than just a little, but was I falling in love with him? I just didn't know, but didn't want to leave Vermillion without getting this resolved.

The night wrapped around me like a cloak. The heat and humidity had not abated. In the distance, lightning flashed yet produced no thunder. Heat lightning. Storms in the clouds. My brothers and I had often sat on the dock watching the display. It was one of those phenomena that fascinated me, like the Northern Lights. We didn't see those multicolored ribbons of light often this far south, but when we did, I couldn't tear my eyes away.

Not a breath of air stirred. Insects chirped and

buzzed around me, and from the lake below I heard the occasional croaking of frogs. A trickle of sweat slid down my temple.

The cool waters of the lake called. A few minutes of foot dangling off the edge of the dock couldn't hurt. I picked up my glass and strolled toward the steps leading to the dock. I paused for a moment or two to breathe in the heady scent of some flowering bush. The fragrance was familiar, yet elusive. I peered toward the right and saw the blooms shining white in the moonlight dappling through the trees.

Of course, the flowering bush my mother had planted close to fifteen years ago. I didn't remember what variety. A Mother's Day gift from us kids, she'd placed it near the steps so she could have easy access to the blooms. Perhaps in the morning, I'd cut a few flowers for inside.

With my wound still sending the occasional jab of pain to my head, I deemed it prudent to be careful. I gripped the stair rail and cautiously descended several steps. The muted glow of the tier lights helped. I paused on the first landing to gaze over the water. No boaters appeared to mar the smooth surface.

I took another sip of wine and prepared to finish my journey when I looked down, stopped, and stared in front of me.

There, stretched between the landing posts and reflecting the glow from the tier lights, was a fine, but deadly, trip wire.

Chapter Twenty-Five

I backed up until the landing railing hit me just above the waist. Turning, I plopped down onto the last riser of the upper steps. I could still see the wire in the dim illumination of the tier lights. If I hadn't taken it slow but gone on in my usual rapid pace, I'd have fallen headfirst down thirty-seven more steps to the next landing.

I drained the remaining wine in my glass and set it beside me, then rose. Crouching behind the device, I reached out and touched it. Fishing line. Simple monofilament found in every home on the lake. I hooked a finger over it and tugged several times before pulling it free. The ends had been loosely secured.

Standing, I gathered it in my hand, picked up my glass, and retreated up the steps. I paused at the top to look and listen. Not a sound out of the ordinary. Amy's kitchen light now shone, as did the back window at Brad's.

Inside, I poured another glass of wine and sat at the table examining the six-foot length of line. It was dumb luck that I'd been looking down and had seen the light reflecting off of it. Whoever had planted it either didn't see or hadn't considered the tier lighting.

In daylight, the clear line would have blended in with the colors of nature and the wood. And a person going down to the dock during the day wouldn't be that careful of where they stepped. The line would have struck me an inch or two above the ankle guaranteeing a nasty, if not deadly, fall. And the loose tying would have ripped it from around the post to likely fall through the open steps onto the hillside beneath.

*And if it didn't, the person responsible would make sure to retrieve it.*

When had it been put in place? I'd been on the dock yesterday and certainly hadn't encountered it. It had to have been today. The most obvious question of course was who?

Brad? I didn't want to think so. Besides, he'd been with me all day—well, most of it—although he could have done it while I was out to dinner.

I shook my head. No, I just couldn't see Brad doing this. And he was right about being with us all when the shot was fired. The shot. Could this be a warning from the person who fired it? But why to me?

I stared at the fishing line again. Should I call the police? Instinct told me yes. If nothing else, it would warn the perpetrator to knock it off.

I picked up the phone and called, giving the person who answered the basics. Fifteen minutes later, a cruiser pulled up and Officer Howard emerged. He and I were fast becoming best friends.

"Good evening, Miss Devlin. Hear you had a spot of trouble. Someone tried to push you down the steps?"

"Sort of." I explained what I'd found on the landing and handed him the line.

"Simple four-pound test. You probably have it around here."

"I'm sure I do."

"And it was tied around the posts?"

"Not very tight, though. It could have pulled loose as soon as my legs hit it."

"You still might have had a nasty fall. Let me get a flashlight and go have a look, but I doubt we'll find anything."

I doubted it, too. He spent ten minutes on the landing while I waited at the top of the steps. As I suspected, he found nothing.

"Could the shooter of last night be responsible?" I asked.

He frowned. "Let's hope not. And why target you?"

"That was my question, too. I don't think I've pissed anyone off lately."

"I'll notify the marine patrol to keep an eye on the docks on this side of the lake. In the meantime, lock your doors and be careful."

He left and I did as suggested. To be on the safe side, I even put the safety bar in the sliding glass door to the deck. I added this latest incident to my journal, and then went to bed.

I tossed and turned until finally giving in to medication. My head hurt and I needed a dreamless sleep. I popped the pain pill and pulled the sheet up to my chin, then let my mind wander while waiting for the pill to take effect.

Officer Howard's comment about the marine patrol troubled me. With the woods as cover, anyone could gain access to the docks and houses via water and not be seen.

*Why not? Come up in a small boat with a trolling motor, set up the trip wire, and leave. If anyone saw the perpetrator, they'd assume he was a fisherman looking for a sweet spot to drop his line.*

Once again I asked myself why and who? Unfortunately, the pill put me under before I could answer.

\*\*\*\*

I slept like the dead. Perhaps not a very nice allusion, but apt. The pill had once again done its job.

In the bathroom, I removed the bandage from my stitches and inspected the wound. The swelling had receded as had the angry redness. The shaved area looked hideous and the hair around it still bore signs of blood in spite of careful washing. I decided the hell with doctor's orders. I was washing my hair. Half an hour later, I clicked off the blow dryer satisfied my hair was clean and the wound undamaged.

I had my morning coffee on the deck. At this time of day, the trees and part of the house shaded it from the sun. A cardinal sent out a melodious call to his or her mate. Off in the distance, a reply was returned. In this peace and quiet, it was hard to imagine the events of recent days.

With coffee kick-starting my brain and no headache, I returned to my thoughts of last night. Who and why? Was Officer Howard correct to think the person or persons had come by boat? Had it been tied loosely to give me a scare rather than injure? Then I had another thought.

*Oh my God, is something similar adorning Brad and Amy's dock steps?*

Unable to resist, I walked down the stairs and through the bushes to Amy's. The draperies on her patio doors were closed indicating she'd not yet risen. I hustled to the dock stairs and descended.

This side of the lake was on high ground, which explained why the treads to the docks were often zigzagged down the hillside. I paused at the first landing, but saw nothing. The second landing revealed more of the same. I turned, retraced my route home and across the yard to Brad's.

Ten minutes later and slightly out of breath I resumed my seat on the deck to finish my coffee. I'd found nothing at his place either. Which meant somebody wanted me out of the way.

*Most docks look alike, especially in this area. What if Brad or Amy was the target after all? In the dark, the person could have made a mistake.*

The idea didn't sit well with me. But who on earth would want to hurt either of them? It made no sense. And maybe I was overanalyzing the whole thing.

Maybe it was a sick joke, something a ten-year-old would think funny, like with the shot. Aim to miss, and then make sure the fishing line would pull loose with the first step. *I might fall a ways, but could always catch myself by grasping the rail.*

I shook my head. Not even I believed it. But I was confused as hell.

"Mind if I join you?"

My head jerked in the direction of the deck steps. Brad stood at the bottom. Sweet warmth infused my body from head to toe.

"Please, do. Coffee?"

"Sounds wonderful," he said as he climbed.

I rushed inside and poured us both a cup with shaking hands. The fact he was here and smiling gave me hope my stupidity of the day before was forgiven. Little doubts still nagged, but I ignored them. Constant questioning was part of my nature.

I set the cup in front of him at the bistro table and resumed my seat.

"Brad, about yesterday. I want to apologize. I know you wouldn't do anything to hurt me. Let's call it temporary insanity due to the knock on the head. You're as honest and above board as the day is long. Am I forgiven?"

He sipped his coffee and didn't make eye contact.

"Of course, you're forgiven. I'm the one who should be apologizing."

Now *he* had me confused. The expression on his face was pure shame. Good grief, had he done something after all?

"Why should you apologize?"

"Because I haven't been honest with you. You were right. I'm not here just by chance." He inhaled a deep breath and let it out slowly. "Jenny, let's talk about Abby Wallace."

"Abby? Whatever for?"

"I met her out in Los Angeles about eleven or twelve years ago. My first wife was a party animal and the two had connected at some affair. One night, for reasons I can't remember, I attended one of those silly get-togethers. Abby came up and introduced herself asking if I remembered her. The name was familiar, but that was all. Her hair was short, cut in a hip style of the time, and she wore this black mini-skirt with a low-cut red top of some sort. We talked and drank most of the evening. She came on to me, and since my marriage wasn't on the firmest ground, one thing led to another and we ended up in bed at her place."

He gulped his coffee while I stared. A slight

sickness churned my stomach. He'd committed adultery with Abby Wallace? For some inexplicable reason I felt betrayed, which was silly since I wasn't his wife. Besides, who was I to judge? I'd been unfaithful during my marriage.

"The affair only lasted a few weeks, and then she was gone. I felt guilty as hell, and made an effort to repair the damage by concentrating on my wife. Didn't work. Her group of friends informed her about Abby and me. She filed for divorce."

"Yeah, I can understand why." He shot me a look and I nodded. "My husband did the same. Remember? I don't blame him. I was stupid. Go on. What brought you here?"

"I heard about the accident from my mother, and I had to admit, I wasn't surprised. During our time together in California, Abby ran wild—drinking, drugs, shoplifting as a form of entertainment. Eventually, I forgot about her."

He finished his coffee and I took the cup in for a refill. I still wasn't sure how he fit into the picture with Amy, but knew I was about to find out.

After taking a sip, he resumed his story.

"My career took off. Over the next eight years I had five bestsellers, another marriage, another divorce, and no time to call my own. I was sorry about the divorce, but as for the rest of it, I was having the time of my life. Then, two years ago, it disappeared."

"What disappeared?"

"My ability to tell a story. Some people call it writer's block. I'm a best-selling author. Damn near anything I turn in would be published, but I refused to turn in crap. Then one sleepless night, a thought came to me. What if a man on the run picked up a hitchhiker, had a fatal accident in which the hiker died, and the man on the run took over his identity? It wasn't a particularly fresh idea, but in the back of my mind, I could see the conflict of being someone you didn't know. And then I thought what if my character did know the person killed? And *then*, I remembered Abby and Amy."

"So, you decided to use their story as the basis for yours?"

He nodded. "I wrote a proposal and sent it in to my agent. He sold it in less than a week. I got the advance and realized I needed more information, so I contacted Trevor to track down Amy and the circumstances of the accident. There was very little on the accident, but when I discovered she still lived part-time here at the lake, I figured I had it made. I'd get to know her, maybe take her out to dinner a few times."

"So you could pump her for information."

I don't know why I sounded so outraged. I'd been doing the same thing. Maybe I expected more from Brad. Or maybe I wondered why he hadn't come clean with me when I'd confessed to my arrangement with Mark Bridges.

"I'd only been here a couple of weeks when you showed up. The party at her place was the first chance I'd had to actually make contact. She was a recluse, and I couldn't get anywhere close to her."

"So, you used me. But why? Didn't your private investigator give you enough details?"

He shook his head. "There was little on Amy other than she was an illustrator. I thought maybe that might be my entry, but my books don't require an illustrator."

"What about the accident?"

"All Trevor learned was that there had been a boating accident with one death. It happened ten years ago here in Vermillion, a small town with only a weekly paper. After a month, other stories of local interest prevailed. Plus, the family was intensely private. After a memorial service, there was no information other than having Abby declared legally dead the following year. Not even the police report gave out much information."

"Why didn't you tell me this that night at dinner when I told you why I was here?"

"Your arrangement disturbed me—made me open my eyes. For the first time, I felt dirty, sleazy. I couldn't take advantage of a woman who had survived a tragedy and still held out hope her sister was alive. That phone conversation you overheard was me telling my agent to squash the deal. Last night, he called to tell me the publisher will sue if I don't produce something even though I told them I'd return the advance."

I could relate to the dirty part. I'd felt the same way that day in the office after agreeing to Mark Bridges' plan. Both of our interests in Amy came with ulterior motives. I wasn't proud of my part. And Brad terminating what was no doubt a lucrative book deal told me he wasn't either.

I placed my hand over his. "So, let's help Amy. I talked to her uncle earlier."

"What did he say?"

I gave him the lowdown on Amy's agreeing to return to therapy.

"Probably not a bad idea," he said.

"There's more."

I also told him about the dark-haired woman buying back the ring and about the trip wire on the landing.

"My God, you could have been killed!" Concern and outrage glowed from his eyes. "What the hell's going on and what is the Vermillion Police Department doing about it?"

"The best they can, I imagine. They don't have a whole lot to go on."

"I don't like it!"

"I don't either."

He frowned and stared across the lawn toward Amy's. "How much detail did you go into when writing that journal of yours?"

"As much as possible. I treated it like a lawyer with a deposition."

"Let's take a look and review this piece by piece. I have an awful feeling something's going to happen. Something bad."

I gaped. "What makes you say that?"

"My gut. Come on, let's go read."

****

While I made fresh coffee, Brad ran into town for takeout sustenance. On a caffeine and sugar high from the now empty box of a dozen donuts, we finished the last page of my electronic journal.

"Is there anything else you can think of?" he asked.

"Not offhand."

He frowned. "How did Mark Bridges know to contact you?"

"He said he'd talked with my parents and that they'd bragged about how proud they were of me or something along those lines. I guess he remembered and tracked me down."

"You're a lawyer. What's your basic assumption on this?"

I sighed and stared out the window. "I'm not sure. If Amy is right and Abby is alive—and I think she is—why wouldn't she contact her sister? And how does the blonde fit into the equation? Is it Abby in disguise? And what about the dark-haired woman in the red sports car. Abby *not* in disguise?"

"Maybe the blonde doesn't fit into the equation. Maybe Amy is mistaken about the ring. For God's sake, it's been ten years and according to her Abby was wearing it the night she died."

"Therefore, logically, if she no longer exists then neither does the ring. So, that leaves us with nothing." I licked my forefinger, dipped it into the powdered sugar residue in the bottom of the donut box and popped it into my mouth. "You know, the clerk at the pawn shop could have been mistaken, too, about the blonde. She could have been in the store when a dark-haired woman sold it and he got confused."

"That's possible. On the other hand, if Abby is alive, but still under a cloud of amnesia, then we have to find her, if for no other reason than to tell that asshole Bridges what he can do with himself."

I laughed, and then sobered. "But then there's the waitress who saw the blonde with the ring. If Abby has amnesia, then why bother with a disguise? What's the purpose?"

"And if she hasn't got amnesia, then this takes on a whole different scenario—one that could be sinister."

"Brad, you knew Abby better than me. What was she like in L. A.?"

"Wild, funny, daring, always willing to push the boundaries."

"She had a warrant out in Texas for drug trafficking. How deeply was she into that stuff when you knew her?"

He leaned back and crossed his arms over his chest.

"She'd blow a little weed right before we'd make...uh, right before...and then take a small hit of coke afterward."

"So she wasn't hard core?"

"Not that I knew of. She treated it like a recreational sport. Same with sex."

"Yet the warrant says drug trafficking specifically. Did she deal, too?"

"I never thought about it before. She didn't have a job, but always seemed to spend money. I just assumed someone was paying her bills or she was one of those people who'd leech off of others until they wise up and tell her to hit the road. I remembered the Wallaces as being rather well-to-do, so perhaps she lived off an allowance."

"Did you do drugs with her?"

I don't know why I asked, but I was developing an intense dislike of Abigail Wallace. And the fact Brad had been her lover rankled.

"Like I said, I smoked some pot and snorted a line or two occasionally. She wasn't around long enough to do much more. When she left town, I quit. The highs were great, but the come downs sucked. Besides, as a writer, I needed a clear head. A plot won't gel if you're impaired. I often wondered how Hemingway managed with his drinking."

I wasn't interested in Ernest Hemingway. I didn't like his writing anyhow.

I nibbled on a morsel of donut remains. "Let's assume for the moment that this is all in Amy's head. Suppose she was in Vermillion one day and saw a woman who looked like her sister. That would explain why nobody else saw the resurrected Abby. With the ten-year anniversary of the accident looming, she goes into high fantasy mode. The blonde is an innocent bystander misidentified by the pawn shop clerk. I did not see a Peeping Tom, but a table umbrella closed against the wind. I wasted a perfectly good day running around looking for a woman who is dead. Doesn't get any nuttier than that. The whack on my head was from a homeless person living in the cabin and frightened of discovery. The shot was an accident. I'm afraid I can't explain the trip wire."

Brad was silent, staring at my computer screen with a blank expression.

"No, it can't be," he muttered.

"What can't be?"

He looked at me with a frown. "Let's suppose the other way—that Amy is right—only take it another step further."

"Such as?"

"Jenny, the Abby I knew was fun-loving, but could also be cold and calculating. She would use and abuse people if it suited her purpose. Oh, this is too fantastic to be believable. It's like something I'd write."

My patience was stretching thin. "Can you please tell me what you're talking about?"

He jumped to his feet. "Just a minute. Let me sort this out in my head."

He paced my kitchen, and I imagined him doing this as he wrote trying to untie a tricky plot twist. I was ready to explode with curiosity when he finally returned to his seat.

"Try this on for size. Amy is right. Abby survived, but the accident was the perfect cover to get out from under the warrant."

"That thought crossed my mind, too. Go on."

"So, she makes her way to God only knows where, and then on the anniversary of her supposed death, returns."

"Why?"

He smiled. "Revenge."

## Chapter Twenty-Six

*Diary of Amy Margaret Wallace*

Today, I'm both excited and apprehensive.

My sleep was interrupted last night by what I thought were footsteps on the front porch. Feeling foolish, I peeked out my bedroom window, but saw nothing other than the moonlight casting shadows across the lawn.

This morning in the middle of the dining room table, a white jeweler's box with an envelope under it almost made my heart stop. I reached for it with shaking fingers and flipped open the hinged lid.

It was Abby's ring.

## Chapter Twenty-Seven

"Revenge? Why?" I asked totally confused.

"Bear with me on this one. I have a lot of theories bouncing around in my head. Try this scenario," Brad said. "Abby and Amy go out in the boat. A storm springs up, the boat is destroyed, and supposedly Abby along with it. But what if she wasn't killed? What if she survived, but kept quiet because of the warrant? Maybe after a few years, she discovered the warrant had been rescinded because she'd been declared dead. Abby had one hell of a sense of timing. Suppose she chooses the tenth anniversary of her so-called death to get even?"

"Even for what? It was an accident." The author in Brad was emerging, but I was a lawyer and needed facts.

"Was it?"

I sat back and stared. "What are you getting at?"

"Remember the other night when Amy had that sort of meltdown and said she hated Abby? What if it was true? What if she rendered Abby unconscious, and then went out in a storm and deliberately rammed into an object. Abby would drown in a tragic accident."

"Brad, that's nuts. Amy wouldn't hurt a fly."

"Isn't that what Norman Bates said in *Psycho*?"

"My God, you've been around her. She's just not capable of doing something like that. Besides, the boat exploded."

"Maybe that part was an accident. All right, how about this? The accident happened just the way we were told. Only Abby didn't die—Amy did. Abby assumed her identity."

He finished with a sly smile. This was his book plot.

"Why? Because of the arrest warrant?" I asked.

He nodded. "Exactly."

"So, if she's living happily as Amy Wallace, why screw everything with Abby sightings?"

His face fell. "Haven't figured that out yet."

"Let me play devil's advocate. Abby and Amy may have been identical twins, but you knew Abby. Could she draw well enough to illustrate books?"

"I have no idea, but it isn't unusual for twins to share the same abilities."

"But Abby and Amy were polar opposites."

He leaned forward. "Personality-wise, not necessarily ability or talent-wise."

"Okay, you've got me there. But there's one other thing."

"What?"

"Hair."

"Hair?"

"At the time of the accident, Abby's was cut in a short, spiky style. Amy had long hair. No way could that be changed to switch identities."

"And you know Abby had short hair how?"

"From the portrait. Amy said the artist worked from photographs. And she used a recent photo of Abby supposedly taken that last weekend."

"We only have her word for that. Maybe Amy had short hair at the time of the accident."

"She did say she had tried going short on a couple of occasions, but she also stated the wind pulled her hair loose. Of course, she might say that to throw me off." His revelations disturbed me, yet I couldn't let it go. "Brad, assuming the identity of a person with the opposite personality of yours is tough. Sooner or later, the real person comes out. She'd never fool Amy's friends for long."

"What friends?"

"And then there's Mark Bridges. Surely, he'd notice."

"Not if she was being real careful."

"Yeah, but what about her parents? Parents can always tell which twin is which."

"Grieving parents?"

"A mother always knows," I insisted.

"Or maybe Abby confessed to them about the warrant and they helped her by covering up. A six-month stay in a sanitarium is a great place to hide."

His logic was giving me doubts. "Maybe, but I doubt it. No, Abby did not assume Amy's identity. However, what if I was right about Abby and the blonde being the same person? It's Abby in a blonde wig."

Brad leaped to his feet. "Or she's blonde and wears a black wig for Amy's benefit for the Abby sightings."

"No, she wears a blonde wig as a disguise whenever it wasn't convenient for Amy to see Abby." My heart pumped hard. "But she had to stay somewhere. And what about the man in the boat? Is he her accomplice or just someone she picked up?"

"Abby collected men like prizes. Besides, she needed someone to keep tabs on Amy. And according to the boat rental records, he had a Texas driver's license. I wonder if he's originally from Dallas."

"The warrant named Abby as an accomplice. You think he was…"

He drew a deep breath. "I sure do. And I think I know where they stayed."

"Oh, my God, you mean…" I let the sentence trail off.

He nodded. "The cabin."

"There wasn't one person staying there, but two."

Brad frowned. "Let me revise that. I think the guy was acting as Abby's eyes and ears. No way would she camp out for even one night in that place. Abby liked her creature comforts."

"Then where was she staying?"

"Who knows? If she had a blonde wig, why not a red one, too? We never asked questions about a redhead."

"So, the guy was the one who bopped me alongside the head. And he used a motorcycle as transportation."

"And he left the campground when first I, and then you, showed up as Amy's neighbors. He wanted to keep an eye on all of us. And I'll bet he fired the shot and set the trip wire, too. I haven't worked out why yet."

"To keep us focused on something other than asking questions about Abby Wallace and blonde?"

"I'll also bet he was actually in the cabin when you went snooping. He slipped out the back door, grabbed a branch, and when you got too close to the motorcycle, attacked."

"Brad, we don't have one iota of proof about any of this."

He rubbed his hand across his chin. "Jen, how long has Amy been here in Vermillion?"

"This summer?" I shrugged. "I'm not sure, but I had the impression she arrived sometime last month. Maybe just after Memorial Day. Why?"

He ignored my question. "And she had her first Abby sighting about a month ago?"

"According to Bridges, about that. Why?"

"God, it's so simple, it's scary," he muttered.

I reached the end of my patience. "What's simple and why do you want to know when Amy came to Lake Wildwood?"

"Knowing Abby, if she knew Amy was here, and needed a place to stay that was a cut above a derelict cabin in the woods, why not use the house in St. Louis?"

My mouth dropped open. "Oh God, that would explain why we couldn't find her registered at any motel or such here. And while I saw the woman in the boat several days running, those longer gaps between Abby sightings would fit."

Brad ran a hand through his hair. "For all we know, she did use a different disguise to stay here for the holiday. It was a busy time. Who's going to remember one person, blonde, brunette or redhead, out of several thousand?"

"But St. Louis is a three-hour drive. That's a long commute."

"Not in a little red sports car. I rode with Abby once or twice. She drove like a maniac. She'd make it in two."

"And the state troopers are thick along the interstate between here and St. Louis. Speed traps all over the place. Maybe she got a ticket."

The possibility of tracing Abby gave me a boost. Here would be concrete proof of her existence. I wondered how long it would take to find out if she'd been given a citation.

Brad threw instant cold water on my theory. "It would take forever to trace. She probably wouldn't have a driver's license under her real name."

I slumped back into my chair. "So what's next? And why is Abby doing this? Does she want to drive her sister crazy? Is that the revenge?"

"I don't know. Like I said, these are all theories that rattle around in my writer's imagination, but someone needs to go to St. Louis and investigate. I'll call Trevor and see if he can use his skills to pry information out of various state agencies, like the Highway Patrol. Meanwhile, let's go under the assumption Abby is still alive. I can visit Amy's place in St. Louis. Ask the neighbors a few questions."

"Won't they think it odd a total stranger asking questions about Amy Wallace?"

"I'll say I'm a client, an author, and that we were supposed to meet at her place to discuss some illustrations."

"Brad, if Abby was using the family home, wouldn't the neighbors have noticed a red sports car zipping in and out?"

"Amy is practically a recluse. If they did notice anything, they probably assumed she'd bought a new car. Or maybe Abby parked it in the garage and only arrived and left after dark. Still someone might have seen something. Jen, I need you to keep an eye on Amy."

"How?"

"Get her out of Vermillion for the rest of the day. Isn't there some kind of resort just south of Springfield with restaurants and entertainment?"

"You mean Branson?"

"Yeah, that's the place. Take her there for the day, or better yet stay the night. Have a leisurely breakfast and take your time returning. It'll give me a chance to ask questions in St. Louis and Trevor time to finish his job."

"That's a good idea. She might relax more in Branson, and nobody is likely to follow us there, at least I hope not."

Brad checked his watch. "It's almost noon. By the time I throw a few things into a bag, call Trevor, and hit the road, it'll be too late to do much in the city. I'll investigate tomorrow morning and try to get back here by nightfall." He sent me a sharp glance. "Will you be all right?"

"In Branson? Sure, assuming Branson is Amy's cup of tea. What do I do if she doesn't want to go?"

"Have her pick a spot to visit for a day or so. Anywhere as long as it's not Vermillion. You're a lawyer. You can convince her."

"I'm in an office ninety-nine percent of the time. I rarely deal with courtrooms or juries."

He pulled me into his arms and laid a mind-blowing kiss on my lips. My stomach clenched with anticipation and heat radiated from my skin. In spite of the urgency of finding Abby, I couldn't see how starting the trip to St. Louis an hour from now would matter.

His lips trailed from my mouth, up my cheeks, and

to the wound on my head.

"You convinced me," he said in a hoarse voice.

"Convinced you of what?" My voice was on the hoarse side, too.

Brad stepped back, drew a finger down to my jaw, and then lightly kissed the tip of my nose.

"That maybe its time to take another chance."

I slipped my arms around his neck, and kissed his chin. I hoped I knew what he meant, but asked anyway.

"A chance on what?"

"Love? A relationship? I'm not sure. Human beings were not created to live alone. We need that soul mate to make our lives complete, and it's my opinion everyone has a soul mate. They just have to find each other."

I remembered having said that to Amy not too long ago. "Why you old romantic, you."

He laughed lightly and kissed me before putting more space between us.

"I guess I am at that." He looked at his watch again. "I'd better get rolling. We'll discuss this subject when I get back from St. Louis."

"In the lawyer world, we call that a continuance."

He grinned, and then the smile slowly faded. "Be careful wherever you and Amy go. I don't want to lose you."

"I have no intention of getting lost."

****

An hour later, I waved goodbye as Brad pulled out of his driveway. I'd packed a small duffle bag for him while he'd called his private investigator friend.

"Trevor's on it," he reported, slinging the bag onto the passenger seat. "Give me a call from Branson. Keep me up to date. I'll let you know what I find out as soon as I can. And be careful!"

"I will, I will. You be careful driving."

He kissed me, slid behind the wheel slamming the door an instant later, and starting the engine.

"Don't worry, I will."

He waved, turned the car around, and roared off. I had the feeling Abby Wallace wasn't the only one with a penchant for fast driving.

I walked back home. Amy's car was in her driveway. I needed a good excuse to ask her to join me in a road trip, but drew a blank until I fingered the stitches. I had it.

Brad's faith in me bolstered my confidence. If all else failed, I'd beg.

I crossed the lawn and knocked on Amy's door. She opened with a huge smile on her face. Her blue eyes sparkled. It was a one-hundred and eighty degree turnaround from the day before.

"Jenny! Come in. How are you feeling? Better, I hope." She eyed my head, stepping back from the threshold. "The shaved area is a little odd, but I guess that's to be expected. When do the stitches come out? How many did you have again? I can't remember. Hope there's no scar to mess up your hair style. Can I get you anything? Iced tea? Coffee?"

I followed her to the kitchen. She sounded as though she'd indulged in a couple of pots of coffee. The words tripped out of her mouth with little rhyme or reason. She babbled, and Amy Wallace did not babble. Something was up. After her depression yesterday, I wondered if she'd taken some kind of medication. Or perhaps none.

"Well, you're certainly in a good mood today. Much better than when I last saw you."

She waved a hand. "I guess I am. I did a lot of thinking last night and finally came to the conclusion my Uncle Mark is full of it. He's been pressuring me about a lot of things lately. I even pretended to go along with his wishes, but changed my mind, so this morning I called and told him to get off my back. I'd live my own life the way I wanted to. Felt good. Maybe I'm growing a spine after all these years."

"Uh, good for you." I wasn't sure how to ease into my request, but Amy solved the problem for me.

"So, what's on your mind?" she asked, pouring two glasses of tea.

I slid onto a stool at the breakfast bar and sipped. "Well, I don't know about you, but I'm ready for a change of scenery. So, I decided to go to Branson. Ever been there?"

"You know, I haven't. I hear it's a nice place."

"Why don't you come with me?"

She hesitated. "Oh, I don't know. I have a lot to do."

"We can leave this afternoon, stay overnight, and take in the sights tomorrow."

She bit her lip and wrinkled her forehead in thought. I plunged on.

"I'd really like you to come. My treat. It's my way of saying thank you for all your help the other day at the hospital. I don't know what I would have done if you hadn't scraped me off the road." When she still hesitated, I pulled out the guilt card. "I still get a throbbing headache every once in a while, and I thought maybe you could share the driving. It's only a two-hour drive, but if you can't go, I guess I can make it."

"Oh, well if you need me then I guess I can come, but I have to be home by tomorrow night, no later than nine. I…I'm expecting a…a phone call."

I suspected her stammering was a little white lie, but didn't care. She'd agreed to go.

I gulped my tea and set the glass on the counter. "That's terrific. Can you be ready in say an hour? I don't think Branson demands fancy clothes."

"No problem. Thanks for inviting me. It does sound like fun and I love country music. I'll meet you at your place."

Relieved, I slid off the stool and headed for the door. She'd agreed, and that's all that counted.

****

We rolled into Branson a little after five and pulled up to a hotel located near the action in the center of town. The recession had prevented the "no vacancy" signs from being displayed, so we had no problem getting two rooms. I drew the line at sharing. I needed my privacy and couldn't talk freely on the phone to Brad with Amy in the room.

The drive down had proven uneventful. No headache at all, and to be truthful, I hadn't expected one.

Amy's upbeat demeanor continued. She tapped her foot and snapped her fingers to the country music on the radio, even singing along on a couple of songs. The smile never left her face. She was a completely different person, and for a moment I recalled Brad's theory about Amy having been killed and Abby impersonating her sister. Then, I dismissed the notion. Abby Wallace didn't sound like the type to like Toby

256

Keith or Lady Antebellum.

I grabbed a quick shower and changed clothes before calling Brad. I left a message in his voice mail saying we'd arrived and where we were staying, and then joined Amy in the lobby.

"I was talking to the desk clerk and he told me about a restaurant called Beer for My Horses just two blocks away. He said the food was good and the entertainment top notch. Want to give it a try?"

"Beer for My Horses?"

She laughed. "Its part of a lyric and the title of a Toby Keith and Willie Nelson hit of a few years ago."

Her enthusiasm hadn't waned and I wondered again if she was on some type of medication.

"Let's go. I like horses—beered up or not. What's the entertainment?"

She led the way out of the hotel and down the street. "The desk clerk was a fountain of information. I understand it has a band—pretty good, too. They do an early show at seven and a late one at ten. In between sets and after the show, a DJ plays music and people dance."

It wasn't my idea of a fun time, but it didn't matter as long as Amy was pleased. Country music wasn't my thing; however, I'd sacrifice.

Beer for My Horses was located on a corner and resembled an old trading post—or what I assumed was an old trading post—with a roof covering the sidewalk and shutters next to multi-paned windows. Inside, a hostess showed us to a table for two near the dance floor. A bandstand with amplifiers and musical instruments stood off to the side. Above, on a balcony, a glassed in area suggested this was the DJ's domain.

The menu was surprisingly eclectic with moderate prices. While we read, a waitress took our drink order. I requested red wine, while Amy asked for a draft Bud. I stared. Beer? All I'd ever seen her drink was wine. I was seeing a whole different side of Amy.

I cleared the surprise from my throat. "What sounds good to you?"

"The Drunken Steak with whiskey sauce sounds great, but then so does the Country Catfish. I can get catfish at home. I can get steak at home, too, but the whiskey sauce sells it," she said with a laugh. "What about you?"

Beer and now whiskey? This trip had turned into an eye-opener.

"I have no idea." I spoke the truth. Everything sounded delicious.

The waitress brought our drinks, and we ordered—she the steak while I opted for an herb crusted pork chop. We both asked for baked potatoes with all the glop on top, and a house salad.

Amy smiled and sipped her beer. "So, Jenny, what kind of law is it you do again?"

"Contract law. I deal mostly with authors and occasionally mediate between publishing houses, agents, and writers. It can be dull, but lucrative if the writer is a name."

"Have you done any famous authors?"

"I hammered out Byron Allday's first contract."

"The science fiction novelist? I love his stuff. Wow, tell me more."

I drank some wine and filled her in on a few of the details of Byron's personality, all the while speculating on if she was really interested or just making conversation.

*First country music, then beer, then whiskey sauce, and now sci-fi? A very strange evening indeed.* If Amy was sucking down happy pills, I didn't see it, but the change in personality concerned me.

While we chatted, the band members ambled in and began setting up for the entertainment. A quick glance around the room showed it to be two-thirds full. I had a feeling the older generation and families liked the early set since most of the patrons were past forty and a number of children sat with their parents.

*The place probably gets going after ten.*

"Is there anything you'd like to do tomorrow?" I asked when the thrill of contract law ran out.

"I haven't read the brochure yet, but from what I've heard this place has it all. I wouldn't mind taking in a museum or two and of course, the shops are said to be excellent. Do you have any preferences?"

*Yeah, bed and a nice long talk with Brad.* I must have looked at my watch a dozen times so far wondering what he was doing and if he'd received any information from his private investigator buddy.

"No, I don't care." The shopping appealed. The museums did not.

The waitress brought our food just as the band started playing. We each requested another drink and dug in. The food was delicious. My pork chop was thick and juicy, and if Amy had any problems with her whiskey coated steak, she didn't voice them.

The band serenaded us throughout the meal. The lead singer played guitar, occasionally relinquishing the spotlight to a tall woman whose red hair was teased almost to the ceiling. Not being an aficionado of country music, I had no idea if they were any good, but Amy applauded and grinned at the end of each song as did the rest of the audience. The set ended with the fiddle player knocking out *The Devil Went Down To Georgia* to a thunderous ovation.

Our meal also ended. To my surprise, Amy ordered another beer. Not to be left out, I kept pace with another glass of wine. She smiled and the urge to talk to her like a sister emerged. Would Amy even be interested? In her present state of mind, I wasn't sure. I dropped my gaze into my glass. The ambient light threw the wine into various shades of red. Now, I was the one in need of help.

"Amy, there's something I want to tell you. Something personal. You opened up the other night about the accident and Abby's death. I need to talk about my divorce."

Her gaze swept the room. "Sure, what about it?"

I gave her the same gory details I had Brad. She listened, nodding at the appropriate times. "Do you think I should track down my ex and tell him I'm sorry? Or has too much time passed?"

She shrugged and sipped her beer. "We all make mistakes. God knows, I have. But saying 'I'm sorry' just makes *us* feel better. Doesn't really help the other person. Your ex has probably moved on with his life. You should do the same. What's done is done."

Her words made sense, but I expected more sympathy or diplomacy from her. My feelings were slightly hurt. Once again I wondered if she had taken some kind of medication. Her behavior was confusing—up one day, down the next. Years ago she'd have been called maniac-depressive. Now, I think the term is bi-polar. I didn't know how to deal with it. On the charitable side, perhaps my confession had made her uncomfortable. Just because I may have felt sisterhood, didn't mean she returned the feeling. A voice boomed from a loudspeaker interrupting my thoughts.

"All right, ladies and gents, let's see how good y'all can dance!"

Music just barely below earsplitting level blasted and within a few minutes the dance floor was jammed. Amy and I watched until the song changed as did the dance. Everyone lined up and danced the same steps. I'd heard about line dancing, but had never actually seen it. It reminded me of the Electric Slide and the Macarena of years ago.

I was about to call it a night when two men walked up to the table.

"Ladies, would you like to dance?" one of them asked.

I opened my mouth to refuse when Amy opened hers first.

"I'd love to!" She took the guy's hand and clamored to her feet. "My foot's been tapping for a long while."

I stared in complete astonishment.

"Ma'am?" the other man asked.

"I haven't got a clue how to dance this way."

He laughed and held out his hand. "Nobody does at first. I'll teach you."

Too stunned by Amy's behavior to think of an excuse I followed him. I stumbled and bumbled my way through several songs, before returning to our table with the others. It had been years since I'd been picked up in a bar, and was wondering how to get out of what could be a sticky situation. On the up side, I'd been engrossed in work for so long that a man asking me to dance was flattering.

"Thank you very much for the dance, ladies. We're moving on to The Wild, Wild West down the street. If you'd like to come, you're welcome."

"That sounds like fun," I said hastily. "But it was a long drive down and we have a full day tomorrow before we have to leave. Thanks for the dance lesson."

They laughed and waved before leaving.

"Jenny, are you tired? Does your head hurt?"

"I am a bit tired."

She immediately rose. "And here I am dancing and keeping you up. *And* you drove the entire way. I'll drive back tomorrow. Are we settled with the waitress?"

"Yes, we're fine, and you aren't keeping me from anything. I actually had a good time."

We said goodnight in the hallway outside our respective rooms. I entered, tossed my purse on the dresser, and yanked my phone out. I had a message from Brad. With the music in the restaurant, I'd never heard it ring.

Without bothering to listen to the voicemail, I dialed. He answered on the second ring.

"Are you all right? When you didn't answer I got concerned."

"I'm fine, but wait until you hear about my day."

I gave him the low down on Amy and the evening's activities, omitting my dancing with another man. Why stir a pot that's ready to boil?

"That's downright bizarre," he said when I finished. "She sounds like she's higher than a kite."

"I know and it worries me."

"And you say she was like that at the lake?"

"She was bouncing off the walls. Do you think she could be taking drugs of some sort?"

"You mean illegal?"

"I don't know. That doesn't sound like Amy at all."

"No," he said slowly. "But it does sound like Abby."

"I thought we abandoned the theory of switching places."

"I know, but it bothers me. Keep an eye on her. Don't let her wander off by herself."

"I won't. How about you? Anything to report?"

"Trevor did some preliminary work on the warrant. It was rescinded six months after issue. The reason was death of the accused."

"That makes sense. The police would have traced Abby to St. Louis, found her parents, and learned of the accident."

"And guess who else was named in a warrant? Roger Corry."

I drew in a sharp breath. "Just like we suspected. The same guy at the marina."

"Yep. He was convicted and sent to the slammer nine years ago for importation with intent to distribute. He was released last year."

"And hooked up again with Abby. Brad, what's going on? Why is she doing this?"

"I don't know yet. Trevor's still researching Abby, but there's little to go on after the accident. She obviously changed her name and kept her nose clean. I'll talk to the neighbors in Webster Groves tomorrow. Maybe one of them can add something. See if you can extend your visit."

"Amy's already said she has to be home tomorrow night. Something about a phone call. I think it might be work oriented," I said.

"Be careful. Don't want you to get hurt again. My heart couldn't take it," he said in a soft tone.

My heartbeat sped up. "I promise. I miss you."

"Miss you, too. Hope this is all over soon. We need to talk."

Talk? As in serious? As in relationship? My heart thumped in both fear and anticipation.

"We will. Soon. I promise that, too."

I hung up and stared at the phone. I hadn't expected this, but in the middle of a mystery, had I managed to fall in love?

Chapter Twenty-Eight

*Diary of Amy Margaret Wallace*

At the moment I'm in Branson and so excited I could burst! I opened the note with the ring. It was from Abby!

I was right all along. Abby is alive and I won't be lonely any more. She'll be at the lake house tomorrow night at nine. She knows Uncle Mark is in Vermillion and asked that I not tell anyone about this until she talks to me first.

I spent the whole morning cleaning until Jenny dropped by with an invite to accompany her to Branson. I decided I needed the distraction. It would be something to do, to keep me occupied while I waited.

My head is spinning. Wait until Uncle Mark hears. He'll be the one needing a shrink!

I wonder if anyone else remembers that tomorrow is the tenth anniversary of the accident.

Chapter Twenty-Nine

"According to the map, it should be just around this corner," Amy said, consulting the brochure in her hand.

For some reason, she was gung-ho on seeing the Titanic museum. To me, the words Titanic and Branson just didn't go together.

We turned the corner and I stopped to stare. "Good God!"

The museum was a two story replica of the famous ship. It managed to look both stunning and tacky at the same time.

Amy laughed. "Oh my goodness. Come on, this has got to be terrific."

I followed her enthusiastic step. Her good spirits from the day before had not worn off. She still laughed and bubbled with conversation, much of which was just talking. She reminded me of a coiled spring about to snap. I vowed to keep a close eye on her the rest of the day.

The museum was better than expected. In my mind, Titanic represented a dividing line between the classes at the beginning of the twentieth century. The ship's destruction marked the end of an era. Never again would such privilege be enjoyed by the rich. A world war and the income tax saw to that.

Next, Amy dragged me to the Ripley's Believe It

Or Not museum. This was more fun. The place was a monument to strange behavior and happenings, some natural, some manmade.

We lunched at a Mexican restaurant. While sipping a margarita, I decided to probe her sudden change in spirits. I didn't buy the crap she'd handed out yesterday about feeling liberated for having told off her uncle. Did she take medication? Had she over-medicated? Under-medicated? Or had she decided uppers just made her feel good?

"You know, this is the most animated I've seen you—ever. I remember you as quiet and shy when you were a kid. I liked looking after you. No trouble at all."

Amy laughed and sipped her drink. "You mean as opposed to Abby. She was all fire. I could never outshine her, so I kept to myself. That's not to say I never won an argument. I can be very stubborn at times."

"Well, I never suspected you'd pick up a guy in a honky-tonk."

A shocked expression crossed her face. "Oh, I didn't pick him up. He picked me up, and all we did was dance for a while. You got picked up, too. What will Brad say?"

What indeed? And why hadn't I confessed to it last night? Because I didn't want to rock the possible romance or relationship boat?

"I can't see how Brad would see that as a threat."

Amy pointed a finger at me. "Ah-ha! So you admit there's something between the two of you."

"He's pretty special, that's for sure," I admitted.

"Tell me about him. I'd like to know more."

As I listed Brad's positive qualities, it dawned on

me that she hadn't answered my question about the sudden change in attitude. Since it was so out of character, I tackled the subject head on.

"So, that's where it stands as of now. I think a relationship is forming. I'm not sure. Gotta take it slow. But tell me about what's going on with that contract you talked about last week. Did you nail it down? Or is that what the phone call is all about?"

Amy didn't answer at first, but stared into the frozen concoction in her glass.

"More or less." She didn't make eye contact. "My agent is supposed to call with news of whether I'm illustrating this big project. It's…it's one of those big books that lie around on coffee tables. The subject matter is endangered wildlife or something along those lines. According to the author, there'll be illustrations of extinct animals and birds. If I get it, I'll be busy for close to a year."

On the surface, the explanation sounded legitimate, so why did I have the feeling she was making it up as she went along?

Our lunch arrived. I'd ordered the cheese enchiladas, while Amy indulged in chicken fajitas. The food was good and the conversation dwindled as we ate. It gave me time to think—about Brad.

By now, he should be out in Webster Groves interviewing neighbors. If Abby was alive and using the family home as a base, then someone must have seen her. Yet the Abby sightings had mostly come in Vermillion.

*We're missing something. Something important, but damned if I can figure out what.*

And while I realized private investigations took

time, I chafed at the lack of news on that front. Assuming Abby was alive, where had she been all those years? What was she doing? And why had she hooked up with a no-account scumbag like Corry again?

Then I remembered Brad's comments about Abby's personality not being the most pleasant. Good twin, bad twin? I could see that. But even as kids, I'd never connected it to criminal activity on Abby's part. Mischievous, yes. Thoughtless, yes. Uncaring about others? Definitely. But criminal? No.

*However, we all grow, and not always in a good way.*

Thinking about Abby brought me around to the more earthy side of Brad. Ever since I'd met him, he'd been an object of my appreciation. I'd been attracted from the first glimpse of that fine rear end and those well-developed muscles.

Attraction was one thing, but investing emotion was harder. Yet somehow, I'd done it. Maybe it was time to put Jim and my infidelity behind me. I'd screwed up. Brad had screwed up with Abby and two failed marriages. Maybe the ensuing years had matured both of us.

Could I try again? Should I try again—with Brad? *I don't want to wake up one day at age fifty, alone in the bed and spending my time writing and reviewing contracts.* I wanted a white picket fence, kids, and carpools before it was too late.

I finished my meal and looked up to find Amy staring at me.

"You seemed deep in thought."

"Just thinking."

"About Brad?" she asked in a teasing tone.

"A little."

"I think someone's in love." Her sing-songy voice oozed amusement.

"Could be. I screwed up my marriage big time. I can't let that happen again. This time I want to be sure."

"Plus Brad has two ex-wives floating around. I can see how you'd want to stand on solid ground. I'd like to get married, have kids, and live happily ever after." Her tone had turned wistful. "Maybe Brad's got a friend I can try on for size."

Her bizarre terminology had me staring. It was so just not her. Lithium? Prozac? Something less legal? I was confused and not sure how to handle it. Once again I wished Brad would call.

"What's next on the agenda?" I asked when the waiter presented the check. I tossed a couple of bills on the table and waved him away with a hefty tip.

"I promise not to drag you to any more museums. Why don't we hit the shops?"

"Sounds like a plan to me."

I don't know what I expected to find in the line of shopping, but was pleasantly surprised at the diversity of stores. Gift, retail, and specialty shops stood side-by-side, and while the prices weren't cheap, neither were they exorbitant. I bought a skirt and a couple of tops, while Amy selected a pair of form-hugging Capris and several Ts and tank tops in bright colors, including red.

"Red?" I asked.

"Uh, yeah, I guess so. It's time I came out of my shell," she said with a laugh.

Shell or not, I couldn't see her wearing any of this. Her neutral mental palette just wouldn't allow it.

By five o'clock my feet were killing me. Amy

seemed to have developed the energy of ten tourists, but even she had to call it a day.

"If I don't want to miss see…uh, taking my phone call, we'd better get on the road," she said with a glance at her watch. A small smile played on her lips.

*She's lying. I just don't know about what.*

"That suits me. How about a quick dinner?"

"Okay, but very quick."

We chose a bar and bar food—wings for me, a burger and fries for her. After checking out of the hotel this morning, we'd chucked our bags into the trunk before exploring Branson. Now, with the shopping bags tossed into the back seat, Amy insisted on driving home.

"You don't have to do that. I'm fine. Not a sign of a headache."

"No, no, you were nice enough to invite me along at your expense, so the least I can do is drive home."

Since she refused to take no for an answer, I slid into the passenger seat. I vaguely remembered the ride to the hospital as being fast and frantic. I'd assumed it was in response to my injury. She drove just as fast and frantic on this twisting two lane road leading to Lake Wildwood. Ten miles out of town, she flipped on the radio.

"Do you mind if I switch channels? I'm tired of country."

"Go ahead."

She twiddled the dial until settling on an urban rock station, and turned up the volume. Hip-hop blasted my eardrums, while she tapped her fingers on the steering wheel in time to the music.

"Hip-hop? You've got to be kidding."

She sent me a sharp look. "Don't try to pigeonhole me. All my life people have done that. Amy does this, Abby does that. I have a lot of different tastes no one suspects."

I'm sure my astonishment at her outburst showed on my face. She laughed.

"I'm sorry, Jenny. Chalk it up to my newfound freedom from taking orders."

"Sure, no problem."

I stared out the passenger side window at the scenery whipping past. I was not only bothered, but scared as well. Something *just wasn't right*.

Amy pulled into my driveway a few minutes before eight.

"Thank you so much for everything, Jenny. I had a terrific time, but gotta scoot now. I have a lot to do before nine."

She grabbed her bags, hugged me, and "scooted" home.

I hustled inside, too, dropped my duffle by the sofa, and whipped out my cell. I hadn't heard from Brad all day. Curiosity was burning a hole in my chest. I pushed his speed dial number.

"Brad," I almost yelled in my anxiety when he answered. "Any news?"

"Some. I talked to a couple of neighbors, but those closest to her work during the day, so I had to wait until just a while ago."

"And?" I tried, but couldn't keep the impatience from my voice.

"Most neighbors didn't notice anything unusual in the last month or so. Lights were occasionally on in the house, but that's all."

"Timers," I said shortly.

"Agreed. Then I hit pay dirt with a neighbor across the street. One day several weeks ago, she happened to look out her front window when she noticed a red car pull into the drive and park in the garage. The driver was a dark-haired woman."

"Oh, my God. Abby?"

"I think so. I also spent some time on the internet looking up twin behavior and such. It was interesting, but technical. I'll tell you later. How did your day go?"

I gave him a brief rundown of the day including Amy's outburst in the car.

"It was so unlike her, Brad. And I know she's lying about a phone call. I have no idea what's going on, but whatever it is she's sure in a state."

"Look, I'm on the road. I should be there by ten, maybe sooner. Wait up for me, okay?"

"You got it."

I hung up and unpacked, then ran a bath. While soaking, I mulled over the information Brad had come up with, and my reactions to Amy over the past twenty-four hours.

I toweled off still in a pensive mood. *It's so odd—almost as if she's not Amy anymore.*

Then I stopped cold. Not Amy? I remembered the theory Brad and I had bounced around—the one about Amy having died, not Abby. My God, *could* it have been Abby all these years?

Brad's concern about Amy's behavior last night mirrored mine. Suddenly, I straightened, my heart pounding. A whole new supposition flashed through my mind.

Oh my God, what if Abby is impersonating her

sister? Only the switch hadn't come ten years ago, but more recently. In ten years, Abby's hair could have grown long. She *could* have shown up at the family home in St. Louis for a reconciliation. The million dollar question now was where the hell is Amy? The answer was obvious. *In a shallow grave somewhere between here and St. Louis.*

I hurriedly dressed, and then sat on the sofa to think. Could the greedy, self-absorbed, Abby actually kill her sister? I didn't want to think so.

*But I bet the boyfriend could without a second thought. However, if it's Abby, then why call attention to herself with silly sightings? It doesn't make sense. Maybe I'm too close to it. Maybe I'm stretching my imagination to the breaking point. Besides, pulling off a charade of switching places would test even Meryl Streep's abilities.*

The most likely explanation was the one given in the car—Amy was always being underestimated. Those quiet, shy ones sometimes had a lot of depth. The old cliché, still waters run deep, had a lot going for it. So, why didn't I buy it?

*Stop over-analyzing!*

My newest theory on the Abby/Amy conundrum didn't make sense, mainly because I couldn't answer the question, "why?" Brad and I had discussed so many possibilities we were getting lost in the process. Amy had either taken, or stopped taking, some kind of medication. End of story.

I glanced at my watch—almost nine-fifteen. I wondered if Amy had received her phone call. I also wondered where Brad was now. With his lead foot, I imagined him pulling into my driveway any moment.

Unable to sit still, I paced. Then I poured a glass of wine and tried to settle down on the deck. A light from Amy's kitchen stabbed the darkness. Insects chirped. The air was still as death. The suffocating calm pressed against my skin. My heart raced for no reason. To the southwest, thunder rumbled with a muted menace.

I returned inside to the coolness of the air conditioning. A storm was brewing. Maybe my anxiety had to do with the closeness of the weather. I stared at my cell, tempted to call Brad. I swallowed the last of my wine and almost choked when the phone rang. Caller ID identified Brad. I fumbled to answer.

"Hello?" My voice sounded scared, breathy.

"Jen, we've got it all wrong."

"What are you talking about?"

"What's the date today?"

"Ah, the 8$^{th}$?"

"That's right. And when did the accident happen?"

"On the 9$^{th}$ of July." I paused. "A little after midnight." A chill raced up and down my spine.

"Jen, get Amy out of there. Abby Wallace is alive, and she has a plan. She doesn't want to drive her sister crazy. She wants to kill her!"

## Chapter Thirty

*Diary of Amy Margaret Wallace*

Fifteen minutes. In another fifteen minutes Abby will be here. The champagne is chilled just the way she likes it. I even daubed her favorite perfume, Midnight Madness, behind my ears in honor of the occasion. I can hardly wait. I'm wearing the ring, too.

This will be the last entry in my journal. I'll give it to Uncle Mark. He can read it and see what an ass he's been. Oh, how Abby will laugh. She didn't like him that much. Used to make fun of him always trying to keep up with her and her friends.

Five minutes to go. I'm so nervous I can barely write. Finally! Abby's coming home!

Chapter Thirty-One

*...She wants to kill her!*

I sucked in a deep breath. "Why do you think that?"

"Trevor just called. He found little on Abby Wallace, so he turned his attention to her parents. When Constance Wallace died, she left everything in trust to her daughter, Amy. Even with the shitty economy, Amy's sitting on close to ten million big ones. Jen, it's all about the money."

I ran a hand through my hair, seeing the logic in his assumption. My heart beat in slow heavy thumps. Ten million bucks! Means, motive, and opportunity.

"But Abby's been declared legally dead. Does she plan on just materializing? That would look suspicious if Amy happens to turn up as a corpse."

"But doable. She returns saying she read about Amy's death in the paper or something, and is ready to claim her inheritance. Her identity won't be a problem. Mark Bridges will confirm it. Hell, the whole world will confirm it—she looks just like Amy. She claims the money, gets the trust rescinded, and goes on her merry way."

"With the sleazy boyfriend in tow," I added. "Brad, what are we going to do? Call the police."

"I will, I will. But Amy comes first. Get her out of Vermillion. It doesn't matter where. Head back to

277

Branson. Stick her in a motel."

"On what excuse? If I tell her Abby is alive and wants to kill her, she'll think I'm nuts. She's not going to go anywhere with me, especially with this newfound independence. Or worse yet, she'll want to stay to prove I'm wrong about her sister wanting to kill her. She'll want to see Abby for herself."

"Convince her. Or don't tell her about Abby. Tell her the boyfriend wants to harm her. Use the revenge theory. *Just get her out of there*. I'll call the police as soon as I hear from you and know you're safe."

"All right, I'm on my way."

"Call when you have her in the car. I'll meet you someplace. I'm thirty minutes away. Now, *go!*"

I hung up and took a moment and several cleansing breaths to steady my nerves.

*The phone call! Oh my God, the phone call. It's got nothing to do with work. Abby's been in contact with her. Maybe even arranging to meet. No wonder Amy's higher than a kite. Am I too late?*

A quick glance at my watch showed the time as close to nine-thirty. Somehow, Abby keeping to an exact time schedule didn't seem in character. I still might be able to do this.

I dashed across the lawn to Amy's, my heart literally in my throat. I had no idea what to say, but Brad's information convinced me Amy Wallace was in danger. If I could get her out of Vermillion, perhaps to my house in St. Louis, then she'd be safe from Abby and her boyfriend.

Amy's car was the only one parked in the driveway. I breathed a sigh of relief—no motorcycle.

Thunder rumbled close by as I leaped up the porch

steps and jerked the screen door open. Not bothering with being polite, I barged in, and then skidded to a stop.

A dark-haired man stood by the fireplace, a beer bottle tilted to his lips. A woman sitting on the sofa looked up.

My breath caught in my throat and my hand fisted against my chest as if to stifle the hard thudding heartbeats.

The woman winked, lifted her champagne glass in a salute, and sipped.

I stared unable to take in everything I saw.

Abby Wallace stared back and smiled. She cradled the champagne glass in her hands. "Well, well, looks like we have company, dear."

I turned my attention to the man. It was the same one I'd seen off and on over the past couple of weeks.

He set his bottle on the mantel and picked up a gun sitting next to it. His gaze raked me from head to foot while I stood frozen in place unable to move, to think, to react—except with fear. I shook with it.

"And you are the nosy neighbor. I thought that whack on the head would have cured you from meddling in things that don't concern you." He gestured toward a chair. "Have a seat."

I did as instructed, but ignored him, focusing my attention instead on Abby.

"Abby, you're...you're alive." It was all I could think to say, and then added, "Where's Amy?"

She laughed and drained her glass, then refilled it from the bottle sitting on the coffee table. She tilted her head back as she drank.

"Of course I'm alive—and kicking, as you can see.

What brings you here on this soon to be stormy night?"

Out of the corner of my eye I caught the flash of lightning. Thunder rolled a few seconds later.

"Ah," Abby said cocking her head and casting a glance at her companion. "How familiar. I think this might be the perfect night for a boating accident, don't you, Roger?"

He grinned and nodded, bracing his foot on the hearth and leering at me again with a smirk.

Tremors rippled through my body from head to toe. She hadn't answered my question. Where was Amy? Had they killed her already? I glanced at the portrait over the fireplace, and then back at Abby. The hair, short and spiky was the same. I *had* seen her in Stone City that day.

She followed my glance. "I like the portrait. I think I'll keep it when I inherit everything. Be a nice souvenir."

"Where's Amy?"

"Not far away."

My heart plunged to my toes. *Please God, don't let her be dead!*

I thought about Brad. With any luck, he'd be here soon. When I didn't call, he'd come looking for me. And he wouldn't charge in like I'd done. He'd see the clown holding the gun on me and call the cops, if he hadn't already. The sliding glass doors to the deck were open making for a perfect entry. All I had to do was keep these two occupied for a while. The boyfriend, Roger, didn't look all that smart, and I figured the cops could take him down fast.

I licked my dry lips and forced words from my even drier mouth.

"How...how did you survive the accident? Where have you been all these years?"

Abby shrugged. "Don't remember much about the accident or how I survived. All I recall is ending up in some cabin up in the hills. Didn't even know my name. I stuck around for a while, and then split. Little by little my memory returned. I even remembered Roger. I'd met him on a street corner in Dallas where he was selling some fine Mexican weed. We were *simpatico*. Then he got careless and sold dope to an undercover cop. Since I was in the car, I got caught up in the sting, too. Luckily, I didn't have anything on me, so a couple of lies, a few tears, and they let me go—at least for a while. I knew the cops would hook my name to Roger's sooner or later. This wasn't the first time I'd driven him to a deal. Some bozo coke-snorter would spill his guts for a lighter sentence."

Why was she telling me all of this? Because it didn't matter? Because I'd soon be dead? Maybe another body in a boating accident? Amy and I on a late night cruise with a storm brewing?

My chest constricted with fear. I cleared my throat. "So, you ran like a rabbit for cover at Lake Wildwood." Brad had been right about that.

Abby shrugged. "It seemed the safest place. The cops would eventually trace me to St. Louis. It bought me some time."

"The accident bought you ten years," I said. More thunder rumbled, closer this time.

"Most of which had me in the slammer," Roger said.

I spared him a glance. He frowned, no doubt at the contempt that must be showing on my face.

"And when you got out, you hooked up with your girlfriend again."

"Of course. She contacted me the day after they set me free."

I looked back at Abby who poured herself another glass of champagne.

Why contact Corry at all? Was she actually in love with this low-level dealer? I didn't see Abby Wallace carrying the torch for ten years.

*Something is wrong, really wrong with this, but what? I'm too scared to think straight.*

"Where have you been all these years?" I wanted to look at my watch in the worst way, but refrained. Where was Brad?

"Here and there. I got fake IDs, worked odd jobs, never staying in one place too long, just waiting for Roger's release. Also took time to work this plan out. My sister owes me. If she hadn't been such a scaredy-cat at the helm, we'd have made it back to shore. But no, not Amy. She had to take it slow and cautious."

"And yet the accident gave you perfect cover. Your parents had you declared legally dead and the warrant was rescinded."

She shrugged again and gulped the champagne. "As I said, it gave me time to think."

"So you decided to come back and show yourself only to her, making everyone think she's crazy."

Still holding the gun on me, Roger grabbed his beer from the mantel and drank. Then he said, "That's right. And when they find her body floating in the lake with a boat drifting nearby, they'll figure she went over the edge and killed herself. Abby'll write a good suicide note."

"And then you just show up and claim a multi-million dollar inheritance? Don't you think the cops will be just a tad suspicious, not to mention your uncle?"

Abby laughed and glanced at the open door as the thunder no longer rumbled, but boomed. The storm was closing in. "Good old Uncle Mark."

A car swept up the drive and pulled to a halt. The car door slammed and footsteps hurried up the porch stairs. I half rose from my seat. *Brad! No! Run!*

"Help!" I screamed, hoping to alert him to the danger.

Mark Bridges entered the room, his gaze sweeping from side to side. He advanced toward Roger, his hands in his pockets as if he had all the time in the world.

"Hello, Abby," he greeted in a cool tone. "Roger, put the gun away and sit down."

"No fuckin' way."

"I said, put the gun down. Now!" Bridges said in a steely tone. "I'm sure Jenny is no threat. Especially when she hears what we have to tell her."

Roger scowled, but tossed the gun onto the hearth, then ambled the few feet to the sofa and sat on the arm next to Abby.

I stared in total astonishment. Mark? Mark was in on this? And then I saw everything clearly.

"It really *is* all about the money, isn't it?"

Lightning flashed again and the thunder cracked closer than a few minutes ago. The breeze freshened flowing in through the open doors, the smell of rain not far off.

Mark sighed. "It's always about the money."

"You've been embezzling."

"I'm afraid so. Abby popped into my house a few months ago demanding her share of the estate. When I tried to put her off, she guessed immediately what I'd done. But instead of threatening to turn me in, she came up with a plan to split what was left."

"So, you all decided to play with Amy's mind. Little Abby sightings to make people think she was hallucinating at best or crazy at worst. You even suckered me into the scheme."

"Yes, I needed an outside witness. Someone with no connection to the family other than a casual friendship years ago. Abby remembered and Googled you. Took me a while to track you down, and your greedy boss played right into my hands."

"And him?" I asked indicating the boyfriend.

"Had to have someone fire the shot at the house while I was here. Gave me an alibi. Amy, of course, helped by declaring it was an accident." Mark shook his head. "Good old Amy. Always seeing the best in people."

Thunder pealed again, louder this time. The patter of raindrops hit the deck outside.

Mark turned to Abby. "Where's Amy?"

"I slipped a couple of Valium into her wine. When she got drowsy, I helped her to the bedroom. She's in la-la land and will be for quite a while."

"Excellent," he said with a smile, and thrusting his hand into his slacks pocket.

"You were never going to institutionalize Amy, were you?" I said. "You always intended to kill her."

"Yes, I'm afraid so," he replied, and pulled a gun on us.

Roger's eyes widened and he lunged for his gun on

the hearth, six feet away.

"Don't!" Mark barked. "Stay right where you are."

Roger stared at the gun, but complied.

Heartbeats drummed in my ears and an odd sensation of floating encased me. The room brightened with another flash of lightning, but I didn't hear the thunder. I was too scared. And if Brad didn't hurry, I'd be dead. Out of the corner of my eye, I caught movement on the sofa.

"You, too, Abby! Don't move an inch," her uncle demanded.

I glanced at Abby for her reaction. To my surprise, she didn't look frightened or even outraged at the turn of events. She poured another glass of champagne. A smile on her lips and the expression in her eyes showed amusement—and excitement.

"Let me guess, Uncle Mark. You're going to kill us all and take the money for yourself?"

"Had it planned that way from the start. I supplied the money for the gun the punk has and the rifle. All bought on the street, of course. The way I figure it, the cops will think he tracked his former girlfriend to St. Louis, followed her to Lake Wildwood, and killed everybody."

Abby grinned as though enjoying the show. "And what's his motive, dear uncle? Why kill me?"

Mark grinned back. "Revenge for dumping him now that you're rich again. And it'll be such a shame your neighbor took this time to drop by."

Roger lunged for his gun, but Mark didn't bat an eye. He fired. The sound exploded against my eardrums. A blossom of red spread across the left side of Roger's white T-shirt. He stared at the stain, and then at Mark with a dazed expression. His eyes rolled back in his head and without uttering a sound, he collapsed, hitting the hearth on his way to the floor.

A gasping sob forced its way through my chest and past my throat. Oh my God! He meant it. He was going to kill us all. Black dots danced in my peripheral vision and I couldn't breathe. If my heart pounded any faster, it would burst from my chest. I wanted to puke.

Mark walked over Roger's body—I had no idea if he was dead or alive—scooped the gun off the bricks and into his hand. He returned the gun he'd been holding to his pocket. For the first time I noticed he wore thin latex gloves.

I could see the scenario now. He'd kill us with Corry's gun, call 9-1-1, and explain to the police how he'd heard the shots, rushed in with *his* gun, and killed the murderer in self-defense.

*And because he's a lawyer and has a good reputation, they'll believe him. The son of a bitch will get away with it.*

A gust of wind blew papers from the dining table onto the floor. Lightning flashed, and the thunder boomed again as the rain came down harder.

Then from outside a car door slammed. Brad! Oh, no! Not Brad, too! He must have seen Bridges' car out front. Not suspecting him of complicity, he'd walk right in! I wanted to scream a warning again, but no coherent words formed in my brain. I was mute—incapable of uttering a sound.

I didn't hear anyone on the porch until Brad entered the room, shaking raindrops from his hair. He took in the situation in a glance, and snapped his head toward me.

"Ah, one more joining the party," Mark said, his voice smooth as aged scotch.

"I should have known," Brad said in a calm tone. "You had control of the trust. If I was writing this, you'd be the embezzler."

Bridges laughed. "And you'd be right. Too bad another bestseller won't get written."

Brad walked over to my chair and kissed the top of my head. "Are you all right?"

"As right as anyone about to die can be, I suppose." My voice came out in a croak. I calmed down now that Brad was here. At least we'd die together.

He transferred his gaze to the woman on the sofa. "Hello, Abby. Nice to see you again."

She raised an eyebrow and the glass of champagne. "Brad, you're looking good."

He looked back to Amy's uncle. "You didn't count on all this, did you?"

"Have to admit, you were a surprise. I figured Jenny would see Amy rushing around trying to find Abby, report back to me, and then go home. Didn't count on you romancing her into staying."

"Also didn't count on me liking Amy or thinking perhaps she wasn't hallucinating," I replied, contempt dripping from my voice.

Bridges cast a nasty glance toward Abby. "I told Abby to get the hell out of town for a while, but no, she had to keep showing herself to Amy. Stupid bitch."

Abby chuckled. "Uncle Mark, you are too much. The first thing that'll happen is Aunt Maggie will demand an audit of the trust, and then your little ship will sink."

"I'll handle your father's sister. There are ways.

Now, everybody on your feet."

I rose, my legs shaking so hard I had to use Brad's arm for support. I was about to die. I knew it. I didn't want to die. I didn't want Brad to die. I wanted to spend a damned long time with him by my side—alive. I didn't really care one way or the other about the scheming Abby Wallace.

Then a blinding flash lit the room. Simultaneously, an ear splitting detonation of thunder shook the house. The smell of singed wood scorched my nostrils. The lights went out.

Brad threw me to the floor and rushed past me. In the darkness, I heard body to body impact. A shot was fired. Abby cried out. The bodies hit the floor. Brad had tackled Bridges and from the grunts and swearing, I'd have to say I was missing one hell of a good fight. A chair and a couple of tables overturned.

In the ensuing lightning flashes, I caught glimpses of them grappling like wrestlers. Outside, the rain came down in torrents banging on the deck and roof like a demented drummer.

I scrambled to my hands and knees and thought about heading toward the door. Self-preservation is a strong instinct, but when someone you might love is in danger, that instinct takes a back seat. I ignored instinct and tried to find a weapon. My hand made contact with a lamp. I grabbed it and rose.

All I could see between the flashes of lightning were two forms. Then the fight ended. One of those silhouettes got to his feet. I raised the lamp over my head.

"Jenny, it's all right."

I lowered the lamp at Brad's voice. "Thank God."

"Here give it to me. I have to tie him up."

The lights blinked, blinked again, and came back on as the emergency generator kicked in. The lamp in my hand, its shade gone, glowed sending a harsh beam of light onto the fight scene.

Bridges was out cold on the floor a few feet from Roger's body. Brad, his hair disheveled and a bruise forming on his jaw, secured his captive's hands behind his back with the cord.

For the first time I looked toward Abby. She sat still as a statue on the sofa, the champagne glass still in her hand, staring at me with consternation on her face.

"You've screwed everything," she said in a soft tone.

Suspicion gathered in my mind. "Yeah, I guess I have."

"Is my uncle dead?"

"No, just unconscious." Brad answered. Even as he spoke Bridges groaned.

"And Roger?"

Brad bent over next to Abby's boyfriend and placed two fingers on his neck.

"He's alive, but barely."

Brad whipped out his phone. "I'm calling nine-one-one"

Abby and I stared at each other like two gladiators about to duel as he gave the police the information.

He hung up and said in a hard voice. "Where's Amy?"

"Amy's very safe. She's not dead yet," Abby murmured.

"Brad, search the house. I'll stay here."

"Are you sure? What if she tries to escape?"

"She won't. Not now. Besides, if Amy's drugged someone may need to carry her. Right, Abby?"

She didn't answer, just stared with a bewildered expression.

Brad hesitated before hurrying down the hallway. Abby and I continued to eye each other. He was back within seconds.

"She's not in her room. I'll check downstairs."

"You almost pulled it off, didn't you?" I asked as he rushed down the steps.

"Almost."

"You don't seem to care that your boyfriend might die."

She smirked and shrugged. "What do I care? He's a loser."

Brad returned with a worried look. "I can't find Amy. She's not in the house. Think she might be in the boat?"

"No, I don't think so."

"Then where is she?"

I walked over to stand in front of Abby who stared into space, a smile lifting her lips.

"She's in the house."

"No, she isn't!"

I reached out and stoked the top of Abby's head, then grasped and pulled the wig off. Dark hair tumbled around her face.

I stared and said in a gentle tone, "Hello, Amy."

Chapter Thirty-Two

"What the hell?" Brad said.

I jerked my head toward the fireplace. "The answer's ten feet away."

His gaze traveled to the portrait understanding creeping into his face.

"Put them in the same hairstyle and no one could tell them apart," I said.

"Why, Amy?" Brad asked in a gentle tone.

On the floor, Bridges lifted his head to stare. "A...Amy? Is that you?"

Amy paid no attention to her uncle, but focused on Brad.

"Why couldn't you leave well enough alone? I had this planned out to the last bullet."

"What...what's going on?" Bridges asked.

"The murder of Amy Wallace," I replied. "An elaborate suicide."

Bridges stared. "And Abby?"

"Dead, and has been for ten years."

In the distance sirens screamed. Amy smiled and stared into space.

"Abby's really dead?" Bridges asked, his eyes disbelieving and confused.

"Yep, and Amy fooled you into believing she was alive," I said.

Brad shook his head. "But why?"

"I don't know. I'm not a psychologist." The sirens had reached the Wallace driveway. "Cops are here."

While Brad ran outside to advise the police about the situation, I sat next to Amy on the sofa and wrapped my arm around her shoulders. In the short time I'd been on Lake Wildwood, I'd come to care very much about her.

"Amy? Are you all right?"

She didn't answer, but continued to stare at nothing. On the floor, Bridges flopped like a fish.

"Untie me, dammit!"

The electric cord, especially with the lamp attached, held and he went nowhere. The naked bulb shattered, the shards embedding themselves in the carpet as he struggled. I figured he was as confused as the rest of us.

Brad returned with the authorities. Three paramedics rushed to Roger Corry. Officer Howard and another man jerked Bridges to his feet.

"I demand you untie me," he blustered. "This is all a mistake and I can explain."

"Fine. Explain it at the station." Howard freed Amy's uncle from the cord and slapped handcuffs on his wrist.

"Officer, you don't know the trouble you're in for this."

"What trouble? You're a thief and almost a murderer," Brad commented. He glanced at the men administering to Corry. "Is he going to make it?"

One shook his head. "Not sure yet. He's lost a lot of blood and it looks like the bullet's close to his heart. Pulse is weak, respirations shallow, and BP is barely registering."

A fourth medic stopped in front of Amy and me. "Are you all right?"

"I'm fine, but she's…"

He didn't need further explanation. Amy still stared, unmoving. He clapped his hands in front of her eyes. She didn't blink or indicate her awareness of his presence.

"What's wrong?" I asked.

"I don't know. Catatonic maybe. We need to get her to the hospital."

"Amy, this man is going to take good care of you. I'll come visit tomorrow." I looked up. Tears filled my eyes. "Be gentle with her. Please. She's my best friend—almost a sister."

He nodded and helped an unresisting Amy to her feet. Still staring, she followed him out the door without so much as a word.

The remaining paramedics placed Corry, IV needles stuck in both arms, on a gurney and rushed him out. Bridges followed, still protesting his treatment.

"If the two of you are up to it, I'd like to get your statements at the station stat," Officer Howard said.

Brad nodded. "We're right behind you."

Alone, Brad turned and folded me into his arms. "God, I was never so terrified in my life as when I walked through that door. I kept waiting for your call, and finally called you. When you didn't answer, I figured you were having trouble convincing Amy, so drove straight here. When I saw Bridges' car out front, I thought maybe he was helping you. Can't believe I walked right in. In my books, Joe Archer would never be that stupid."

"If it's any consolation, I did the same thing. Only

Bridges wasn't here yet. I rushed right in to find who I thought was Abby and her boyfriend swilling champagne."

"I still don't understand all of this. How did you realize Amy was Abby?"

I buried my nose in his shoulder and clasped my arms around his waist.

"There was something out of whack the last twenty-four hours. While I was waiting for you to get back, I kept thinking it was like something out of a movie. We talked while you searched the house. Abby wouldn't have said I'd screwed everything in such a soft tone. She'd have cursed a blue streak and been at my throat. But she just sat there. Then it hit me. What if Abby wasn't Abby? The minute I touched her hair I knew it was a wig."

"What was the purpose of the charade?"

"I don't know, but its obvious Amy Wallace is seriously disturbed."

He pulled back and kissed me. I kissed him back releasing all of the fear that had built over the past hour. I wanted him to make everything all right. To my astonishment, I wanted him to be there for me—always. I wanted him.

He broke off the kiss when two officers reentered the house.

"I'm sorry, folks, but I'm going to have to ask you to leave. We need to gather evidence. This is a crime scene."

Brad smiled and whispered in my ear. "Vermillion PD's version of a forensics team. Let's get to the station and give our statements."

With our arms around each other's waists, we

walked outside. The storm, so instrumental in saving our lives, had moved on. Only a light drizzle remained. The air smelled fresh and clean—like a new beginning.

I breathed in deeply, glad to be alive.

\*\*\*\*

I've heard it said that fear is the most powerful of all emotions. It triggers the fight or flight instinct, and when over, leaves the victim exhausted.

I was living proof of that. Time lost all meaning. Once at the station, my body craved a soft bed and to sleep for a week. Instead, I had to tell the police everything that had happened tonight.

I signed my statement and met Brad in the waiting area where he talked with Officer Howard.

"Can we go home now?" I asked, stifling a yawn.

The policeman smiled. "Yes, you're free to go. If we have any further questions, I'll be in touch."

"What about Bridges?" Brad said.

"He called his lawyer right off the bat, and is still proclaiming his innocence, but from a cell."

I snorted. "Yeah, right. He was embezzling from Amy's trust and going to kill us all."

"How's Corry?" Brad asked.

Howard shrugged. "Touch and go. He went into emergency surgery once they got him stabilized. No word yet."

"And Amy?" I inquired.

"She's been taken to the hospital and is currently under suicide watch. I imagine she'll be moved soon to a private psychiatric facility. The doctors sedated her pretty heavily, and we're trying to get in touch with her next of kin, some aunt down in Florida."

"So, she's not under arrest?"

"Not at this time. She's done nothing illegal, although that could change the more we investigate."

I sighed. Poor Amy. "Has she spoken?"

"We haven't gotten a statement from her yet."

"No, I mean just spoken—said anything. When the paramedics took her away, she was staring into space like in a trance, not saying a word."

"Not to my knowledge."

Brad placed his arm around my shoulders, hugged me close, and then kissed the top of my head.

"Amy has deep psychological problems. I'd say pretending to be her dead sister proves that." He extended his hand. "Thanks for all your help, Officer Howard. If you need us, don't hesitate to call."

We exited the police station and drove home.

"I can't believe any of this happened," I said, laying my head back on the headrest.

"I don't know why we never considered Mark Bridges as an embezzler. All the signs were there."

"He damn near had a heart attack when Amy wanted an advance on her trust to buy the ring. And he flat out refused to sell any of her portfolio."

"If he was embezzling from the trust, he was also probably screwing with her investments. My guess is someone will initiate an immediate audit."

I rubbed my fingers over my forehead trying to ease the headache forming behind my eyes. I felt as if I'd lost a friend. Amy wasn't really Amy any more. I wondered if in the recesses of her mind, she knew.

"With Amy incapacitated, I'm sure the courts will appoint a guardian, probably the aunt."

We pulled into my driveway. The police were still at Amy's and I wondered what else they had found.

Would they also ask for a warrant to search the Webster Groves house?

At the moment, I didn't care. My head pounded. I swallowed a pain pill, stumbled into the bedroom, undressed, and fell into bed. Brad slid in next to me, kissed my temple, and cradled me in his arms. I may have been exhausted, but not so much as to not appreciate his warmth and the security it brought.

****

The tantalizing aromas of fresh-brewed coffee and bacon frying tickled my nose. A moment later, the sound of the latter sizzling in the pan brought me to full consciousness. Rolling over, I drew a deep breath and stretched. My hand patted the sheets next to me, still warm from Brad's body. He couldn't have been up too long.

I rose, showered, and dressed quickly. By the time I entered the kitchen, the food was done and Brad had his phone against his ear.

"Okay, thanks for the update." He hung up and turned to smile at me. "Feeling better?"

"I'll feel even better once I eat. God, I'm hungry. I can't even remember whether or not I ate last night. Who were you talking to?" I asked.

"Officer Howard called to tell me Bridges' lawyer arrived early this morning. Arraignment's this afternoon. He could make bail and be out of here by evening."

"That's assuming a judge will even grant bail." I paused as a snippet of a phone conversation came back to me. "He slipped up, you know. Bridges, I mean. The day of the ring incident, he called to ream me a new one and mentioned a brunette in a red sports car. I never told him that detail until later.

"And I also should have realized he wasn't likely to have remembered a casual conversation with my parents from years ago concerning their pride in my accomplishments. He made it sound as if he'd just spoken with them, yet he hadn't been in Vermillion in years."

"So, how *did* he know to contact you?"

I shook my head. "Before you barged in, he said Abby—or rather Amy—had remembered and Googled me. I dare say a private investigator or even Amy herself tracked me down. Any word on Corry?"

Brad nodded, took the stool next to me, and proceeded to eat.

"Howard informed me Corry is hanging in there. They retrieved the bullet, but while he's in and out of consciousness, he's still too weak to make a statement."

"Bad news for Bridges. I'd love to know how all this came about."

He shook his head. "Bridges won't talk and is probably hoping Corry bites the big one before saying anything."

"And poor Amy is in no condition to tell us either."

"The police did a thorough search of Amy's last night. In the bottom drawer of a dresser downstairs, they discovered a long blonde wig."

I sipped some coffee. "This is so confusing. Amy was pretending to be Abby *and* disguising Abby at the same time."

"She had to. Too many eyes in Vermillion might recognize her as Abby. And she couldn't very well sell the ring as Amy. I'm sure in her mind, it all made sense."

"Now that I think of it, I never saw the blonde or the brunette I thought might be Abby while Amy was around." I whacked the countertop with my hand. "She was so convincing. I didn't suspect a thing. I feel foolish not to have seen through the charade."

"Don't be. She even fooled her uncle into believing she was Abby. Any discrepancies in behavior could be explained away as ten years is a long time. She could have matured or he could have forgotten."

"Corry admitted last night he was the one who hit me. And I wonder if Amy was responsible for the trip wire. She must have walked into the house that day we were at the marina. I forgot to lock the door or put my computer into hibernation. She hadn't counted on the electronic journal. She saw it and read what I'd written."

"So, she rigged up a trip wire in the hope that sooner or later you'd go down to the dock," Brad said. "Only Amy wasn't sure how to do it, which explains why it was tied so loosely. I wonder if she meant your fall to be fatal."

"The only person Amy wanted dead was Amy. Corry would have tightened it enough to kill me, but Amy couldn't do that. She either wanted me to catch myself or see the wire."

"Thank God for small favors."

His tone sent a warm glow throughout my body. I don't know how it happened, but in a few short weeks, I'd come to realize the man meant a lot to me. I wanted him in my future, but wasn't sure about permanently. My past actions during my marriage still haunted me. I wondered if he felt the same.

*And how the hell do I bring up the subject? By*

*being straight forward and telling him?*

"And the sighting you had of Abby in Stone City was perfect," Brad said, his voice bringing me out of semi-romantic thoughts.

"She never went on an Abby hunt. She put on the short brunette wig, waited for me to make an appearance, and then allowed me to see her to confirm a woman in a red sports car." I bit off a chunk of bacon. "I wonder what happened to the car."

"It's probably in some farmer's barn near here."

"And that day in Victoria's, she saw a red sports car flash by and used it as an opportunity to suck me in to her theory Abby was alive." I shook my head and pushed my empty plate away. "It worked. I saw the car, but didn't get much of a look at the driver. Later, it was enough to make me think."

"All in all, it was one hell of a revenge and suicide plot. I just wish we knew the whole story."

"Maybe Amy will be well enough soon to fill us in."

Brad poured us both another cup of coffee. He paused with a thoughtful expression. "Jen, I know this is probably not the time or the place, but can we talk?"

My heart rate increased. "Sure, let's go into the living room."

He collected the dishes and set them in the sink, then followed me. I sat on the sofa, my fingers nervously plucking at the cording on a pillow. I was afraid to look him in the eye.

Brad didn't sit, but paced in front of the fireplace, a frown on his face.

"Jen, three years ago, my life was in shambles. My second marriage had disintegrated and I acknowledged

I wasn't good husband material. It's pretty sobering to know you haven't got what it takes to maintain a lifetime relationship. Then, my career took a nosedive. I couldn't sell a book. My concentration was shot. So, I decided to simplify my life."

I cleared the lump from my throat. "No complications."

"More or less. I refused party invitations, pared the people I spent time with to a few good friends. I got more selective with the women I dated. But none of it helped with the writing. The spark had gone."

"Until you got an idea for a twin story and came here."

"I was suddenly enthused again, but it had nothing to do with my project and everything to do with a change in scenery." He ceased pacing and smiled. "One day, there I was fixing some porch steps when I looked up and saw you. I can't explain it, but it was like an invisible cord had suddenly attached itself to me forcing me to tag along."

I looked up in surprise. "You...you felt it, too? I noticed you the minute I pulled up. Later, when you came to the door, I knew there was some—I don't know—spark between us. It scared me. I'd so screwed up my marriage, I was afraid to get involved on a serious level."

"The more I got to know you, the more I realized you might be something very special." He came over and sat next to me. Taking my hand in his, he brought it to his lips. "I began to realize just how damned special the day you were attacked. My fear for you grew when you found the trip wire, but last night I finally owned up that if Mark Bridges had succeeded in killing you, I would have wanted to die, too."

Tears filled my eyes. "Oh, Brad, last night I was terrified you'd come barging in and when you did, I…well, I just can't describe the fear. I was certain we would all die, and I'd never get to say how much I care for you."

"Jenny, I want to make this work between us. With two failed marriages and countless broken relationships, I'm a huge risk. I'll understand if you don't want to take me on, but God Almighty, I care about you, too."

"Maybe the right woman never came along. Am I the woman? I don't know. I wasn't the best of wives either."

"I believe good people stray from their spouses because something is lacking. I have no idea what it was in my case, but this feels right. I think I love you, Jenny Devlin. Psychic mumbo-jumbo aside, I think our halves finally found each other. Will you take a chance?"

"A chance?" I pulled away slightly. "Brad, I'll admit I've got serious feelings for you. But even after six years, the guilt at what I did to my ex-husband is still with me. I'm not sure I can take that final leap of faith into another marriage just yet. I'd like to explore this relationship at a slow pace. This time I want to be damned sure. Am I sounding like a jerk?"

He sighed and smiled. "No. Not at all. Marriage? I'm not sure about that yet either. I'm not the easiest person to live with. There might be times when I simply don't want to talk to you because I'm in full writer mode. I can closet myself in a room for literally days living on bottled water and candy bars. I think slow and careful is the way to go. If you can ease your guilt and learn the art of living with a self-centered author, then we should give this a shot."

"And you might have to learn how to be less isolated from others in your life. Get out of that room once in a while for a decent lunch with your…significant other."

"Touché. You're right. Life is a compromise. And relationships are give and take. I'll try if you will."

I kissed him lightly on the chin. "You know, I've discovered an interesting fact about us."

He cocked an eyebrow. "Yeah? What?"

"Authors and lawyers have a lot in common."

He kissed the tip of my nose. "And what would that be?"

I planted my lips on his chin. "We both talk too damned much."

Brad laughed, swept me into his arms and carried me down the hall to the bedroom.

Perhaps this was meant to be. For the first time in a long while, I envisioned a future. A future I never expected to find.

He quickly stripped my clothes off and tossed me onto the bed. His clothing also found the floor and, with a devilish grin, covered my body with his.

I thought no more.

Chapter Thirty-Three

*Two months later*

The afterglow of making love warmed my soul as Brad and I sat on my front porch sipping wine. It was nearly dinnertime. Wine and Brad had made a lovely appetizer. Labor Day was just around the corner and another summer would officially end. We'd both stayed on here in Vermillion for the remainder of the season.

We were cautiously exploring our relationship and so far, things were going well. I'd learned how to back off when he wanted to work, and he was slowly coming around to the idea of not isolating himself for days at a time.

He'd also made the sacrifice of moving in with me in St. Louis. "Guess we're going to have to make this work now," he'd said with a grin.

My boss was more than disappointed about the turn of events. All those billing hours lost. He also lost me. I decided to strike out on my own. All I needed was a computer and a few clients to start.

Brad was supportive. "Great idea, hon. Authors hate reading contracts, and while my agent does most of the work, he still sends it through a lawyer before I sign. Might as well be you."

"And your agent has how many clients?" I cooed.

Brad was working like a fiend on two stories at

once. The first dealt with our ordeal and Amy. The twin story had legs, and from what I'd read, was damned good. Luckily, his agent hadn't contacted the publisher about rescinding the advance.

"His comment was, 'I knew you'd come to your senses,'" Brad reported.

His other story was the one he'd begun before the Amy situation heated up. The body floating under the dock with an ice pick in the back was a man. Brad refuses to let me in on the killer or the motive.

I sipped from my wine glass and sighed in pure bliss.

Brad squeezed my hand. "Happy?"

"Don't you see the grin on my face?"

He laughed. "I'll bet it mirrors mine. I got a call today from my realtor out in Los Angeles. He's got an offer on my condo—a nice one, too."

"Did you counter?"

"Not yet."

The lawyer in me rose. "Negotiate, dear. Get the best deal possible."

"I knew you'd say that."

I laughed and sipped more wine. A car drove into the Wallace driveway. The driver, a woman, emerged, stared at the house, and then glanced our way. She hesitated before striding across the lawn toward us.

Pausing at the foot of the steps, she said, "Hello. Are you Jenny Devlin?"

I rose. "Yes."

She smiled and extended a hand. "I'm Margaret Reynolds, Amy's aunt. Her father was my older brother."

I shook her hand and introduced Brad. "Please, sit

down." I indicated a chair. "Can I get you something to drink?"

"No, thanks."

"How's Amy?" I asked, resuming my seat.

She sat and brushed a lock of hair from her eyes. "Doing as well as can be expected. I have power of attorney now, so the doctor keeps me well-informed on her progress."

"Do you know what happened? How this all came about?" Brad asked.

"There are still some holes, but by and large the story is coming out." She fingered a pleat in the skirt of her dress. "I live in Orlando. About a year or so ago I was in St. Louis and spent a few days with Amy. I hadn't seen her in a couple of years, but she seemed withdrawn, distant. When I asked her what was wrong, she said Mark was pressuring her into signing a power of attorney. His excuse was he planned on traveling a lot and it would be easier for him to transfer her investments from place to place, especially since she stayed here in the summer. I thought it smelled like bullshit, if you'll excuse the language. You know, I wouldn't mind a bottle of water."

Brad rose and entered the house, returning in less than a minute. He handed her the bottle. She twisted the cap off and drank half of it immediately before continuing.

"I never liked Mark Bridges. There was always something about him that sent up red flags. I warned my brother, Bill, not to trust him. I didn't voice my suspicions to Connie, my sister-in-law, about *her* brother."

"What kind of red flags?" I asked.

"Always telling everyone how well his investments were doing. He'd come here to visit and try to drum up business. I found it in bad taste. And he also buttered up the ladies. I'll say this, the man oozed charm."

"Funny. That's how he once described Abby," I commented.

"Not surprised. They were cut from the same cloth. Both were finaglers and manipulators." She paused and frowned, then sipped from the bottle again. "I know this is going to sound sick and depraved, but in the back of my mind I always wondered if Mark Bridges wasn't in love with Abby."

"His niece?" I said with a gasp.

She waved a hand. "Oh, nothing happened, but he hung around with her and her friends here at the lake. It gave me the creeps."

I remembered Amy telling me how Abby had laughed at their uncle for trying to insinuate himself into the younger crowd.

She shook her head. "Abby was always wild, but nothing Bill and Connie couldn't handle."

"And then Abby left town," Brad added.

Mrs. Reynolds nodded. "After the accident, I hired a private investigator to dig into those years Abby was gone. He came up with lots of stuff from minor drug use to a ton of unpaid speeding tickets, and a shoplifting charge. Then she met Roger Corry. He was real trouble. Had a record a mile long. Later, I gave the report to my sister."

So, the aunt, not Amy had instigated the investigation. Amy had probably discovered the report after her mother's death. I'd only seen a small portion of that report—the part Amy wanted me to see.

"How did he come back into the picture?" Brad inquired.

"According to Amy, Abby drank a buttload of wine that last night and talked about him and the trouble she was in. Amy had a name and used it later."

"What sent her around the bend?" I asked.

"The last time I saw Amy, I voiced my suspicions of Mark's honesty. I didn't like this business about the power of attorney. I suggested she get an independent audit of the trust and her investments. I don't know if she did, but with my suspicions and the anniversary of Abby's death approaching, plus the guilt that had festered for a decade, she snapped." She finished her water, and shook her head. "I feel like I precipitated the whole charade. She hired a private investigator to inquire about Corry. From there she contacted Roger, pretended to be Abby and set the whole thing in motion. Amy hired a lawyer here in Vermillion and made a new will leaving everything to me. Bridges was the previous beneficiary. She also had her loving uncle investigated."

"Suicide. She wanted to die, but couldn't bring herself to do it. Instead, she assumed her dead sister's identity and confronted her uncle knowing he was a crook and would do it for her," I said.

"As Abby, she suggested killing off Amy, and then splitting the trust with Mark," Brad said.

"And once Amy was dead, Mark would be holding the bag on an untouchable inheritance, because, of course, Abby had died years ago. Plus, a new will put yet another person in his way," I said.

Mrs. Reynolds nodded. "That's about the size of it."

I took another sip of wine and eyed Margaret Reynolds. "You know about Roger Corry, I suppose. He died of complications a few days after he was shot, but not before spilling everything he knew about Abby and her uncle."

Margaret rolled the empty bottle between her hands.

"The weasel will cop a plea. Amy set the whole thing up. She'd finally be put out of her guilty misery, and Mark would be in jail. She didn't give a damn about Corry. I talked to the prosecutor down here. He said Bridges was stunned that sweet, quiet little Amy had hoodwinked him. He honestly thought he was dealing with Abby."

"My guess is Amy kept contact with him as Abby to a minimum. The less he saw of her, the less he might question. I take it Bridges is singing like a bird," I said.

"Murder charges were never brought after Corry died on the theory he was going for his gun. Called it self-defense," Brad told her.

"He cut a deal on the embezzlement before Corry made his statement. He knew it would be over the minute someone audited the trust and Amy's investments, not to mention other people who trusted him with *their* money. Scheming son of a bitch," Margaret said with a snarl.

"How did she make contact as Abby? Walk right up and say, 'Hi, Uncle Mark?'" Brad asked.

"Believe it or not, that's exactly what she did. He says one night someone knocked on his door and when he opened it, there stood Abby. The speech patterns and mannerisms convinced him she was real. She retold incidents from the past only he and Abby would know."

"Or so he thought," I murmured. "It never occurred to him Abby may have told Amy."

"No one knows a twin like a twin," Brad replied.

Margaret nodded. "He claims Abby demanded her share of the trust. When he tried to put her off, she threatened an audit."

"And an audit would bring out the truth," I murmured.

Margaret nodded. "He says 'Abby' thought up the scheme to kill Amy and split the money. And he also claims she was the one who suggested Corry to help."

"Why bring in Corry at all?" I said.

"Supposedly to harass Amy. Plus she needed someone to drive the boat. Remember, Amy wasn't that familiar with boats," Brad answered.

I recalled Amy towing Corry behind the boat not far from my dock. "She knew enough to keep Corry believing."

"Corry was an idiot," Amy's aunt said. "The dollar signs he saw masked any inconsistencies with the Abby he'd once known."

"And don't forget, Corry and Abby weren't together all that long before he was sent to prison. What I can't believe is Mark Bridges thinking he could pull this off," Brad muttered.

"I can't believe Amy pulled it off," I replied.

"Sweet, pliable Amy whose disturbed mind worked like a steel trap," Brad answered.

"I don't think this was Bridges' first foray into murder," Margaret said.

Stunned, I could only stare. "What?"

"I've been living in the house in Webster Groves. The sanitarium Amy's at is only a few minutes away.

One day I went through her desk and found a bunch of correspondence from Connie to various lawyers. My brother died four years after Abby, and as I said, Bridges was overseeing the estate. I guess my harping on keeping tabs on him had paid off. Bill must have voiced his concerns to his wife. Connie was initiating an audit. In the pile of letters, I discovered an e-mail from her brother protesting. Three days later she was killed by a hit and run driver."

"Bridges?" Brad asked.

"I think so, but there's not one iota of proof. The case went cold and after this length of time I doubt any new evidence will surface."

"His own sister?" I said, disbelief in my voice.

Brad shrugged. "Why not? He was perfectly willing to kill his own nieces. And he wasn't in the least bit shocked by the so-called Abby's suggestion they kill Amy."

Margaret shook her head. "Abby was a lot of things. She lied, cheated, stole, and manipulated people to do her bidding. However, she wasn't a killer. And she never hated her twin. She'd have taken every last dime Amy had, but wouldn't physically harm her." She set the empty water bottle on the floor. "There's something else you should know. I found Amy's diary and read it before turning it over to her psychiatrist. It begins shortly after she came down here for the summer. She detailed everything. Somewhere along the line, she began to believe her fantasy."

"You mean she wrote it convinced she had seen Abby?" I asked, confused. I'd never dealt with mental illness before and had trouble grasping the convoluted thinking.

"She needed validation for what she was doing," Brad said. "I guess we'll never know how her mind worked."

"You mean, pretending to be Abby eventually had her believing Abby was alive?" I asked, still confused.

"I think she began to think like Abby, feel like her. Maybe even *be* her for brief periods," Margaret said.

I remembered the trip to Branson and the changed personality. Physically, I was with Amy—mentally and emotionally, it was Abby.

"My poor niece never got over Abby's death or that she was responsible. Even those months in the sanitarium after the accident didn't help. She merely suppressed the hope her sister had survived."

"So, the tenth anniversary and the knowledge her uncle was cheating her all came together in one giant mental breakdown," I said, shaking my head.

"Guilt is a tremendous motivator," Brad concluded.

"In Branson I kept thinking how Amy had suddenly seemed to change character."

"She knew the end was near and let the Abby persona take over. She'd need it to achieve the end result," Brad concluded.

"What I can't understand is why bring me into any of this? During the confrontation, Bridges said it was 'Abby' who suggested contacting me. Why bring in an outside source? To legitimize 'Amy's' so-called hallucinations? It doesn't make sense," I said.

"Maybe it was a last ditch cry for help," Brad answered. "*Maybe* she hoped you would uncover the scheme and she wouldn't have to die."

Margaret rose. "Right now, my niece is in deep therapy trying to deal with guilt complexes and death wishes. She drifted in and out of reality and became Abby for the sole purpose to kill herself—period. Taking her uncle down was an extra."

"Such an elaborate scheme," I lamented. "It would have been so much easier to simply aim the car at a tree."

"But Amy couldn't do that," Brad said in a soft tone. "She wanted to die, but not by her own hand."

"Jenny, I want to thank you for being Amy's friend."

"No thanks needed. What began as a simple assignment turned into true friendship. I contacted her publisher and got a list of the books she's illustrated. I bought them all. She does such beautiful work—so much soul and vulnerability came through. The wildlife leaps right off the pages and into my living room. I wish I had an Amy Wallace original to hang on the wall."

Margaret smiled. "I'm sure there must be some around the house in St. Louis. I'll check."

"Oh, I didn't mean…"

"I'm sure Amy would be only too happy to part with one or two. You've done so much for her." She hesitated. "I have no idea when or even if she'll be released from the sanitarium, but would you both stop by occasionally to say hello? I think it would mean a lot to her."

"We'd be honored," I said. "In a way I feel like she's the sister I never had. I wish we'd gotten to know each other sooner. Maybe none of this would have happened if she'd had a friend. Of course, we'll go see her."

Brad glanced at me. "We wouldn't abandon her."

Margaret waved goodbye and retraced her steps back to Amy's house.

"Poor Amy," Brad murmured as we went inside. "I wonder if her mental illness stemmed from the accident or if it's been with her forever."

"Hard to tell. I guess always being in the shadow of your sister could stomp your self-esteem into the dirt. In her mind, nothing she ever did was quite good enough." I sighed. "I hope she makes a complete recovery."

Brad pulled me into his arms. "Me, too. I like Amy." He kissed me, and then asked, "What's for dinner?"

"I have no idea. You were my appetizer earlier."

He nuzzled my ear. "In that case, you could be my entrée."

"And we'd both be each other's dessert?"

"Why not?"

"I guess I can live on love for a while."

"Until the honeymoon's over, huh? Uh, I'm speaking metaphorically, of course."

I punched him lightly on the arm. "Swine, maybe someday."

"O-o-o, you hit me. I like it."

He swung me up into his arms and carried me toward the bedroom. I had no problem visualizing our future together. We'd joke, laugh, love, and upon occasion argue. But most of all, we'd love. That "someday" might not be so far away after all.

I looked forward to the rest of our lives.

## A word from the author...

I was born in Indianapolis, Indiana, but lived for many years in Memphis, Tennessee, which I now consider home. I have two adult children and seven grandchildren. At present, I reside in Ft. Lauderdale, Florida, with my husband, Bruce, and a cantankerous dog named Lucky.

I've been a serious writer since 2002 and belong to Romance Writers of America, Florida Romance Writers, and River City Romance Writers along with Mystery Writers of America.

I love writing and hope readers enjoy the journey along with me.

~*~

**Other Suzanne Rossi titles**
**available from The Wild Rose Press, Inc.**

*ALONG CAME QUINN*
*ALL IN THE FAMILY*
*A TANGLED WEB*
*NEARLY DEPARTED*
*HEAR NO EVIL*
*THE REUNION*
*DEADLY INHERITANCE*
*DEATH IS THE PITS*
*THROUGH MY EYES*
*A NOVEL DEATH*
*RENDEZVOUS WITH DEATH*

www.ingramcontent.com/pod-product-compliance
Lightning Source LLC
Chambersburg PA
CBHW071533260626
47170CB00002B/609